ABSOLUTION BY MURDER

The Sister Fidelma Mysteries:

Absolution by Murder
Shroud for the Archbishop*

*forthcoming

ABSOLUTION BY MURDER

A Sister Fidelma Mystery

Peter Tremayne

St. Martin's Press ❧ New York

ISBN 0-312-13918-7

First published in Great Britain by Headline Book Publishing

10   9   8   7   6   5   4   3   2

To Dorothea

Sister Fidelma's World

The Sister Fidelma mysteries are set during the mid-seventh century AD.

Sister Fidelma is not simply a religieuse, a member of the community of St. Brigid of Kildare. She is also a qualified *dálaigh*, or advocate of the ancient law courts of Ireland. As this background will not be familiar to many readers, this foreword provides a few essential points of reference designed to make the stories more readily appreciated.

Ireland, in the seventh century AD, consisted of five main provincial kingdoms: indeed, the modern Irish word for a province is still *cúige*, literally 'a fifth'. Four provincial kings— of Ulaidh (Ulster), of Connacht, of Muman (Munster) and of Laigin (Leinster)—gave their allegiance to the *Ard Rí* or High King, who ruled from Tara, in the 'royal' fifth province of Midhe (Meath), which means the 'middle province'. Even among these provincial kingdoms, there was a decentralisation of power to petty-kingdoms and clan territories.

The law of primogeniture, the inheritance by the eldest son or daughter, was an alien concept in Ireland. Kingship, from the lowliest clan chieftain to the High King, was only partial hereditary and mainly electoral. Each ruler had to prove himself or herself worthy of office and was elected by the *derbfhine* of their family—three generations gathered in conclave. If a ruler did not pursue the commonwealth of the people, they were impeached and removed from office. Therefore the monarchial system of ancient Ireland had more in common with a modern day republic than with the feudal monarchies of medieval Europe.

Ireland, in the seventh century AD, was governed by a system of sophisticated laws called the Laws of the *Fénechas*, or land-tillers, which became more popularly known as the Brehon Laws, deriving from the word *breitheamh*—a judge. Tradition has it that these laws were first gathered in 714 BC by the order of the High King, Ollamh Fódhla. But it was in AD 438 that the High King, Laoghaire, appointed a commission of nine learned people to study, revise and commit the laws to the new writing in Latin characters. One of those serving on the commission was Patrick, eventually to become patron saint of Ireland. After three years, the commission produced a written text of the laws, the first known codification.

The first complete surviving texts of the ancient laws of Ireland are preserved in an eleventh-century manuscript book. It was not until the seventeenth-century that the English colonial administration in Ireland finally suppressed the use of the Brehon Law system. To even possess a copy of the law books was punishable, often by death or transportation.

The law system was not static and every three years at the Féis Temhrach (Festival of Tara) the lawyers and administrators gathered to consider and revise the laws in the light of changing society and its needs.

Under these laws, women occupied a unique place. The Irish laws gave more rights and protection to women than any other western law code at that time or since. Women could, and did, aspire to all offices and professions as the coequal with men. They could be political leaders, command their people in battle as warriors, by physicians, local magistrates, poets, artisans, lawyers and judges. We know the name of many female judges of Fidelma's period—Bríg Briugaid, Áine Ingine Iugaire and Darí among many others. Darí, for example, was not only a judge but also the author of a noted law text written in the sixth century AD. Women were protected by the laws against sexual harassment; against discrimination; from rape; they had the right of divorce on equal terms from their husbands with equitable separation laws and could demand part of their husband's property as a divorce settlement; they had the right of inheritance of personal property and the right of sickness benefits. Seen from today's perspective, the Brehon Laws provided for an almost feminist paradise.

This background, and its strong contrast with Ireland's neighbours, should be understood to appreciate Fidelma's role in these stories.

Fidelma was born at Cashel, capital of the kingdom of Muman (Munster) in south-west Ireland, in AD 636. She was the youngest daughter of Failbe Fland, the king, who died the year after her birth and was raised under the guidance of a distant cousin, Abbot Laisran of Durrow. When she reached the 'Age of Choice' (fourteen years), she went to study at the bardic school of the Brehon Morann of Tara, as many other young Irish girls did. Eight years of study resulted in Fidelma obtaining the degree of *Anruth*, only one degree below the highest offered at either bardic or ecclesiastical universities in ancient Ireland. The highest degree was *ollamh*, still the modern Irish word for a professor. Fidelma's studies were in law, both in the criminal code of the *Senchus Mór* and the civil code of the *Leabhar Acaill*. She therefore became a *dálaigh* or advocate of the courts.

Her role could be likened to a modern Scottish sheriff-substitute, whose job is to gather and assess the evidence, independent of the police, to see if there is a case to be answered. The modern French *juge d'instruction* holds a similar role.

In those days, most of the professional or intellectual classes were members of the new Christian religious houses, just as, in previous centuries, all members of professions and intellectuals were Druids. Fidelma became a member of the religious community of Kildare founded in the late fifth century AD by St. Brigid.

While the seventh century AD was considered part of the European 'Dark Ages', for Ireland it was a period of 'Golden Enlightenment'. Students from every corner of Europe flocked to Irish universities to receive their education, including the sons of the Anglo-Saxon kings. For example, Aldfrith, who became king of Northumbria from AD 685-705, was educated at Bangor and achieved a reputation in Ireland as a poet in the Irish language. Three of his poems still survive in ancient texts. At the great ecclesiastical university of Durrow, at this time, it is recorded that no less than eighteen different nations were represented among the students. At the same time, Irish male and female missionaries were setting out to reconvert a pagan Europe to Christianity, establishing churches, monasteries and centres of learning throughout Europe as far east as Kiev, in the Ukraine; as far north as the Faroes, and as far south as Taranto in southern Italy. Ireland was a by-word for literacy and learning.

However, the Celtic Church of Ireland was in constant dispute with Rome on matters of liturgy and ritual. Rome had began to reform itself in the fourth century, changing its dating of Easter and aspects of its liturgy. The Celtic Church and the Eastern Orthodox Church refused to follow Rome but the Celtic Church was gradually absorbed by Rome between the ninth and eleventh centuries while the Eastern Orthodox Churches have continued to remain independent of Rome. The Celtic Church of Ireland, during Fidelma's time, was much concerned with this conflict.

The first Fidelma mystery, *Absolution By Murder*, is set against the most famous debate between the representatives of the Celtic and Roman Churches at Whitby in AD 664.

One thing that marked both the Celtic Church and Rome in the seventh century was that the concept of celibacy was not universal. While there were always ascetics in both churches who sublimated physical love in a dedication to the deity, it was not until the Council of Nicea in AD 325 that clerical marriages were condemned but not banned. The concept of celibacy in the Roman Church arose from the customs practised by the pagan priestesses of Vesta and the priests of Diana. By the fifth century Rome had forbidden clerics from the rank of abbot and bishop to sleep with their wives and, shortly after, even to marry at all. The general clergy were discouraged from marrying by Rome but not forbidden to do so. Indeed, it was not until the reforming papacy of Leo IX (AD 1049-1054) that a serious attempt was made to force the western clergy to accept universal celibacy. In the Eastern Orthodox Church, priests below the rank of abbot and bishop have retained their right to marry until this day.

The condemnation of the 'sin of the flesh' remained alien to the Celtic Church for a long time after Rome's attitude became a dogma. In Fidelma's world, both sexes inhabited abbeys and monastic foundations which were known as *conhospitae*, or double houses, where men and women lived raising their children in Christ's service.

Fidelma's own house of St. Brigid of Kildare was one such community of both sexes in Fidelma's time. When Brigid established her community at Kildare (Cill-Dara = the church of oaks) she invited a bishop named Conlaed to join her. Her first biography, written in AD 650, in Fidelma's time, was written by a monk of Kildare named Cogitosus, who makes it clear that it was a mixed community.

It should also be pointed out that, showing women's coequal role with men, women were priests of the Celtic Church at this time. Brigid herself was ordained a bishop by Patrick's nephew, Mel and her case was not unique. Roman actually wrote a protest in the sixth century at the Celtic practise of allowing women to celebrate the divine sacrifice of Mass.

Armed with this background knowledge we may now enter Fidelma's world. This story is placed in the year AD 664.

No wild beasts are so cruel as the Christians in their dealings with each other.

Ammianus Marcellinus
(c. AD 330–95)

Chapter One

The man had not been dead long. The blood and spittle around his twisted lips had not even dried. The body swung to and fro in the faint breeze, suspended at the end of a stout hemp rope from the branch of a squat oak tree. The head was twisted at an awkward angle where the neck had been broken. The clothes were torn and if the man had worn sandals then they had since been taken by scavengers for there was no sign of any footwear. The contorted hands, still sticky with blood, showed that the man had not died without a struggle.

It was not the fact that a man had been hanged on a crossroad tree that caused the small party of travellers to halt. The travellers had become used to witnessing ritual executions and punishments since they had crossed from the land of Rheged into the kingdom of Northumbria. The Angles and Saxons who dwelt there seemed to live by a harsh code of penalties for those who transgressed their laws, from an assortment of mutilations of the body to execution by the most painful means devised, the most common and humane being by hanging. The sight of one more unfortunate suspended on a tree no longer troubled them. What had caused the party to draw rein on their mounts, an assortment of horses and mules, was something else.

The party of travellers consisted of four men and two women. Each was clad in the undyed wool *tunica* of the religious, and the hair of the men was shaven at the front, their tonsure marking

1

them as brothers of the church of Columba from the Holy Island of Iona. Almost as one they had halted to sit staring up at the body of the man hanging in gruesome wide-eyed death, the tongue blackened and stretched between the lips in what must have been one last frantic gasp for air. The face of everyone in the party was grim with apprehension as it examined the body.

The reason was not hard to discern. The head of the body was also shaven with the tonsure of Columba. What remained of his clothing proclaimed it to have once consisted of the habit of a religieux, though there was no sign of the crucifix, leather belt and satchel that a *peregrinus pro Christo* would have carried.

The leading traveller had drawn near on his mule and gazed up with a terrified expression on his white features.

Another of the party, one of the two women, urged her mount nearer and gazed up at the corpse with a steady eye. She rode a horse, a fact that signified that she was no ordinary religieuse but a woman of rank. There was no fear on her pale features, just a slight expression of repulsion and curiosity. She was a young woman, tall but well proportioned, a fact scarcely concealed by her sombre dress. Rebellious strands of red hair streaked from beneath her headdress. Her pale-skinned features were attractive and her eyes were bright and it was difficult to discern whether they were blue or green, so changeable with emotion were they.

'Come away, Sister Fidelma,' muttered her male companion in agitation. 'This is not a sight for your eyes.'

The woman addressed as Sister Fidelma grimaced in vexation at his anxious tone.

'Whose eyes is it a sight for, Brother Taran?' she responded. Then, edging her horse even closer to the corpse, she observed,

'Our brother is not long dead. Who can have done this terrible deed? Robbers?'

Brother Taran shook his head.

'This is a strange country, sister. This is only my second mission to it. Thirty years have passed since we first began to bring the word of Christ to this Godforsaken land. There still be many pagans about with scant respect for our cloth. Let us move on – quickly. Whoever did this deed may have remained in the vicinity. The abbey of Streoneshalh cannot be too far distant and we want to reach it before the sun drops below those hills.'

He shivered slightly.

The young woman continued to frown, displaying her irritation.

'You would continue on and leave one of our brethren in this manner? Unblessed and unburied?'

Her voice was sharp and angry.

Brother Taran shrugged, his obvious fear making him a sorry spectacle. She turned to her companions.

'I have need of a knife to cut our brother down,' she explained. 'We must pray for his soul and accord him a Christian burial.'

The others cast uneasy glances at each other.

'Perhaps Brother Taran is right,' replied her female companion, apologetically. She was a large-boned girl, sitting heavy and awkward on her mount. 'After all, he knows this country – as do I. Was I not a prisoner here for several years, taken as a hostage from the land of the Cruthin? Best to press on to seek the shelter of the abbey of Streoneshalh. We can report this atrocity to the abbess there. She will know how to deal with the matter.'

Sister Fidelma pursed her lips and exhaled in annoyance.

'We can at least deal with our departed brother's spiritual needs, Sister Gwid,' she replied shortly. She paused a moment. 'Has no one a knife?'

Hesitantly, one of her male companions moved forward and handed over a small knife.

Sister Fidelma took it and dismounted, moving across to where the rope that held the body was tied to a lower branch to keep it in place. She had raised the knife to cut it when a sharp cry caused her to turn sharply round in the direction of the sound.

Half-a-dozen men had emerged on foot from the woods on the far side of the road. They were led by a man mounted on a horse – a burly man with long unkempt hair curling from underneath a polished bronze helmet and merging into a great bushy black beard. He wore a burnished breastplate and carried himself with some authority. His companions, clustered behind him, carried an assortment of weaponry, mostly staffs and bows with arrows strung but not drawn.

Sister Fidelma had no knowledge of what the man shouted, but it was clearly an order, and it took little guessing that it was an order for her to desist in her task.

She glanced at Brother Taran, who was patently apprehensive.

'Who are these people?'

'They are Saxons, sister.'

Sister Fidelma gestured with impatience.

'That I can deduce for myself. But my knowledge of Saxon is imperfect. You must speak with them and ask who they are and what they know of this murder.'

Brother Taran turned his mule and, in stumbling fashion, called out to the leader of the men.

The burly man with the helmet grinned and spat before letting forth a volley of sounds.

'He says his name is Wulfric of Frihop, thane to Alhfrith of Deira, and that this is his land. His hall lies beyond the trees.'

Brother Taran's voice was nervous and he translated in a worried staccato.

'Ask him what this means?' Sister Fidelma's voice was cold and commanding as she gestured towards the hanging body.

The Saxon warrior rode closer, examining Brother Taran with a curious frown. Then his bearded face broke into an evil grin. His close-set eyes and furtive look reminded Fidelma of a cunning fox. He nodded his head as if amused as Taran spoke hesitantly and replied, spitting on the ground again in emphasis as he did so.

'It means that the brother was executed,' translated Taran.

'Executed?' Fidelma's brows drew together. 'By what law does this man dare execute a monk of Iona?'

'Not of Iona. The monk was a Northumbrian from the monastery on the Farne Islands,' came the reply.

Sister Fidelma bit her lip. She knew that the bishop of Northumbria, Colmán, was also abbot of Lindisfarne and that the abbey was the centre of the church in this kingdom.

'His name? What was the name of this brother?' demanded Fidelma. 'And what was his crime?'

Wulfric shrugged eloquently.

'His mother probably knew his name – and his God. I did not know it.'

'Under what law was he executed?' she pressed again, trying to control the anger she felt.

The warrior, Wulfric, had moved so that his mount was close to the young religieuse. He leant forward in his saddle towards her. Her nose wrinkled as she smelt his foul breath and saw his blackened teeth grinning at her. He was clearly impressed that, young as she was, and woman that she was, she did not seem afraid of him or of his companions. His dark eyes were speculative as he rested both hands on the pommel of his saddle and smirked towards the swinging body.

'The law that says a man who insults his betters must pay the price.'

'Insults his betters?'

Wulfric nodded.

'The monk,' Taran continued to translate in nervous fashion, 'arrived at Wulfric's village at noon seeking rest and hospitality on his journey. Wulfric, being a good Christian,' – had Wulfric emphasised this point or was it merely Taran's translation? – 'granted him rest and a meal. The mead was flowing in the feasting hall when the argument broke out.'

'An argument?'

'It seems that Wulfric's king, Alhfrith . . .'

'Alhfrith?' interrupted Fidelma. 'I thought Oswy was the king of Northumbria?'

'Alhfrith is Oswy's son and petty king of Deira, which is the southern province of Northumbria in which we are now.'

Fidelma motioned Taran to continue his translation.

'This Alhfrith has become a follower of Rome and has expelled many monks from the monastery of Ripon for not following the teachings and liturgy of Rome. Apparently, one of Wulfric's men engaged this monk in discourse on the rival merits of the liturgy of Columba and the teachings of Rome. The discussion turned to argument and argument to anger and the monk said heated words. The words were considered insulting.'

Sister Fidelma stared at the thane in disbelief.

'And for this the man was killed? Killed for mere words?'

Wulfric had been stroking his beard impassively and now he smiled, nodding again as Taran put the question to him.

'This man insulted the thane of Frihop. For that he was executed. Common man may not insult one of noble birth. It is the law. And it is the law that the man must remain hanging here for one full moon from this day.'

Anger now clearly formed on the features of the young sister. She knew little of Saxon law and in her opinion it was blatantly unjust, but she was wise enough to know how far to exhibit her indignation. She turned and swung herself easily back on to her horse and stared at the warrior.

'Know this, Wulfric, I am on my way to Streoneshalh, where I shall meet with Oswy, king of this land of Northumbria. And there I shall inform Oswy of how you have treated this servant of God and one who is under his protection as Christian king of this land.'

If the words were meant to give Wulfric any apprehension, they did not.

The man simply threw back his head and roared with laughter as her speech was translated.

Sister Fidelma's keen eyes had not ceased to keep watch not only on Wulfric but on his companions, who stood fingering their bows while the exchange was taking place, glancing now and then at their leader as if to anticipate his orders. Now she felt it time for discretion. She nudged her horse forward, followed by a relieved Brother Taran and her companions. She purposefully kept her mount to a walking gait. Haste would betray fear and fear was the last thing to show such a bully as Wulfric obviously was.

7

To her surprise, no attempt was made to stop them. Wulfric and his men simply remained looking after them, some laughing amongst themselves. After a while, when enough distance had been placed between them and Wulfric's band at the crossroads, Fidelma turned with a shake of her head to Taran.

'This is, indeed, a strange pagan country. I thought that this Northumbria was ruled in peace and contentment by Oswy?'

It was Sister Gwid, who like Brother Taran was of the Cruthin of the north, those whom many called the Picts, who answered Fidelma. Sister Gwid knew something of the ways and the language of Northumbria, having been for several years a captive within its borders.

'You have much to learn of this savage place, Sister Fidelma,' she began.

The condescension in her voice died as Fidelma turned her fiery eyes on her. 'Then tell me.' Her voice was cold and clear like the crystal waters of a racing mountain stream.

'Well.' Gwid was more contrite now. 'Northumbria was once settled by Angles. They are no different to the Saxons in the south of this country; that is, their language is the same and they used to worship the same outlandish gods until our missionaries began to preach the word of the true God. Two kingdoms were set up here, Bernicia to the north and Deira to the south. Sixty years ago, the two kingdoms were joined as one and this is now ruled by Oswy. But Oswy allows his son, Alhfrith, to be petty king of his southern province, Deira. Is this not so, Brother Taran?'

Brother Taran nodded sourly.

'A curse on Oswy and his house,' he muttered. 'Oswy's brother, Oswald, when he was king, led the Northumbrians to invade our country when I was but new born. My father, who was a chieftain of the Gododdin, was slain by them and my mother cut down before him as he lay dying. I hate them all!'

Fidelma raised an eyebrow.

'Yet you are a brother of Christ devoted to peace. You should have no hate in your heart.'

Taran sighed. 'You are right, sister. Sometimes our creed is a hard taskmaster.'

'Anyway,' she continued, 'I thought Oswy was educated at Iona and that he favoured the liturgy of the church of Colmcille? Why then would his son be a follower of Rome and an enemy to our cause?'

'These Northumbrians call the Blessed Colmcille by the name Columba,' intervened Sister Gwid pedantically. 'It is easier for them to pronounce.'

It was Brother Taran who answered Fidelma's question.

'I believe that Alhfrith is at enmity with his father, who has married again. Alhfrith fears that his father means to disinherit him in favour of Ecgfrith, his son by his current wife.'

Fidelma sighed deeply.

'I cannot understand this Saxon law of inheritance. I am told that they accept the first-born son as the heir rather than, as we do, allow the most worthy of the family to be elected by free choice.'

Sister Gwid suddenly gave a shout and pointed to the distant horizon.

'The sea! I can see the sea! And that black building on the horizon there – that must be the abbey of Streoneshalh.'

Sister Fidelma halted her horse and gazed into the distance with narrowed eyes.

'What say you, Brother Taran? You know this part of the country. Are we near the end of our journey?'

Taran's face expressed relief.

'Sister Gwid is right. That is our destination – Streoneshalh, the abbey of the Blessed Hilda, cousin to King Oswy.'

Chapter Two

The raucous voice, raised in apparent distress, caused the abbess to lift her eyes from the table, where she had been studying a page of illustrated vellum, and frown in annoyance at being disturbed.

She sat in a dark, stone-flagged chamber, lit by several tallow candles placed in bronze holders around the high walls. It was day, but the single, high window admitted little light. And the room was cold and austere in spite of several colourful tapestries covering the bleaker aspects of its masonry. Nor did the smouldering fire set in a large hearth at one end of the room give much warmth.

The abbess sat still for a moment. Her broad forehead and thin, angular features set in deep lines as her brows drew together. Her dark eyes, in which it was almost impossible to discern the pupils, held an angry glint as she positioned her head slightly to one side, listening to the shouting. Then she eased her richly woven woollen cloak around her shoulders, letting her hand slip momentarily to the ornately wrought gold crucifix hung on a string of tiny ivory beads around her neck. It was obvious from her clothing and adornments that she was a woman of wealth and position in her own right.

The shouting continued outside the wooden door of the chamber and so, suppressing a sigh of annoyance, she rose. Although she was of average height, there was something about her carriage that gave her a commanding appearance. Anger now intensified her features.

There came an abrupt banging on the oak door and it swung open almost immediately, before she had time to respond.

A woman in the brown homespun of a sister of the order stood nervously on the threshold.

Behind her a man in beggar's clothes struggled in the grip of two muscular brothers. The sister's posture and flushed face betrayed her nervousness and she seemed at a loss to frame the words that she so obviously sought.

'What does this mean?'

The abbess spoke softly, yet there was steel in her tone.

'Mother Abbess,' began the sister apprehensively but before she had time to finish her sentence the beggar shouted again, incoherently.

'Speak!' demanded the abbess impatiently. 'What is the meaning of this outrageous disturbance?'

'Mother Abbess, this beggar demanded to see you, and when we tried to turn him away from the abbey he started to shout and attack the brethren.' The words came out in a breathless gallop.

The abbess compressed her lips grimly.

'Bring him forward,' she ordered.

The sister turned and gestured to the brothers to bring the beggar forward. The man had ceased to struggle.

He was a thin man, so thin he looked more like a skeleton than a man of flesh. His eyes were grey, almost colourless, and his head was a thatch of dirty brown hair. The skin stretched tautly over his emaciated form was yellow and parchment-like. He was dressed in tattered clothing. It was obvious that the man was a foreigner in the kingdom of Northumbria.

'What do you want?' demanded the abbess, regarding him in distaste. 'Why do you cause such a commotion in this house of contemplation?'

'Want?' The beggar repeated the word slowly. Then he broke into another language, a staccato of sound so fast that the abbess bent her head slightly forward as she tried to follow him.

'Do you speak my language, the language of the children of Éireann?'

She nodded as she translated his words in her mind. For thirty years now the kingdom of Northumbria had been taught Christianity, learning and literacy by the Irish monks from the Holy Island of Iona.

'I speak your language well enough,' she conceded.

The beggar paused and bobbed his head several times in quick succession as if nodding agreement.

'Are you the Abbess Hilda of Streoneshalh?'

The abbess sniffed impatiently.

'I am Hilda.'

'Then hear me, Hilda of Streoneshalh! There is doom in the air. Blood will flow at Streoneshalh before this week is over.'

Abbess Hilda stared at the beggar in surprise. It took her a moment or two to recover from the shock of his statement, delivered in a flat, matter-of-fact tone. His agitation had departed from him. He stood calmly, staring at her with eyes like the opaque grey of a muggy winter's sky.

'Who are you?' she demanded, recovering herself. 'And how do you dare prophesy in this house of God?'

The beggar's thin lips cracked into a smile.

'I am Canna, the son of Canna, and I have read these things in the skies at night. There will soon descend on this abbey many of the great and learned, from Ireland in the west, Dál Riada in the north, Canterbury to the south and Rome in the east. Each will come to debate on the merits of their respective paths to an understanding of the One True God.'

Abbess Hilda made an impatient gesture with a thin hand.

'This much even a house-churl would know, soothsayer,' she responded in annoyance. 'Everyone knows that Oswy, the king, has summoned the leading scholars of the Church to debate whether the teachings of Rome or those of Columba of Iona should be followed in this kingdom. Why bother us with this kitchen prattle?'

The begger grinned viciously. 'But what they do not know is that there is death in the air. Mark me, Abbess Hilda, before the week is out blood will flow under the roof of this great abbey. Blood will stain the cold stone of its floor.'

Abbess Hilda allowed herself to sneer.

'And I suppose, for a price, you will avert the course of this evil?'

To her surprise, the beggar shook his head.

'You must know, daughter of Hereri of Deira, that there is no averting the course of the stars in the sky. There is no way, once their path is discerned, that the path can be altered. On the day the sun is blotted from the sky, blood will flow! I came to warn you, that is all. I have fulfilled my obligation to the Son of God. Take heed of my warning.'

Abbess Hilda stared at the beggar as he closed his mouth firmly and thrust his chin out in defiance. She bit her lip for a moment, disturbed by the man's manner as much as by his message, but then her features re-formed in an expression of annoyance. She glanced towards the sister who had disturbed her.

'Take this insolent churl and have him whipped,' she said curtly.

The two brothers tightened their hold on the beggar's arms and dragged him, struggling, from the chamber.

As the sister turned to leave, Abbess Hilda raised a hand as if to stay her. The sister turned expectantly. The abbess bent forward and lowered her voice.

'Tell them not to whip him too hard and, when they have done, give him a piece of bread from the kitchens, then let him depart in peace.'

The sister raised her eyebrows, hesitated as if to dispute her orders and then nodded hurriedly and withdrew without another word.

From behind the closed doors, the Abbess Hilda could hear the strident voice of the son of Canna still crying:

'Beware, Abbess! On the day the sun is blotted from the sky, blood shall flow in your abbey!'

The man strained forward into the cutting wind, leaning against the dark oak of the ship's high prow, his narrowed eyes searching the distant coastline. The wind moaned softly as it ruffled his dark hair, causing his cheeks to redden and tugging at his brown, homespun woollen habit. The man clutched at the rail with both hands, even though the rise and fall of the deck beneath his feet was gentle over waves made restless by the wailing coastal wind. The seas were choppy, with little white feathers seeming to dance across the grey seascape.

'Is that it, captain?'

He raised his voice to call to the muscular and elderly seaman who stood just behind him.

The man, bright eyed with gnarled features, his skin tanned

almost mahogany by a lifetime of exposure to the sea winds, grimaced.

'That it is, Brother Eadulf. That is your destination. The coast of the kingdom of Oswy.'

The young man addressed as Brother Eadulf turned back to examine the coastline with enthusiasm animating his features.

The vessel had been hugging the coastline now for two days, moving slowly northward and trying to avoid the more tempestuous waves of the North Sea plains. Its captain had been content to steer for the more sheltered bays and coves as he sought a safer haven in the calmer inshore waters. Now he had been forced to head seaward to circumvent a great headland whose long coastline faced out towards the north-east and the open blustery sea.

The captain of the vessel, Stuf by name, from the kingdom of the South Saxons, moved closer to the young monk and pointed.

'Do you see those cliffs there?'

Brother Eadulf ran his curious eyes along the dark sandstone cliffs, which averaged three to four hundred feet in height and gave an impression of formidable steepness. They were guarded by a narrow belt of sand or a scar of rugged rock at their base.

'I do.'

'There now, do you see the black outline on the top of those cliffs? Well, that is the abbey of Hilda, the abbey called Streoneshalh.'

From this distance, Brother Eadulf could not make out much beyond the small black outline that the man had indicated. It stood just before what seemed a crevice in the cliff.

'That is our harbour,' the captain said, as if reading his thoughts. 'That is the valley of a small river named the Esk which empties into the sea just below the abbey. A small township has arisen there in the last ten years and, because of the proximity of Mother Hilda's abbey, the people are already calling it Witebia, "the town of the pure".'

'How soon before we reach it?'

The old captain shrugged. 'Perhaps within the hour. It depends on this shoreward breeze and the running tide. There is a dangerous reef near the harbour entrance that cuts into the sea here for nearly a mile. Nothing dangerous – if one is a good sailor.'

He did not add 'as I am' but Eadulf interpreted the hidden meaning.

Brother Eadulf reluctantly drew his eyes away from the cliff-rimmed coastline.

'I'd better inform His Grace.'

He staggered a little as he turned, then bit his lip to quell the curse that came unbidden to his tongue. He was coming to think of himself as a sailor. Had he not twice crossed the great sea between Britain and the land of Éireann and then only recently crossed the sea between Britain and Gaul, returning from a two-year pilgrimage to Rome itself? But he had discovered that he needed to adjust from land to sea on every voyage. During the three days they had now been sailing from the kingdom of Kent, Brother Eadulf had taken one full day to gain his sea legs. Indeed during the first day he had been sorely ill. He had lain on a straw palliasse, groaning and vomiting until he thought he would surely die of nausea and fatigue. Only on this the third day had he been able to stand without feeling bilious and let the pungent sea breezes clear his head and lungs, making him feel vaguely human again. But every now and then a capricious wave would still send him staggering, to the amusement of Stuf and his crew.

17

Stuf reached out a strong brown calloused hand to steady the young monk as he nearly lost his footing.

Brother Eadulf sheepishly smiled his thanks before turning away.

Stuf watched him go with a grin at his awkward gait. Another week and maybe the young religieux would make a passable sailor, he thought. He would soon have his muscles toned up again by active work. They had obviously been made flaccid by too many years at prayer in darkened cloisters away from the sun. The young monk had the build of a warrior. Stuf shook his head disapprovingly. Christianity was turning Saxon warriors into women.

The old captain had sailed with many cargoes along these shores but this was the first time he had sailed with a party of Christians. A curious group of passengers, by the breath of Woden. Stuf made no secret of the fact that he preferred to worship the old gods, the gods of his fathers. Indeed, his own country of the South Saxons was only now reluctantly allowing those who taught of the God with no name, whose Son was called Christ, to enter their kingdom and preach. Stuf would have preferred the king of the South Saxons to continue to forbid them to teach there. He had no time for Christians or their teachings.

When his time came, he wanted to go to the Hall of Heroes, sword in hand, shouting the sacred name of Woden, as countless generations of his ancestors had done before him, rather than whimper the name of some foreign god in the outlandish tongue of the Romans and expire peacefully in a bed. That was no way for a Saxon warrior to pass into the other life. Indeed, a Saxon was denied any form of afterlife unless he went sword in hand to the Heroes' Hall.

So far as Stuf could make out, this Christ was supposed to be a God of peace, of slaves and old men and women.

Better a manly god, a warrior god, like Tiw or Woden, Thunor, Freyr and Seaxnat, who punished their enemies, welcomed warriors and slew the weak and feeble.

Yet he was a man of business. A ship's master. And the gold of the Christians was as good as anyone's, so it was none of his concern that his cargo was a group of Christian religious.

He turned, back against the wind, and spat over the side, raising his colourless yet bright eyes to the great sail above him. Now was the time to haul down the sail and set the thirty-eight slaves who manned the oars pulling towards the coast. He moved aft along the eighty-foot-long vessel, shouting orders as he went.

Brother Eadulf made his way to the stern to find his companions, a half-dozen men now stretched out on straw palliasses. He spoke to a rotund and jovial-looking man with greying hair.

'We are within sight of Witebia, Brother Wighard,' he said. 'The captain says we should be landing within the hour. Should I tell His Grace?'

The rotund man shook his head.

'His Grace continues to feel unwell,' he replied mournfully.

Brother Eadulf looked concerned.

'Better to get him to the bows where the air might restore him to health.'

Brother Wighard shook his head emphatically.

'I know you have studied the art of the apothecary, Eadulf. But such cures can also kill, my brother. Let His Grace rest a while longer.'

Eadulf hesitated, torn between his own knowledge and belief

and the fact that Wighard was not someone to be disregarded. Wighard was secretary to Deusdedit, Archbishop of Canterbury. And it was Deusdedit who was the subject of their conversation.

The archbishop was elderly and had been ordained by Eugenius I, Bishop of Rome and Father of the Universal Church, to be the head of Rome's mission to the Anglo-Saxon kingdoms in Britain.

But no one could converse with Deusdedit without first obtaining Wighard's approval. Wighard's cherubic-like features hid a coldly calculating mind and an ambition that was keen as a sharpened sword. Thus much had Eadulf discovered during the few days he had been in proximity with the Kentish monk. Wighard was extremely jealous of his position as secretary and confidant of the archbishop.

Deusdedit himself had the honour of being the first Saxon ever to hold the office that Augustine of Rome had inaugurated at Canterbury when he had arrived to convert the pagan Saxons to Christ scarcely seventy years before. Only missionaries from Rome had held the office of chief of Rome's missionaries to the Anglo-Saxons. But Deusdedit, a West Saxon whose original name had been Frithuwine, had proved himself learned, patient and zealous for the teachings of Rome. Frithuwine had been baptized in the new faith as he who had been given, *deditus*, to God, *Deus*. The Holy Father had no qualms in appointing him as his spokesman to the Anglo-Saxon kingdoms and, for nine years now, Deusdedit had guided the fortunes of those Christians who looked to Rome for their spiritual authority.

But Deusdedit had not been in the best of health since the start of the voyage and had spent most of the time apart from the rest being attended only by his secretary Wighard.

Eadulf hesitated before Wighard, wondering whether he

should be more forceful in applying his knowledge of medicine. Then he shrugged.

'Will you then warn His Grace that we will be landing soon?' he asked.

Wighard nodded reassuringly.

'It shall be done. Let me know, Eadulf, if there is any sign of a welcoming reception on the foreshore.'

Brother Eadulf inclined his head. The great sail was already down and stowed and now the groaning oarsmen were heaving on the large wooden oars that propelled the sleek ship. For a few moments, Eadulf stood soaking in the activity on board as the vessel seemed to fairly skim over the waters towards the shoreline. He found himself thinking that it was in just such ships that his ancestors, hardly any time ago, must have crossed the limitless seas to raid and finally settle on this fruitful island of Britain.

The overseers moved down the rows of slaves as they grunted and strained against their oars, encouraging them to greater efforts with cracking whips and oath-filled screams. Now and then there came a sharp cry of pain, as the tongue of a whip made contact with unprotected flesh. Eadulf watched the sailors running hither and thither on their unaccountable tasks with an ill-concealed feeling of envy. He suddenly shook himself as he registered the thought.

He should envy no one, for he had turned his back on his inheritance as hereditary *gerefa*, or magistrate, of the lands of the thane of Seaxmund's Ham when he had reached his twentieth birthday. He had forsworn the old gods of the South Folk, in the kingdom of the East Angles, and followed the new God whose teachings had been brought to them from Ireland. He had been young and enthusiastic when he had fallen in with an

21

Irishman who spoke terrible Saxon but had succeeded in making his purpose known. The Irishman, Fursa by name, had not only taught Eadulf how to read and write his native Saxon, a language which Eadulf had never seen written before, but Fursa imparted to him a knowledge of Irish and Latin in addition to converting him to the knowledge of Christ, the Son of the God with no name.

So apt a pupil had Eadulf become that Fursa had sent him with letters of introduction to his own land of Ireland, firstly to a monastery at Durrow, where students from all four corners of the world were educated and trained. For a year Eadulf had studied in Durrow among the pious brethren there but, finding an interest in the cures and healing powers of the Irish apothecaries, he had gone on to study four years more at the famous college of medicine at Tuaim Brecain, where he had learnt of the legendary Midach, son of Diancecht, who had been slain and from whose three hundred and sixty-five joints and sinews and members of the body three hundred and sixty-five herbs had grown, each herb with the virtue to cure that part of the body from which it had grown.

That learning had awakened in him a thirst for knowledge and a discovery that he also had the ability to solve riddles; puzzles that were like an unknown language to some became an easy conundrum for solution to him. He supposed that the ability had something to do with his having acquired through his family, which held the position of hereditary *gerefa*, an oral knowledge of the law of the Saxons. Sometimes, though not very often, he would regret that, had he not forsworn Woden and Seaxnat, he too would have become *gerefa* to the thane of Seaxmund's Ham.

Like many another Saxon monk he had followed the

teachings of his Irish mentors on the liturgical usages of their church, the dating of the Easter celebration, so central to the Christian faith, and even the style of their tonsure, the shaving of the head to denote that their lives were dedicated unquestioningly to Christ. Only on his return from Ireland had Eadulf encountered those religious who looked to the Archbishop of Canterbury for authority which came from Rome. And he had discovered that Rome's ways were not those of the Irish nor, indeed, of the Britons. Their liturgy was different, the dating of Easter and even the style of their tonsure differed sharply from Rome.

Eadulf had decided to resolve this mystery and so undertook a pilgrimage to Rome where he had stayed two years studying under the masters in that Eternal City. He had returned to the kingdom of Kent bearing the *corona spinea*, a Roman tonsure, on his crown and eager to offer his services to Deusdedit, dedicated to the principles of the Roman teaching.

And now the years of argument between the teachings of the Irish monks and those of Rome were soon to be resolved.

Oswy, the powerful king of Northumbria, whose kingdom had been converted by the Irish monks from the monastery of Columba on the Holy Island of Iona, had decided to summon a great meeting at Streoneshalh abbey where advocates of both the Irish and Roman practices were to argue their cause and Oswy was to sit in judgment and decide, once and for all, whether his kingdom would follow the Irish or whether it would follow Rome. And everyone knew that where Northumbria led, the other Anglo-Saxon kingdoms, from Mercia and East Anglia to Wessex and Sussex, would follow.

Churchmen were gathering on Witebia from the four corners of the earth and soon they would be locked in debate in the hall of the abbey of Streoneshalh, overlooking the tiny harbour.

Eadulf gazed with excitement as the ship steered closer to the towering cliffs and the black outline of the impressive abbey of Hilda of Streoneshalh grew clearer in his vision.

Chapter Three

The Abbess Hilda stood looking down from her window at Streoneshalh to the small harbour at the mouth of the river below the cliffs. The harbour was a flurry of activity, with tiny figures scurrying here and there bent on the tasks of off-loading the several ships that rode at anchor within its shelter.

'His Grace the Archbishop of Canterbury and his party are safely landed,' she observed slowly. 'And I have news that my cousin, the king, is arriving at noon tomorrow. That means our deliberations can begin, as planned, tomorrow evening.'

Behind her, seated before the smouldering fire in her dark chamber, was a hawk-faced man with swarthy features and a slightly autocratic expression. He looked like a man used to command and, moreover, used to being obeyed. He was clad in the robes of an abbot and wore the crucifix and ring of a bishop. His tonsure, whereby the front of his head was shaved back to a line running from ear to ear, immediately proclaimed that he followed the ways of Iona rather than those of Rome.

'That is good,' he said. He spoke in Saxon, slow and accented. 'It is auspicious to start our deliberations on the first day of a new month.'

Abbess Hilda turned from the window and smiled nervously at him.

'There has never been a gathering of such importance, my lord Colmán.'

There was a suppressed tone of excitement in her voice.

Colmán's thin mouth twitched in a slight sneer.

'I suppose that is true for Northumbria. Speaking for myself, I can recall many important synods and assemblies. Druim Ceatt, for example, where our saintly Colmcille presided, was an important assembly for our faith in Ireland.'

The abbess decided to ignore the slightly condescending tone of the Abbot of Lindisfarne. It had been three years since Colmán had arrived from Iona to succeed Finán as bishop of Northumbria. But the two men were totally dissimilar in attitudes. The saintly Finán, though considered by some a man of fierce temper, was sincere, courteous and eager to teach, treating everyone as equals. He it was who had succeeded in converting and baptizing the fierce pagan king Peada of the Middle Angles, a son of the scourge of all Christians, Penda of Mercia. But Colmán was a man of different temperament to Finán. He seemed to treat both Angles and Saxons patronisingly, his tone and words often sneering at the fact that they were but newly come to the teachings of Christ and implying that therefore they should accept everything he said without question. Nor did he disguise his pride in the fact that it was the monks of Iona who had had to teach the Angles of Northumbria the art of lettering and how to read and how to write. The new bishop of Northumbria was an authoritarian and made his dislike of anyone who questioned his authority immediately known.

'Who will be making the opening arguments for the teachings of Colmcille?' asked Hilda.

The abbess made no secret that she followed the teachings of Colmcille's church and disagreed with the arguments of Rome. As a young girl, Hilda had been baptised by the Roman Paulinus, who had been sent from Canterbury to convert the

Northumbrians to Christ and Rome when she was a babe in arms. But it had been Aidán, the first saintly missionary from Iona, who had succeeded in the conversion of Northumbria where Paulinus had failed and who had persuaded Hilda to enter the religious life. Such was her aptitude for piety and teaching that Aidán had ordained her abbess of a foundation at Heruteu. Her enthusiasm for the faith caused her to have built a new abbey called Streoneshalh, 'the great hall by the seashore', seven years before. During the seven years, a complex of magnificent buildings had grown up under her guidance. Northumbria had never seen such an impressive structure. And Streoneshalh was now regarded as one of the most important centres of learning in the kingdom. Because of its renown, the king, Oswy, had chosen it as the venue for his debate between the followers of Iona and those of Rome.

Colmán folded his hands complacently before him.

'I have, as you know, gathered here many people of knowledge and talent to argue the case of our Church,' he said. 'Foremost among them is the Abbess Étain of Kildare. At times like these I find that I am but a plain-spoken man with little guile or scholarship. In such debates the plain-spoken advocate is at a disadvantage against those who use wit and humour to convince their audience. The Abbess Étain is a woman of much wisdom and she will open the proceedings on our behalf.'

Abbess Hilda nodded approvingly.

'I have already conversed with Étain of Kildare. Her wit is as quick and sharp as she is attractive.'

Colmán sniffed disapprovingly. The Abbess Hilda raised a delicate hand to hide her smile. She knew that Colmán had little time for women. He was one of the ascetics who argued that marriage was incompatible with spiritual life. Among most of

27

the Christian clergy of Ireland, and among the Britons, marriage and procreation was not regarded as a sin. Indeed, many of the religious houses were communities of brothers and sisters in Christ who cohabited, working together for the furtherance of the faith. Hilda's own foundation of Streoneshalh itself was a 'double house' in that both men and women lived and dedicated their lives and children to the work of God. But while Rome accepted that even their chief apostle Peter had married, and that Philip the apostle not only married but begat four daughters, it was known that the bishops of Rome favoured Paul's preference for celibacy for all their religious. Had not Paul written to the Corinthians that while marriage and procreation was no sin, it was not as good as celibacy among the brethren? Yet most Roman clergy, even bishops, presbyters, abbots and deacons, continued to be married in the traditional manner. Only ascetics sought to deny themselves all the temptations of the flesh and Colmán was such a man.

'I suppose, even with Deusdedit of Canterbury here, that Wilfrid of Ripon will open for the Roman faction? I am told that Deusdedit is no great orator.' Colmán was changing the subject.

Abbess Hilda hesitated and shook her head.

'I have heard that Agilbert, the Frankish bishop of Wessex, will head their council.'

Colmán raised his eyebrows in surprise.

'I thought that Agilbert had taken offence with the king of Wessex and left for Frankia?'

'No. He has been staying with Wilfrid at Ripon for several months. After all, it was Agilbert who converted and baptised Wilfrid to the faith. They are close friends.'

'I know of Agilbert. A Frankish aristocrat. His cousin Audo

is the Frankish prince who founded a religious house at Jouarre with his sister Telchilde as its abbess. Agilbert is well connected and powerful. A man to have a care of.'

Colmán seemed about to amplify his warning when there came a knock at the door.

In answer to Abbess Hilda's response, the door swung open.

A young religieuse stood there, hands demurely folded before her. She was tall, with a well-proportioned figure which, the keen eyes of the abbess saw, vibrated youthful exuberance. Rebellious strands of red hair streaked from beneath her headdress. She had an attractive face – not beautiful, thought Hilda, but attractive. The abbess suddenly realised that her scrutiny was being returned by a pair of watchful bright eyes. She could not make out whether they were blue or green in the changing light that seemed to emanate from them.

'What is it, child?' inquired the abbess.

The young woman's chin came up a trifle pugnaciously and she introduced herself in Irish.

'I have just arrived at the abbey, Mother Abbess, and have been asked to report my presence to you and the Bishop Colmán. My name is Fidelma of Kildare.'

Before Abbess Hilda had time to respond, questioning why a young Irish religieuse should be worthy to be asked to make her presence known to them, the Bishop Colmán had risen from his chair and had taken a stride towards the girl with an outstretched hand of welcome. Hilda stared at him, her mouth opening slightly in her astonishment. It was curiously unlike the haughty misogynism of Colmán to rise up to greet a young sister of the order.

'Sister Fidelma!' Colmán's voice was animated. 'Your reputation precedes you. I am Colmán.'

29

The young religieuse took his hand and inclined her head slightly in deference to his rank. Hilda had long since become accustomed to the lack of servility that the Irish displayed towards their superiors, unlike the deep reverence Saxons displayed towards their betters.

'You do me honour, your grace. I was not aware that I was possessed of a reputation.'

The keen eyes of Abbess Hilda saw an amused smile play around the mouth of the younger woman. It was hard to tell whether the girl was being modest or merely mocking. Again the bright eyes – Hilda was sure they were green now – turned inquiringly in her direction.

Colmán turned in some embarrassment at his neglect of the Mother Abbess.

'This is the Abbess Hilda of Streoneshalh.'

Sister Fidelma moved forward and reached to incline her head over the abbess's ring.

'You are most welcome here, Fidelma of Kildare,' Hilda acknowledged, 'though I confess that my lord the Bishop of Lindisfarne has placed me at a disadvantage. I stand in ignorance of your reputation.'

Hilda glanced at the hawk-faced Colmán as if seeking comment.

'Sister Fidelma is a *dálaigh* of the Brehon courts of Ireland,' explained Colmán.

Abbess Hilda frowned.

'I am not acquainted with this expression – *daw-lee*.' She rendered the term as closely as she could in her own phonetics. She stared at the girl as if challenging her to an explanation.

Sister Fidelma's cheeks reddened slightly and her voice was slightly breathless as she sought to explain.

'I am an advocate, qualified to plead before the law courts of my country, to prosecute or defend those summoned to answer to the law before our judges, the Brehons.'

Colmán nodded. 'Sister Fidelma is qualified to the degree of *anruth*, only one degree below the highest qualification in our land. Already, even among the brethren in Lindisfarne, we have heard tales of how she was able to solve a mystery oppressing the High King at Tara.'

Fidelma gave a deprecating shrug of her shoulders.

'My lord bishop does me too much honour,' she said. 'Anyone could have resolved the mystery given time.'

There was no false modesty in her voice, just a plain statement of her opinion.

'So?' Abbess Hilda stared curiously at her. 'A qualified advocate, so young and a woman? Alas, in our culture women could not aspire to such a position, which is reserved only for men.'

Sister Fidelma nodded slowly.

'I have heard, Mother Abbess, that women among the Angles and Saxons suffer many disadvantages compared with their sisters in Ireland.'

'That may be so, Fidelma,' Colmán interrupted with an air of condescension. 'But remember what the Good Book says: "What went you into the wilderness to see, a man clothed in fine garments?"'

Hilda cast a glance of annoyance at Colmán. His comparison of Northumbria to a wilderness was another demonstration of his superior attitudes, which had increasingly annoyed her over the last three years. She nearly made a rejoinder, but hesitated and turned back to Fidelma. She was disconcerted to find the bright green eyes fixed penetratingly on her as if the girl could read her thoughts.

Their eyes locked for some time, as if challenging each other. It was Bishop Colmán who broke the silence.

'And was your journey without incident, sister?'

Sister Fidelma turned, memory suddenly coming back.

'Alas, no. Not many miles from here, where a man called Wulfric claims that he is lord—'

Abbess Hilda frowned.

'I know the man and the place. Wulfric of Frihop, whose hall lies some fifteen miles to the east. What of it, sister?'

'We found a brother hanging from a tree at the crossroads. Wulfric claimed the monk had been executed for insulting him. Our brother wore the tonsure of our Church, my lord bishop, and Wulfric did not conceal that he came from your own house of Lindisfarne.'

Colmán bit his lip and suppressed an intake of breath.

'It must be Brother Aelfric. He was returning from a mission to Mercia and expected to join us here any day now.'

'But why would Aelfric insult the thane of Frihop?' demanded Abbess Hilda.

'By your leave, Mother Abbess,' interrupted Sister Fidelma. 'I had the impression that this was merely an excuse. The argument was about the differences between Iona and Rome and it would seem that Wulfric and his friends favour Rome. This Brother Aelfric was apparently manoeuvred into the insult and then hanged for it.'

Hilda examined the girl sharply.

'You do have a legal, inquiring mind, Fidelma of Kildare. But, as you well know, to hypothesise is one thing. To prove your contention is quite another.'

Sister Fidelma smiled softly.

'I did not mean to present my impression as a legal argument, Mother Abbess. Merely that I think you would do well to have a care of Wulfric of Frihop. If he can get away with the judicial murder of a religious simply because he supports the liturgy of Colmcille then every one of us who comes to this abbey to argue in that cause may be in danger.'

'Wulfric of Frihop is known to us. He is Alhfrith's right hand man and Alhfrith is king of Deira,' Hilda replied sharply. Then she sighed and shrugged and added in a softer tone, 'And are you here to contribute to the debate, Fidelma of Kildare?'

The young religieuse gave a modest chuckle.

'That I should dare to raise my voice among so many eloquent orators who have gathered would be an impertinence. No, Mother Abbess. I am here merely to advise on law. Our church, whose teachings your people follow, is subject to the laws of our people and the Abbess Étain, who will be speaking for our church, asked me to attend in case there is need for some advice or explanation in this matter. That is all.'

'Then you are truly well come to this place, for your counsel is to aid us in arriving at the one great truth,' replied Hilda. 'And your counsel concerning Wulfric will be noted, have no fear. I shall speak concerning the matter with my cousin, King Oswy, when he arrives tomorrow. Iona or Rome, both are under the protection of the royal house of Northumbria.'

Sister Fidelma grimaced wryly. Royal protection had not helped Brother Aelfric. She decided, however, to change the subject.

'I am forgetting one of the purposes of my disturbing you.'

She reached within her habit and brought out two packages.

'I have journeyed here from Ireland through Dál Riada and the Holy Island of Iona.'

Abbess Hilda's eyes grew misty.

'You have stayed on the Holy Island where the great Columba lived and worked?'

'Well, tell us, did you meet with the abbot?' asked Colmán, interested.

Fidelma nodded.

'I saw Cumméne the Fair and he sends greetings to you both and these letters.' She held out the packages. 'He makes a strong plea for Northumbria to adhere to the liturgy practised by Colmcille. Further, as a gift to the abbey of Streoneshalh, Cumméne Finn has sent a gift by me. I have left it with your *librarius*. It is a copy of Cumméne's own book on the miraculous powers of Colmcille, of saintly name.'

Abbess Hilda took her package from Fidelma's hand.

'The Abbot of Iona is wise and generous. How I envy you your visit to such a sanctified place. We owe so much to that miraculous little island. I shall look forward to studying the book later. But this letter draws my attention . . .'

Sister Fidelma inclined her head.

'Then I will withdraw and leave you to study the letters from Cumméne Finn.'

Colmán was already deep into his letter and scarcely looked up as she bowed her head and withdrew.

Outside, in the sandstone-flagged cloisters, Sister Fidelma paused and smiled to herself. She found herself in a curiously exhilarated mood in spite of the length of her journey and her fatigue. She had never travelled beyond the confines of Ireland before and now she had not only crossed the grey, stormy sea to Iona, but travelled through the kingdom of the Dál Riada, through the country of Rheged to the land of the Northumbrians

– three different cultures and countries. There was much to take in, much to be considered.

Pressing for her immediate attention was the fact of her arrival at Streoneshalh on the eve of the highly anticipated debate between the churchmen of Rome and those of her own culture and she would not only witness it but be a part of it. Sister Fidelma was possessed of a spirit of time and place, of history and mankind's place in its unfolding tapestry. She often reflected that, had she not studied law under the great Brehon Morann of Tara, she would have studied history. But law she had studied. Had she not, perhaps the Abbess Étain of Kildare would not have invited her to join her delegation, which had left for Lindisfarne at the invitation of Bishop Colmán.

The summons had come to Fidelma while she had been on a pilgrimage to Armagh. In fact, Fidelma had been surprised at it, for when she had left her own house of Kildare Étain had not been abbess. She had known Étain for many years and knew her reputation as a scholar and orator. Étain, in retrospect, had been the correct choice to take the office of abbess on the death of her predecessor. The word had come to Fidelma that Étain had already left for the kingdom of the Saxons and so Fidelma had decided to proceed firstly to the monastery of Bangor and then cross the stormy strait to Dál Riada. Then from Iona she had joined Brother Taran and his companions, who had been setting out on a mission to Northumbria.

There had been only one other female in the band and that had been Brother Taran's fellow Pict, Sister Gwid. She was a large raw-boned girl, giving an impression of clumsy awkwardness, her hands and feet seemingly too large. Yet she seemed always anxious to please and did not mind doing any work of drudgery no matter how heavy the task. Fidelma had been astonished to find that Sister Gwid, after her conversion to Christ, had studied at Iona before crossing to spend a year in Ireland, studying at the abbey of Emly during the time when Étain had been a simple instructress there. Fidelma was more than surprised to find that Gwid had specialized in Greek and a study of the meaning of the writings of the apostles.

Sister Gwid confided to Fidelma that she had been on her return journey to Iona when she, too, had been sent a message from the Abbess Étain to join her in Northumbria to act as her secretary during the debate that was to take place. No one objected, therefore, to Gwid and Fidelma joining the party led by Taran on the hazardous journey south from Iona to the kingdom of Oswy.

The journey with Brother Taran had simply confirmed Fidelma's dislike of the Pictish religieux. He was a vain man, darkly handsome according to some notions, but with looks which made Fidelma regard him as a pompous bantam cock, strutting and preening. Yet, as a man with knowledge of the ways of the Angles and Saxons, she would not argue with his ability in easing their path through the hostile land. But as a man she found him weak and vacillating, one minute attempting to impress, another hopelessly inadequate – as at their confrontation with Wulfric.

Fidelma gave a mental shake of her head. So much for Taran. There were other things to think of now. New sights, new sounds and new people.

She gave a startled 'oh' as she walked around a corner and collided with a thickset monk.

Only the fact that he reached out strong hands and caught her saved her from stumbling backwards and falling.

For a moment the young man and woman stared at each other.

It was a moment of pure chemistry. Some empathy passed from the dark brown eyes of the man into Fidelma's green ones. Then Fidelma noticed the tonsure of Rome on the young man's crown and realised that he must be one of the Roman delegation and probably a Saxon.

'Forgive me,' she said stiffly, choosing Latin to address him. Realising that he still grasped her forearms, she gently pulled away.

The young monk let go immediately and took a step back, fighting the confusion on his face. He succeeded.

'*Mea culpa*,' he replied gravely, striking his left breast with his right clenched fist, yet with a smile flickering behind his eyes.

Fidelma hesitated and then bowed her head in acknowledgment before moving on, wondering why the face of the young Saxon intrigued her. Perhaps it was the quiet humour that lurked in his gaze. Her experience with Saxons was limited but she had not credited them with being a humorous people. To meet one who was not dour and brooding and took insult at the slightest thing, which, in her experience, all Saxons did, fascinated her. In general, she had found them morose and quick-tempered; they were a people who lived by the sword and, with few exceptions, believed in their gods of war rather than the God of Peace.

She suddenly became annoyed with her thoughts. Odd that a brief encounter could stir such silly notions.

She turned into the part of the abbey made over for the accommodation of those visitors attending the debate, the *domus hospitale*. Most of the religious were accommodated in several large *dormitoria*, but for the many abbots, abbesses, bishops and other dignitaries a special series of *cubicula* had been set aside as individual quarters. Sister Fidelma herself had been lucky to have been allocated one of these *cubicula*, no more than a tiny cell eight feet by six with a simple wooden cot, a table and chair. Fidelma supposed that she had the intercession of Bishop Colmán to thank for such hospitality. She opened the door of her *cubiculum* and paused in surprise on the threshold.

A slightly built, good-looking woman rose from the chair with extended hands.

'Étain!' exclaimed Sister Fidelma, recognising the abbess of Kildare.

The Abbess Étain was an attractive woman in her early thirties; the daughter of an Eoghanacht king of Cashel, she had given up a world of indolence and pleasure after her husband had been killed in battle. Her star had risen rapidly, for she was soon acknowledged to be possessed of such skill and oratorical knowledge that she had been able to argue theology on the same footing with the archbishop of Armagh and all the bishops and abbots of Ireland. It was in tribute to her reputation that she had been appointed as abbess of St Brigit's great foundation at Kildare.

Fidelma moved forward and bowed her head, but Étain took both her hands in a warm embrace. They had been friends for several years before Étain had been elevated to her present position, since when neither had seen the other, for Fidelma had been travelling through Ireland.

'It is good to see you again, even in this outlandish country.' Étain spoke with a soft, rich soprano voice. Fidelma had often thought it was like a musical instrument which could sharpen in anger, become vibrant with indignation or be used sweetly, as it was now. 'I am glad your journey here was safe, Fidelma.'

Fidelma grinned mischievously.

'Should it have been otherwise, when we journey in the name and under the protection of the one true God?'

Étain returned her smile.

'At least I journeyed with temporal assistance. I came with some brothers from Durrow. We landed in Rheged and were joined by a group of brethren from that kingdom of Britons. Then, at the border of Rheged and Northumbria, we were officially met by Athelnoth and a band of Saxon warriors who escorted us here. Have you met Athelnoth?'

Fidelma shook her head.

'I have only arrived here within the last hour myself, Mother Abbess,' she said.

Étain pursed her lips and grimaced disapprovingly.

'Athelnoth was sent to greet and escort me by King Oswy and the Bishop of Northumbria. He was outspoken against Irish teachings and our influence in Northumbria to the point of insulting us. He is an ordained priest but one who argues for Rome. Once I even had to prevent one of our brothers from physically assaulting Athelnoth, so blunt is his criticism of our liturgy.'

Fidelma shrugged indifferently.

'From what I hear, Mother Abbess, the debate over our respective liturgies is causing a great deal of tension and argument. I would not have thought it possible that such emotions would be aroused by a discussion on the correct date of the Paschal ceremony—'

Étain grimaced.

'You must learn to refer to it here as Easter.'

Fidelma frowned.

'Easter?'

'The Saxons have accepted most of our teaching of Christian

faith but as for the Paschal feast they insist on naming it after their pagan goddess of fertility, Eostre, whose rituals fall at the time of the Spring equinox. There is much that is still pagan in this land. You will find that many still follow the ways of their old gods and goddesses and that their hearts are still filled with hate and war.'

The Abbess Étain suddenly shivered.

'I feel there is much that is oppressive here, Fidelma. Oppressive and menacing.'

Sister Fidelma smiled reassuringly.

'Whenever there is a conflict of opinion, then human tensions rise and give way to fear. I do not think we need worry. There will be much posturing during the verbal conflict. But once we have reached a resolution then all will be forgotten and forgiven.' She hesitated. 'When does the debate begin?'

'The King Oswy and his entourage will not arrive at the abbey until noon tomorrow. The Abbess Hilda has told me that, all being well, she will allow the opening arguments to commence in the late afternoon. Bishop Colmán has asked me to make the opening arguments for our church.'

Fidelma thought she saw some anxiety on the Abbess Étain's features.

'Does that worry you, Mother Abbess?'

Étain suddenly smiled and shook her head.

'No. I revel in debate and argument. I have good companions to advise me, such as yourself.'

'That reminds me,' Fidelma replied, 'I had Sister Gwid as my travelling companion. An intelligent girl whose looks give the wrong impression. She tells me that she is to act as your secretary and Greek translator.'

An indefinable expression showed on Abbess Étain's face

for a split second. Fidelma could not make up her mind whether it was anger or a lesser emotion.

'Young Gwid can be an annoying person. A little like a puppy dog, unassertive and too sycophantic at times. But she is an excellent Greek scholar, though I think she spends too much of her time admiring the poems of Sappho rather than construing the Gospels.' She sounded disapproving, but then shrugged. 'Yes, I do have good companions to advise me. But there is something else that makes me feel uneasy. I think it is the atmosphere of hostility and dislike I feel from those of the Roman faction. Agilbert the Frank, for example, who has trained many years in Ireland but has a deep devotion to Rome, and that man Wilfrid, who even refused to greet me when the Abbess Hilda introduced us—'

'Who is Wilfrid? I find these Saxon names hard to understand.'

Étain sighed.

'He is a young man, but one who leads the Rome faction here in Northumbria. I believe he is the son of some noble. By all accounts he has a sharp temper. He has been to Rome and Canterbury and was taken into the faith by Agilbert, who ordained him as a priest. He was given the monastery of Ripon by the petty king of the area, who threw out two of our own brethren, Eata and Cuthbert, who were joint abbots there. This Wilfred seems to be our fiercest enemy, a passionate advocate of the Roman liturgy. Alas, I fear we have many enemies here.'

Sister Fidelma found herself suddenly visualising the face of the young Saxon monk whom she had just bumped into.

'Yet surely not all those who support Rome are our enemies?'

The abbess smiled meditatively.

41

'Maybe you are right, Fidelma. And maybe I am simply nervous after all.'

'A lot depends on your opening arguments tomorrow,' agreed Fidelma.

'There is something more, though—' Étain was hesitant.

Fidelma waited patiently, watching the expression on the abbess's face. It seemed that Étain found it difficult to formulate what she had in mind.

'Fidelma,' she said with a sudden rush, 'I am disposed to take a husband.'

Fidelma's eyes widened but she said nothing. Clergy, even bishops, took spouses; even the religious of houses, whether mixed or not, could have wives and husbands, under Brehon law and custom. But the position of an abbot and abbess was in a different category for they were usually bound to celibacy. Such was the rule at Kildare. It was the Irish custom that the coarb, or successor to the founder of an abbey, should always be chosen in the kindred of the founder. Since abbots and abbesses were not expected to have direct issue, the successor was chosen from a collateral branch. But if, in the collateral branches, no religious was found fit to be elected to such a position, then a secular member of the family of the coarb was elected as lay abbot or abbess. Étain claimed relation to the family of Brigit of Kildare.

'It would mean giving up Kildare and returning to being an ordinary religieuse,' Fidelma pointed out eventually when Étain made no further comment.

Étain nodded. 'I have thought of this long and hard on my journey here. To cohabit with a stranger will be difficult, especially after one has been alone for so long. Yet when I arrived here, I realised that my mind was made up. I have exchanged the traditional betrothal gifts. The matter is now decided.'

Instinctively Fidelma reached out a hand, caught Étain's slim one and squeezed it.

'Then I am happy for you, Étain; happy in your certainty. Who is your stranger?'

Étain smiled shyly.

'If I felt able to tell only one person, it would be you, Fidelma. But I feel that it should be my secret, and his, until after this debate. When this great assembly is over, then you shall know, for I will announce my resignation from Kildare.'

They were distracted by a growing noise of shouting from beyond the window of the *cubiculum*.

'What on earth is that?' demanded Sister Fidelma, frowning at the raucous tones. 'There seems some sort of scuffle taking place beneath the abbey wall.'

Abbess Étain sighed.

'I have seen so many scuffles between our religious and the brethren of Rome since I came here. I presume it is another such. Grown men resorting to personal insults and punches simply because they disagree with each other over the interpretation of the Word of God. It is sad that men, and women, of the cloth become as spiteful children when they cannot agree.'

Sister Fidelma went to the window and leant forward.

A little way off a beggar was surrounded by a crowd of people, mostly peasants so far as she could tell from their dress, although a few wore the brown habit of the brethren. They seemed to be taunting and deriding a poorly dressed man, presumably a beggar from his clothes, whose voice was raised in raucous tones which seemed to drown out their jibes.

Sister Fidelma raised an eyebrow.

'The beggar seems to be one of our countrymen, Mother Abbess,' she said.

The Abbess Étain moved forward to join her.

'A beggar. They suffer greatly from the arrogance of a crowd.'

'But listen to what he says.'

The two women strained to catch the rasping tones of the beggar. The voice was raised loudly.

'I tell you, tomorrow the sun shall be blotted from the heavens and when that time comes there shall be blood staining the floor of this abbey. Beware! Beware, I tell you! I see blood in this place!'

Chapter Four

The tolling of the abbey's great bell announced the approach of the official opening of the synod. At least, Sister Fidelma mused, both sides seemed to accept the Greek term *synodos* to describe this assembly of Christian dignitaries. The synod of Streoneshalh promised to be one of the most important meetings for the churches of both Iona and Rome.

Sister Fidelma took her seat in the *sacrarium* of the abbey, for the chapel, the largest chamber, had been given over for the use of the assembly. There was a general hubbub of what seemed to be countless people all talking at once. The vast stone-walled *sacrarium*, with its high, vaulted roof, acted as a means of increasing the sound by providing an echo. Yet, in spite of the spaciousness, Fidelma had a momentary feeling of claustrophobia at the sight and smells of the numerous religious packed along the pews. On the left side of the *sacrarium*, seated in rows on dark oak benches, there had assembled all those who supported the rule of Columba. On the right side of the *sacrarium* were gathered those who argued for Rome.

Fidelma had never seen so large a concourse of leaders of the Church of Christ before. As well as religious in their distinctive dress, there were many whose rich apparel proclaimed them to be nobles from a variety of kingdoms.

'Impressive, isn't it?'

Fidelma looked up and found Brother Taran slipping into

the seat beside her. She groaned inwardly. She had been hoping to avoid the pretentious brother. His company was a little too exhausting after their long journey from Iona.

'I have not seen such an impressive gathering since I sat at the Great Assembly of Tara last year,' she replied coldly when he asked her what she thought of the gathering. Also impressive, she added silently to herself, was the putrescence of the body odours which were permeating the *sacrarium* in spite of the strategically placed censers in which incense had been lit to fumigate the proceedings. It was a sad reflection on the hygiene of the religious of Northumbria, she thought disapprovingly. Among the brethren of Ireland, bathing was a daily occurrence and every ninth day a visit was made to the communal *tigh 'n alluis*, the sweating house, where a turf fire caused people to sweat profusively before they plunged into cold water and were then rubbed warm.

She suddenly found herself thinking about the Saxon monk she had encountered on the previous evening. He had the odour of cleanliness and a faint fragrance of herbs about him. At least he, among the Saxons, knew how to keep clean. She wrinkled her nose disapprovingly as she peered around, wondering if she could spot the monk on the Roman benches.

Sister Gwid suddenly appeared, red-faced as always, as if she had been running, and slipped on to the bench on the other side of Fidelma.

'You nearly missed the opening of the synod.' Fidelma smiled as the awkward girl struggled to catch her breath. 'But shouldn't you be seated with Abbess Étain, among the benches of the advocates, to help her as her secretary?'

Sister Gwid grimaced negatively.

'She said she will call me if I am needed today,' she replied.

Fidelma turned her attention back to the head of the *sacrarium*. A dais had been raised at one end on which a regal chair had been set. It stood empty and obviously awaited the arrival of King Oswy himself. There were several smaller chairs clustered around, slightly behind it, and these were already filled with an assortment of men and women. Their clothing and jewellery bespoke riches and position.

Fidelma suddenly realised that Brother Taran, for all his failings, might prove useful to her by pointing out who people were. After all, it was his second mission to Northumbria and he was surely well informed.

'Easy enough,' replied the Pict when she indicated the people seated around the regal chair. 'They are all members of Oswy's immediate family. That is the queen just taking her seat now.'

Fidelma looked at the stern-faced woman who was seating herself next to the throne. This was Eanflaed. Taran was nothing loath to give details. Eanflaed's father had been a previous king of Northumbria but her mother had been a Kentish princess and she had been taken to Kent to be brought up to follow Roman ways. Never far away was her private chaplain, a priest named Romanus from Kent, who kept strictly to the dictates of Rome. He was a short, dark man, with black curly hair and features that Fidelma would have described as mean. The eyes were somehow too close together and his lips too thin. In fact, so Taran said, in a knowing tone, rumour had it that it was pressure from Eanflaed, backed by Romanus, which had forced Oswy to initiate the debate at all.

Eanflaed was Oswy's third wife and he had married her just after he had succeeded to the throne some twenty years before. His first wife had been a Briton, Rhiainfellt, a princess of

Rheged, whose people followed the ways and rituals of the church of Iona. But Rhiainfellt had died. His second marriage had been to Fín, daughter of Colmán Rimid, the northern Uí Néill High King of Ireland.

At that information, Sister Fidelma expressed surprise, for she had not known of Oswy's relationship to the High King.

'What happened to that wife? Another death?' she asked.

It was Sister Gwid who had the answer.

'A divorce,' she said, as if approvingly. 'Fín realised how much she hated Northumbria and Oswy. She had a son by Oswy, named Aldfrith, but took the child back to Ireland with her. Her son has been educated at the foundation of the blessed Comgall, the friend of Colmcille, at Bangor. He is now quite a renowned poet in the Irish tongue under the name Flann Fína. Aldfrith has renounced all rights to be considered for the kingship of Northumbria.'

Sister Fidelma shook her head.

'The Saxons have a law called primogeniture, that the first born inherits. Was this Aldfrith, then, the first born?'

Sister Gwid shrugged indifferently, but Taran pointed to the dais.

'See the young man seated directly behind Eanflaed, the one with the blond hair and the scar on his face?'

Fidelma glanced in the direction Taran indicated. She wondered why she felt an instant dislike of the young man whom he had pointed out.

'Well, that is Alhfrith, Oswy's son by Rhiainfellt, his first wife, who is now the petty king of the southern province of Deira. We spoke of him yesterday. The talk is that he is pro-Roman and in rebellion against his father's adherence to Iona. He has already expelled the monks faithful to the rule of

Colmcille from the monastery of Ripon and given it to his friend, Wilfrid.'

'And Wulfric of Frihop is his right hand,' muttered Fidelma. The young man looked surly and aggressive. Perhaps that was cause enough to dislike the arrogant manner in which he sprawled in his chair.

The grim-faced woman next to Alhfrith was apparently his wife Cyneburh, the still-embittered daughter of the slain Penda of Mercia, who had been killed in battle by Oswy. Next to her, of an equally sour disposition, sat Alhflaed, the sister of Alhfrith, who had married Peada, the son of Penda of Mercia. Here Taran grew quite animated in his explanations. Alhfrith, according to him, had been responsible for the murder of Peada a year after Peada had agreed to become petty king of Mercia giving his allegiance to Oswy. Rumour had it that Alhfrith also had his ambitious eye on the kingship of Mercia.

Next to Oswy's current wife, Eanflaed, sat their first-born son, Ecgfrith. At eighteen years of age he was a sullen, brooding young man. His dark eyes were restless and he kept shifting in his seat. Taran said that it was his ambition to fill the throne of Oswy before he was much older and he was filled with envy for his elder half-brother Alhfrith, who was heir to the throne under law. The only other child of Oswy in attendance was Aelflaed. She had been born in the year when Oswy had achieved his great victory over Penda and, as a thank-offering, had been dedicated to God and entrusted to the Abbess Hilda to bring up at Streoneshalh as a virgin devoted to Christ.

Brother Taran informed Fidelma that Oswy had two more children – a daughter, Osthryth, now five years old, and a son, Aelfwine, aged three. These were too young to attend in the *sacrarium*.

49

Finally Sister Fidelma interrupted the enthusiastic brother's monologue on the personalities.

'All this knowledge is too much for me to take in at one sitting. I shall get to know who is who as the debate continues. But there are so many people.'

Brother Taran nodded complacently.

'It is an important debate, sister. Not only is the royal house of Northumbria represented but, see, there is Domangart of Dál Riada together with Drust, the king of Picts, and there are princes and representatives of Cenwealh of Wessex, Eorcenberht of Kent, Wulfhere of Mercia and—'

'Enough!' protested Fidelma. 'I will never master all these outlandish Saxon names. I will call on you when I need your knowledge.'

As Fidelma sat studying the sea of faces the doors of the hall opened and a man entered carrying a banner. This, Taran promptly informed her, was the *thuff*, the standard that always preceded the king to announce his presence. Then came a tall handsome man, well muscled, with flaxen hair and long moustaches, dressed in rich and elaborate clothing with a circle of gold on his head.

So Fidelma, for the first time, caught sight of the king of Northumbria, Oswy. Oswy had become king when his brother Oswald had been slain by Penda and his British allies at Maserfeld and, within a few years, had taken his revenge on Penda, slaughtering him and his followers. And now Oswy was acclaimed *Bretwalda*, a title, Taran told her, that proclaimed him overlord of all the kingdoms of the Angles and Saxons.

Fidelma examined the tall man intently. She knew his previous history well. Oswy and his brothers had been driven from Northumbria when they were children, and their father, the king, had been slain by Edwin, who had usurped the throne. The exiled royal children had been brought up in the kingdom of Dál Riada, converting from paganism to Christianity in the Holy Island of Iona. When Oswy's elder brother, Oswald, regained the throne and brought them out of exile, he had sent to Iona and asked for missionaries to teach his people, bringing them forth from paganism and teaching them how to form letters and read and write. It seemed, to Fidelma, that Oswy would naturally side with the church of Iona.

But, she recalled, in this debate, while Oswy was chief judge, he would probably be under pressure from his heirs and the royal representatives of all the lesser kings who would sit as a jury during the debates.

Behind Oswy, in the procession which made its way from the main doors around the hall to the seats on the dais, first came Colmán , as Oswy's bishop as well as chief abbot; next came Hilda and another woman whose features seemed similar to Oswy's.

'That is Oswy's eldest sister, Abbe,' whispered Gwid, against the quiet that had descended in the hall. 'She was in exile in Iona and is a firm adherent of the liturgy of Colmcille. She is abbess at Coldingham, which is north from here. It is a double house where men and women can dedicate their lives and families to the path of Christ.

'It has a dubious reputation, I hear tell,' Sister Gwid said. Her voice dropped even lower than usual in disapproval. 'There is talk that the abbey is given over to feasting, drinking and other entertainments.'

Sister Fidelma made no response. There were many *conhospitae* or double houses. There was little wrong in that. She disliked the way Sister Gwid seemed to imply that there was something wicked about such a way of life. She knew some ascetics disapproved and argued that all who dedicated their lives to the service of Christ should remain celibate. She had even heard that some groups of ascetics cohabited without sexual contact as a demonstration of the strength of their faith and the supernatural character of chastity, a practice that John Chrysostom of Antioch had declaimed against.

Fidelma was not against religious cohabiting. She shared her belief that the religious should marry and procreate with the majority of those who followed Rome, the churches of the Britons and the Irish and even the eastern churches. Only ascetics believed in celibacy and demanded segregation of the sexes among the religious. She had not suspected Sister Gwid of being an ascetic or supporting their cause. She herself accepted that the time would come when she would find someone to share her work with. But there was plenty of time and she had, as yet, met no man who had attracted her enough to cause her to contemplate making a decision. Perhaps such a decision might never need be made. Life was like that. In a way, she envied the certainty of her friend Étain in making her decision to resign from Kildare and marry again.

She turned to concentrate on the procession.

An elderly man came next, his face yellow and glistening with sweat. He leant heavily on the arm of a younger man whose face immediately put Fidelma in mind of the cunning of a wolf, in spite of its cherubic, chubby roundness. The eyes were too close together and forever searching as if seeking out enemies. The old man was clearly ill. She turned to Taran.

'Deusdedit, Archbishop of Canterbury, and his secretary, Wighard,' he said before she had even articulated the question.

'They walk there as the chief representatives of those who oppose us.'

'And the very old man who brings up the rear of the procession?'

She had caught sight of the last member of the group, who seemed as if he were a hundred, with bent back and a body that looked more like a walking skeleton than a living man.

'That is the man who can sway the Saxons against us,' observed Taran.

Fidelma raised an eyebrow.

'Is that Wilfrid? I thought he was a younger man?'

Taran shook his head.

'Not Wilfrid. That is Jacobus, whom the Saxons call James. Over sixty years ago, when Rome sought to reinforce the mission of Augustine in Kent, they sent a group of missionaries led by one called Paulinus. This Jacobus came with them – which makes him more than four score years in age. When Edwin of Northumbria married Aethelburh of Kent, the mother of Queen Eanflaed there, Paulinus came with her as her chaplain and made an unsuccessful attempt to convert the Northumbrians to the Roman path to Christ. He fled with Aethelburh and the baby Eanflaed back to Kent, where he died twenty years ago when the pagans rose up against them.'

'And this Jacobus? This man James?' pressed Fidelma. 'Did he flee also?'

'He remained behind in Catraeth, which the Saxons call Catterick, living sometimes as a hermit and sometimes attempting to convert the natives to Christ. I have no doubt that he will be called upon as proof that it was Rome who attempted to convert Northumbria before Iona and the argument put forward that Northumbria should be Roman. His venerability and the fact that he is a Roman who knew both Paulinus and Augustine stands against us.'

Sister Fidelma was impressed, in spite of herself, with Brother Taran's knowledge.

The procession had reached its appointed place now and the Abbess Hilda made a motion for all to rise.

Bishop Colmán took a step forward and traced the sign of the Cross in the air. Then he held up his hand and gave the blessing in the style of the church of Iona, using the first, third and fourth fingers to denote the Trinity as opposed to the Roman use of the thumb and the first and second fingers. There was some murmuring from the ranks of the pro-Romans at this but Colmán ignored it, asking a blessing in Greek, in which language the services of the church of Iona were usually said.

Then Deusdedit was helped forward and, in a soft whispering tone that underscored his apparent illness, he gave a blessing in the Roman style and in Latin.

Everyone became seated except Abbess Hilda.

'Brothers and sisters in Christ, the debate is now begun. Is our church of Northumbria to follow the teachings of Iona, from where this land was raised from the darkness into the light of Christ, or is it to follow those of Rome, from where that light originally spread to this, the outer reaches of the world? The decision will be yours.'

She glanced to the benches on her right.

'The opening arguments will now be made. Agilbert of Wessex, are you prepared to make your preliminary statement?'

'No!' came a rasping voice. There was a silence and then a swelling murmur.

Abbess Hilda raised her hand.

A lean dark-skinned man, with thin haughty-looking features

and an aquiline nose, rose to his feet.

'Agilbert is a Frank,' whispered Taran. 'He studied many years in Ireland.'

'Many years ago,' Agilbert began – in a hesitant, thickly accented Saxon, which Fidelma had to ask Taran to translate – 'Cenwealh of Wessex invited me to be bishop in his kingdom. For ten years I fulfilled the office but Cenwealh became dissatisfied, claiming I did not speak his Saxon dialect well enough. And he appointed Wine as bishop above me. I left the land of the West Saxons. Now I am asked to argue for Roman observance. If I am not able to speak to the satisfaction of Cenwealh and the West Saxons, I am not capable of speaking in this place. Therefore, my pupil Wilfrid of Ripon shall open this debate for Rome.'

Fidelma frowned.

'The Frank seems very touchy.'

'I hear he is on his way back to Frankia because he has taken against all the Saxons.'

A small, stocky, younger man, with a red face and a brusque, pugnacious manner, had risen.

'I, Wilfrid of Ripon, am prepared to put forward my preliminary arguments.'

Abbess Hilda inclined her head in acknowledgment.

'And for the cause of Iona, is Abbess Étain of Kildare prepared with her preliminary remarks?'

The abbess had turned to the benches where those who supported the church of Iona were seated.

There was no reply.

Fidelma craned forward and for the first time she suddenly realised that she could not see Étain in the *sacrarium*. The murmuring became a roar.

Abbess Abbe's voice sounded hollowly: 'It seems the Abbess of Kildare is not in attendance.'

There was a commotion around one of the doors of the *sacrarium* and Fidelma caught sight of the figure of one of the brothers. He stood, ashen-faced, chest heaving, as he paused on the threshold.

'Catastrophe!' His voice was high pitched. 'Oh brethren, catastrophe!'

Abbess Hilda gazed at the man with anger on her features.

'Brother Agatho! You forget yourself!'

The monk hurried forward. Even from a distance Fidelma could see panic on his face.

'Not I! Go to the windows and gaze at the sun! The hand of God is blotting it from the sky . . . the sky grows dark. *Domine dirige nos*! Surely this is a portent of evil on this assembly?'

The words were translated hurriedly to Sister Fidelma by Taran, for she could not understand the rapid tongue of the Saxon.

There was a stirring in the *sacrarium* and many of those gathered hurried towards the windows and stared out.

It was the austere Agilbert who turned to those who had still kept their places.

'It is even as Brother Agatho has said. The sun is blotted from the sky. It is a harbinger of evil on these proceedings.'

Chapter Five

Sister Fidelma turned with a look of incredulity to Brother Taran.

'Are these Saxons so superstitious? Do they know nothing of astronomy?'

'Very little,' Taran replied smugly. 'Our people have given them some knowledge but they are slow to learn.'

'But someone should inform them that this is no supernatural phenomenon.'

'They would not thank you for it.' Sister Gwid sniffed disapprovingly from her other side.

'But many of our brethren here are well versed in the science of astronomy and know of eclipses and other phenomena of the sky,' Fidelma pointed out.

Brother Taran motioned her to silence, for Wilfrid, the pugnacious-sounding chief spokesman of the pro-Roman faction, was on his feet.

'Surely, this blotting out of the sun is, indeed, an ill omen, my brethren. But what does it convey? It conveys this simple message – unless the churchmen and women of this country turn from the misconceptions of Columba to the one true universal church of Rome, then Christianity will be blotted from the land as God has blotted the sun from the sky. It is a portent, indeed.'

There was uproar as the pro-Roman faction applauded their agreement while the representatives of the church of Columba shouted their defiance at what they considered an outrageous statement.

A man in his thirties with the tonsure of Columba leapt to his feet, his face working in anger.

'How does Wilfrid of Ripon know this thing? Has God spoken to him directly to explain this phenomenon in our skies? Surely, it can equally be argued that the portent means that Rome should come into line with Columba? Unless those who support Rome's revisions of the true faith turn back to Columba then, indeed, will Christianity be blotted from the land.'

Howls of outrage echoed along the benches of the pro-Roman faction.

'That was Cuthbert of Melrose,' Taran said with a grin. He was clearly enjoying the argument. 'It was Wilfrid who, at Alhfrith's behest, threw him out of Ripon because he followed the custom of Columba.'

Oswy, the king, rose now. The uproar died away almost immediately.

'This argument will achieve us nothing. These proceedings will be suspended until—'

An inarticulate cry prevented him completing the sentence.

'The sun appears again!' exclaimed a voice from one of the observers at the window.

There was another general movement to the windows as several craned their heads towards the blue afternoon sky.

'Indeed, it does. The black shape is moving away,' called another. 'See, here is the sun's light.'

The greyness of the twilight was suddenly gone and the light flooded back through the windows of the *sacrarium*.

Sister Fidelma found herself shaking her head, astounded by the proceedings. She had been educated in a culture whose science had long gazed at the stars and noted their motions.

'It is hard to believe that these people can be in such ignorance of the movements in the heavens. In our monastic and bardic schools any qualified instructor is able to tell the courses of the sun and moon. Why, every intelligent person should know the day of the solar month, the age of the moon, the time of the flow of the tide, the day of the week – and the times of eclipses are no secret.'

Brother Taran grinned derisively.

'You forget that your countrymen and the Britons are renowned through many lands for their knowledge of astronomy. But these Saxons are still barbarians.'

'But surely they have read the treatise of the great Dallán Forgaill, who explained how often the moon stands before the sun, thus blotting out its light from the skies?'

Taran shrugged.

'Only a few of these Saxons are able to read and write. And they were not even capable of those accomplishments until the blessed Aidán arrived in this land. They could not even write down their own language, far less construe the languages of others.'

The Abbess Hilda was banging a staff on the stone floor for attention. Reluctantly, the members of the assembly were returning to their benches. The muttering of their voices began to die away.

'Light has returned and so we may continue. Has the Abbess of Kildare joined the proceedings yet?' Sister Fidelma turned her mind back to the matter in hand and found herself bewildered. The space assigned to the Abbess Étain still remained unfilled.

Wilfrid of Ripon had risen with a smirk.

'If the chief speaker of the church of Columba is not willing to join us, perhaps we should proceed without her?'

'There are plenty more who will speak on our behalf!' shouted back Cuthbert, not bothering to rise this time.

Again the Abbess Hilda banged her staff of office.

Then for the second time the assembly was abruptly interrupted by the great doors swinging open. This time a young sister with white face and staring eyes entered the *sacrarium*. It was obvious that she had been running – her hair was in disarray, spilling beneath her headdress. She paused, her eyes searching the vast chamber. Then she hurried directly to where the Abbess Hilda stood in bewilderment, just below the king.

Wonderingly, Fidelma watched as the sister moved swiftly to the Abbess Hilda, who bent forward so that the woman might whisper into her ear. Fidelma could not see Hilda's face, but she saw the abbess rise and move immediately towards the king, bending and repeating whatever message had been brought.

The *sacrarium* was now silent as the churchmen and delegates sat watching the new drama.

The king rose and left, followed a short while later by Hilda, Abbe, Colmán, Deusdedit, Wighard and Jacobus.

There was sudden uproar in the chamber as those gathered turned excitedly to each other to see if any knew the meaning of this curious behaviour. Voices were raised in speculation.

Two Northumbrian religieuses from Coldingham who were seated behind Fidelma were of the opinion that an army of Britons had invaded the kingdom, taking advantage of the king's preoccupation with the synod. They could remember the invasion of Cadwallon ap Cadfan, king of Gwynedd, which had ravaged the kingdom and caused the slaughter of many during one ill-fated year. But a brother of a house at Gilling, seated in front, interrupted with the opinion that it was more likely that the Mercians were invading, for had not Wulfhere, the son of Penda, sworn to re-establish Mercian independence from Northumbria and already begun to re-assert its dominance south of the Humber? The Mercians were always looking for a chance to avenge themselves on Oswy, who had slain Penda and, for three years, ruled Mercia. And even though Wulfhere had sent a royal representative to the synod it was just the sort of dirty trick the Mercians would play.

Fidelma was intrigued to hear the political speculation but for one not well acquainted with the position of the Saxon kingdoms it sounded very confusing. It was so unlike her native land, where there seemed a clear order under law and where the High King and his court were the final authority in the land. Even though some petty kings might dispute with the High King they at least acknowledged the nominal rule of Tara. The Saxons always seemed to be quarrelling among themselves and using the sword as the only arbiter in law.

A hand fell on her shoulder. A young sister leaned across her.

'Sister Fidelma? The Mother Abbess requires your presence in her chambers immediately.'

Surprised and somewhat bewildered, ignoring the looks of open curiosity from Sister Gwid and Brother Taran, Sister Fidelma rose and followed the young religieuse away from the pandemonium and confusion of the *sacrarium* and along the quieter corridors until she found herself ushered into the chamber of the Abbess Hilda. The abbess was standing before her fire, hands clasped before her. Her face was grey and grave. Bishop Colmán was seated in the chair to one side of the fire as he had been seated on the previous evening. He, too, had an air of solemnity, as if weighed down by a heavy problem.

They both appeared almost too preoccupied to notice her entrance.

'Mother Abbess, you sent for me?'

Hilda seemed to pull herself together with a sigh and glanced at Colmán who responded with a curious gesture of his hand as if motioning her to proceed.

'My lord bishop reminds me that you are an advocate of the law in your own land, Fidelma.'

Sister Fidelma frowned.

'That is so,' she confirmed, wondering what was coming.

'He reminds me that you have acquired a reputation for unravelling mysteries, for solving crimes.'

Fidelma waited expectantly.

'Sister Fidelma,' went on the abbess after a pause, 'I have great need of the talents of one such as you.'

'I am willing to place my poor abilities at your disposal,' Fidelma replied slowly, wondering what problem had arisen.

Abbess Hilda bit her lip as she struggled to frame the sentences.

'I have bad news, sister. The Abbess Étain of Kildare was found in her cell this morning. Her throat was cut – cut in such a manner that one is left with but one interpretation. The Abbess Étain was most foully murdered.'

Chapter Six

The door opened unceremoniously while Sister Fidelma was still in a state of shock at the news. She dimly became aware that Colmán was struggling to rise from his chair and turned to see who could bring the bishop to his feet.

Oswy of Northumbria entered the room.

Events had moved quickly, too quickly for Fidelma to accept that her friend, her colleague for several years, and more recently her abbess, had been cruelly slain. She made a conscious effort to suppress the grief she felt, for the news had grieved her considerably. Yet grief would not help Étain now. Her mind was working rapidly. Fidelma's training and talents were being called upon and grief would only cloud her ability. Grief could be given way to later.

She tried to concentrate her thoughts on the new entrant into the chamber.

Close up, the king of Northumbria did not seem as handsome as he had appeared from a distance. He was tall and muscular but his fair hair was a dirty yellowing grey and he was obviously approaching his three score years. His skin was yellowing and across his nose and cheeks the breaking of small blood vessels had caused bright red lines to weave across the skin. His eyes were sunken, his brow heavily creased. Fidelma had heard it said that every Northumbrian king had died a violent death in battle. It was an unfavourable heritage to look forward to.

Oswy glanced around, almost with a haunted look, and let his eyes settle on Sister Fidelma.

'I have heard that you are a *dálaigh* of the Brehon courts of Ireland?'

To Fidelma's surprise he spoke the language of Ireland almost as a native. Then she remembered that he had been brought up in exile in Iona. She realised that she should not be surprised at his command of her language.

'I am qualified to the level of *anruth*.'

Colmán shuffled forward to explain.

'That means—'

Oswy turned on him with an impatient gesture.

'I know exactly what it means, lord bishop. One qualified to the level of *anruth* is representative of the noble stream of knowledge and can discourse on equal footing with kings, even with the High King himself.' He smiled in self-satisfaction at the embarrassed bishop before turning back to Sister Fidelma. 'Nevertheless, even I am surprised to find such a learned head on such young shoulders.'

Fidelma suppressed a sigh.

'I studied for eight years with the Brehon Morann of Tara, one of the great judges of my country.'

Oswy nodded absently.

'I do not question your qualifications and my lord Colmán has informed me of your reputation. You know that we have need of you?'

Sister Fidelma inclined her head.

'I am told that the Abbess Étain has been murdered. She was not only my abbess but she was my friend. I am ready to help.'

'The abbess was due to open the debate of our assembly on behalf of the church of Iona, as you know. There is much dissension within my land, Sister Fidelma. This matter is delicate. Already rumours are whispered abroad and speculation runs riot. If the abbess was murdered by one of the pro-Roman faction, as seems likely, then there will be such a breach among the people that the truth of Christ may suffer a death blow in the land. Civil war seems likely to rip the people apart. Do you understand?'

'I understand,' replied Fidelma. 'Yet there is something much more serious to be considered.'

Oswy raised his eyebrows in surprise.

'More serious than political repercussions that will reach from Iona, perhaps even the primacy of Armagh, to Rome itself?' he demanded.

'Yes, more serious even than that,' Fidelma quietly assured him. 'Whoever killed Étain of Kildare must be brought to justice. That is the greater right and moral. What others make of it is their concern. The seeking of truth is more serious than any other consideration.'

For a moment or two Oswy looked blank. Then he smiled ruefully.

'There speaks the representative of the law. I have long missed the discourses of the Brehons of your country, the judges who sit above the king and his court. Here, the king is the law and no one can sit in judgment on a king.'

Fidelma grimaced indifferently.

'I have heard of the faults of your Saxon system.'

Abbess Hilda looked shocked.

'My child, remember you speak to the king.'

But Oswy was grinning.

'Cousin Hilda, do not rebuke her. She acts in accordance with her own culture. In Ireland, a king is not a law-maker, nor does he rule by the divine right. A king is only an administrator of a law passed down from generation to generation. Any advocate, such as an *anruth* or an *ollamh*, may argue law with the highest king in the land. Is that not so, Sister Fidelma?'

Fidelma smiled tightly.

'You have a keen grasp of our system, Oswy of Northumbria.'

'And you seem to have a sharp mind and do not appear in fear of any faction,' observed Oswy. 'That is good. My cousin Hilda has undoubtedly asked you to undertake the task of discovering who killed Étain of Kildare? What is your reply? Will you do it?'

The door was flung open abruptly.

Sister Gwid stood framed in the doorway, her large, awkward body strangely contorted. Her hair was askew under her headdress, her mouth was trembling, her eyes were red and bloodshot and the tears streamed down her flaccid white cheeks. For a moment she stood sobbing, staring wildly from one face to another.

'What the—?' began Oswy in surprise.

'Is it true? Oh God, tell me it is not so!' wailed the distressed sister, wringing her large red bony hands in acute distress. 'Is the Abbess Étain dead?'

Sister Fidelma recovered from her surprise first and hurried across to Sister Gwid, taking the tall girl by the arm and withdrawing her from the room. Outside, in the corridor, she signalled to the worried-looking sister who attended the Abbess Hilda and who had apparently tried to prevent Sister Gwid from entering the chamber.

'It is true, Gwid,' Fidelma said softly, feeling sorry for the large girl. She motioned to the hovering anchoress. 'Let this sister take you to your *dormitorium*. Go and lie down awhile and I will come to see you as soon as I can.'

The stocky Pictish sister allowed herself to be guided down the corridor, her great shoulders heaving in renewed anguish.

Sister Fidelma hesitated a moment before turning back into the room.

'Sister Gwid was a student of the Abbess Étain at Emly,' she explained, meeting the questioning eyes of the company. 'She was attending here in the capacity of a secretary to the abbess. I think she had developed a sort of adulation for Étain. Her death is a deep shock. We all have our ways of dealing with grief.'

Abbess Hilda made a sympathetic noise.

'I will go to comfort the poor girl shortly,' Hilda said. 'Let us first agree to this business.'

Oswy nodded. 'What do you say to the proposition, Fidelma of Kildare?'

Fidelma bit her lip and nodded.

'Abbess Hilda has already indicated that she wishes me to make inquiries. I will do this, not for politics but for the morality of law and the fact that Étain was my friend.'

'That is well said,' observed Oswy. 'Nonetheless, politics do come into this matter. This slaughter, especially of one so eminent, may well be a ruse to disrupt our debate. The obvious interpretation is that Étain, as a chief representative of the faith of Colmcille, was feloniously killed by someone who is pro-Roman. On the other hand, perhaps the killer wishes us to think that so that those in the hall will, out of sympathy, support Iona against Rome.'

Sister Fidelma gazed thoughtfully at Oswy. Here was no simple mind. Here was a king who had ruled with an iron hand for over a score of years among the Northumbrians and turned back every attempt by the other Saxon kings to invade and conquer his land and oust him. Now most Saxon kings, nominally at least, regarded him as their overlord and even the Bishop of Rome addressed him as 'king of the Saxons'. She could appreciate the sharpness of his intellect.

'That will be for me to discover then,' she observed quietly.

Oswy hesitated and shook his head.

'Not entirely.'

Fidelma raised an eyebrow questioningly.

'There is a condition.'

'I am an advocate of the Brehon courts. I do not work under any condition excepting my duty to uncover the truth.' Her eyes held a dangerous glint.

The Abbess Hilda's face was scandalised.

'Sister, you really do forget that you are no longer in your own country and that its laws do not extend here. You must treat the king with respect.'

Once again Oswy smiled, glancing at Hilda with a quick shake of his head.

'Sister Fidelma and I understand one another, Hilda. And we respect one another, I am sure. Nevertheless, I must insist that condition be met for, as I have said, this is a matter of politics and the future of our kingdoms and the religion which they will follow depend on the solution to this matter.'

'I fail to understand—' began Fidelma slightly bewildered.

'Let me make it clearer, then,' Oswy broke in. 'There are two rumours already circulating through the abbey. One is that the Roman faction have sought this appalling method to silence one of the most erudite advocates of the church of Colmcille. The other story is that this is a ruse by those who support the teachings of Iona to wreck the synod and ensure Iona and not

Rome governs the liturgy of Northumbria.'

'Yes, this I can follow.'

'My daughter Aelflaed, who has trained under the sisters of Iona, has already spoken of raising warriors to strike at those who would drive them out. My son Alhfrith and his wife, Cyneburh, conspire to use military force to overthrow the supporters of Iona. And my young son' – he paused and gave a bitter laugh – 'my son Ecgfrith, who cares only for power, watches and waits for the main chance, for a weakness to be revealed so that he can use it and seize my throne. Do you see why this matter is of importance?'

Sister Fidelma raised a shoulder and let it fall.

'But I do not understand what condition you have to make. I am capable of investigating this mystery.'

'To demonstrate to both factions that I, Oswy of Northumbria, am being even-handed and unbiased in my dispensation of the law, I cannot allow the death of the Abbess Étain to be investigated by one of the church of Colmcille alone. No more could I allow the matter to be investigated just by one of the church of Rome.'

Fidelma looked puzzled.

'Then what are you proposing?'

'That you, sister, join forces with one who favours the Roman faction. If you investigate jointly no one will be able to accuse us of partiality when the result is made known. Will you agree to this?'

Sister Fidelma stared at the king for a while.

'It is the first time that I have heard it impugned that a *dálaigh* of the Brehon courts would make a biased decision. The motto of our profession is "the truth against the world". Whether the deed was done by one of my church or by that of Rome, the result would still be the same. I am sworn to uphold the truth, however unpalatable.' She paused, then shrugged. 'And yet . . . yet I do see a logic in your suggestion. I will agree. But who will I work with? I confess that my Saxon is almost non-existent and I know that few of the Saxons have any knowledge of Latin, Greek or Hebrew, tongues I have some fluency in.'

Oswy's face had relaxed into a smile.

'In that there is no problem. Among the party of the Archbishop of Canterbury is a young man who is ideally suited to this task.'

Abbess Hilda had turned to her cousin with a look of interest. 'Who is this?'

'A brother named Eadulf from Seaxmund's Ham in Ealdwulf's kingdom of East Anglia. Brother Eadulf has spent five years as a student in Ireland and a further two years studying in Rome itself. He therefore speaks Irish, Latin and Greek as well as his native Saxon. He has a knowledge of law. In fact, had he not become a religieux he would have been hereditary *gerefa* – that, Fidelma, is an officer of our laws. Archbishop Deusdedit informs me that he is an inveterate solver of puzzles. So, would you object to working with such a man, Sister Fidelma?'

Fidelma was indifferent.

'So long as truth is the objective of us both. But how does he feel about working with me?'

'We may ask him, for I sent a message for him to come here and wait outside. He should be here by now.'

Oswy strode to the door and threw it open.

Sister Fidelma's lips parted in surprise as the young monk whom she had encountered in the cloisters of the abbey on the previous evening entered and bowed his head before the king.

Then he raised his eyes and caught sight of Sister Fidelma. His own face momentarily mirrored the astonishment on Fidelma's and then it became an impassive mask again.

'This is Brother Eadulf.' Oswy introduced the newcomer, continuing to speak in Irish. 'Brother Eadulf, this is the *dálaigh* of whom I have already spoken, Sister Fidelma. Do you agree to work with her, bearing in mind what I have told you of the importance of resolving this mystery as soon as possible?'

Brother Eadulf's brown eyes met the fiery green sparkle of Sister Fidelma's.

Again Fidelma felt the curious thrill of contact that she had experienced on the previous evening.

'I am willing.' His voice was a rich baritone. 'If it is agreeable to Sister Fidelma.'

'Sister?' pressed Oswy.

'We should begin at once,' Fidelma said dispassionately, hiding her feeling of confusion under the Saxon's gaze.

'In that I agree,' replied Oswy. 'Your investigation will be done in my name. You may question anyone, of whatever station in life, whom you wish to question and my warriors stand ready to act upon your commands. I would only say, before I depart, that urgency is the priority. For every hour that rumour and speculation runs unchecked in this place, then the enemies of peace will have increasing power and civil war looms ever nearer.'

Oswy gazed from one to another, smiled briefly and left the room.

Sister Fidelma found her mind racing. There was so much to take in, not least the death of Étain.

She suddenly became aware that Abbess Hilda, Colmán and Eadulf were all watching her.

'I am sorry?' She was aware that a question must have been asked of her.

Abbess Hilda sniffed.

'I asked how you wished to proceed.'

'It would be best to view the scene of the outrage,' Brother Eadulf said quickly.

Fidelma found herself clenching her teeth in annoyance at having the question answered for her.

The Saxon was right, of course, but she had no wish to be dictated to. She tried to think of another course of action which she could usefully take, simply to contradict him. She could not.

'Yes,' she replied reluctantly. 'We will go to Abbess Étain's *cubiculum*. Has anything been disturbed there since the body was discovered?'

Hilda shook her head.

'Nothing, so far as I am aware. Shall I accompany you?

'No need,' Fidelma said quickly, lest Brother Eadulf decided to answer for her again. 'We will report as and when we require anything.'

She turned, without looking at Eadulf, and strode from the room.

Behind her, Eadulf bowed to the abbess and to Bishop Colmán and hurried after her.

Colmán pursed his lips as the door closed.

'It is like putting a wolf and a fox together to hunt a hare,' he said slowly.

Abbess Hilda smiled thinly at the bishop.

'It would be interesting to know which you see as the wolf and which as the fox.'

Chapter Seven

Fidelma paused outside the door of the *cubiculum hospitale* that had been assigned to the Abbess Étain. Fidelma had not spoken a word directly to the Saxon monk since they had left Abbess Hilda's chamber and walked through the gloomy cloisters and corridors to the guests' quarters. She now found it hard to gather the fortitude to enter the cell. But while Brother Eadulf had assumed that her lack of communication and hesitation were due to some pique over the fact that she had to work with him in resolving the matter, and was content to let the pique run its course, Fidelma now found herself struggling with the fact that this was the moment that she dreaded.

The moment when she was forced to gaze on the body of her friend Étain in death.

The personal shock of Étain's murder was something she still had to deal with. Étain had been a good friend. Not a close friend, but a friend nevertheless. Fidelma remembered her meeting with her only the evening before when Étain had confided that she was giving up the abbacy of Kildare to marry, to pursue her personal happiness. Fidelma frowned. Marry whom? How could she contact Étain's betrothed and tell him this tragic news? Was he an Eoghanacht chieftain or some religieux she had met in Ireland? Well, time to sort that out when she returned to Ireland.

She stood for a moment taking a few deep breaths, trying to prepare herself.

'If you do not wish to view the body, sister, I can perform this task for you.' Eadulf spoke in a mollifying tone, obviously mistaking her hesitation for trepidation at viewing a body. They were the first words the Saxon monk had addressed directly to her.

Fidelma found herself torn between two reactions.

The first was one of surprise at the fluency of his Irish and at the fact that this was the language in which he chose to address her, in a rich, baritone voice. The second was one of irritation at his slightly patronising tone, which showed his obvious train of thought.

The irritation was the predominant of the two emotions and it gave her the strength she needed.

'Étain was abbess of my house of Kildare, Brother Eadulf,' she said firmly. 'I knew her well. Only that makes me pause, as it would any civilised person.'

Brother Eadulf bit his lip. The woman was quick-tempered and sensitive, he thought; her green eyes were like twin fires.

'Then all the more reason to save you this task,' he said soothingly. 'I am proficient in the art of the apothecaries, having studied at your famous medical school of Tuaim Brecain.'

But his words did not pacify her and only added to her irritation.

'And I am a *dálaigh* of the Brehon courts,' she said stiffly. 'I presume I do not have to explain the obligation that is incumbent with that office?'

Before he could answer, she had pushed open the door of the *cubiculum*.

It was gloomy in the cells, in spite of the fact that it was still light outside. There were two more hours to dark but the grey skies had already produced a twilight which made it impossible to see detail, for the window which lit the cell was small and high in the shadowy stone wall.

'Find a lamp, brother,' she instructed.

Eadulf hesitated. He was unused to being ordered by a woman. Then he shrugged and turned to an oil lamp hanging on the wall, ready for use when it grew dark. It took a moment to strike a tinder and adjust the wick.

Eadulf, raising the lamp in one hand, entered the room behind Fidelma.

The body of Abbess Étain had not been moved but was still sprawled on its back, as it had fallen in death, lying across the wooden cot which served as the bed in the chamber. She was fully clothed except for her headdress. Her hair, long and blond like spun gold, fell in tresses around her head. The eyes were wide and staring to the ceiling. The mouth was open, twisted in an ugly grimace. Blood covered the lower half of the face and the neck and shoulders.

Compressing her lips together, Sister Fidelma moved forward and forced herself to stare downwards, avoiding the cold open eyes of death. She genuflected and muttered a prayer for her dead abbess. '*Sancta Brigita intercedat pro amica mea . . .*' she whispered. Then she reached forward and closed the eyes, adding the prayer for the dead, '*Requiem aeternam dona ei Domine . . .*'

When she had finished she turned to her companion, who had waited just inside the door.

'As we will be working together, brother,' she said coldly, 'let us agree on what we see.'

Brother Eadulf moved closer to her side, still holding the lamp high. Fidelma intoned dispassionately: 'There is a jagged

75

cut, almost a tear, from left ear to centre base of the neck, and another cut from the right ear also to the centre, almost forming a "v" beneath the chin. Do you agree?'

Eadulf slowly nodded.

'I agree, sister. Two separate cuts, obviously.'

'I see no other visible injuries.'

'To inflict such cuts, the attacker would have to hold the abbess's head back, perhaps holding her by the back of the hair, and stab swiftly into the neck by the ear and perform the same stabbing attack again.'

Sister Fidelma was thoughtful.

'The knife was not a sharp one. The flesh is torn rather than cut. That implies a person of some strength.'

Brother Eadulf smiled thinly.

'Then we can rule out any of the sisters as suspects.'

Fidelma raised a cynical eyebrow.

'At the moment, no one is ruled out. Strength, like intelligence, is not solely possessed by man.'

'Very well. But the abbess must have known her attacker.'

'How do you deduce that?'

'There is no sign of a struggle. Glance around the room. Nothing seems out of place. Nothing is in disarray. And, observe, the abbess's headdress is still hung neatly from the peg for her clothes. As you know, among the sisters, it is a rule that the veil should not be discarded before strangers.'

Sister Fidelma had to admit to herself that Brother Eadulf was observant.

'You argue that Abbess Étain had removed her headdress before or when the attacker came to her cell. You imply that she knew the attacker well enough not to replace the veil on her head?'

'Just so.'

'But what if the attacker entered the cell before she knew who it was and then she had no time to reach for her veil before she was assaulted?'

'A possibility that I ruled out.'

'How so?'

'Because there still would have been signs of disturbance. If the abbess had been startled by the entrance of a stranger, she would have attempted firstly to reach her headdress or to struggle with the intruder. No, everything is neat and tidy, even the bed coverings are not disturbed. The only thing spoiling the tranquillity is the abbess lying across her bed with her throat cut.'

Sister Fidelma compressed her lips. Eadulf was right. He had a keen eye.

'It seems logical,' she admitted after some thought. 'But not entirely conclusive. I think I would reserve my judgment on her knowledge of her attacker. But the odds are in your favour.' She turned and gave Eadulf a sudden searching look. 'You mentioned that you are a physician?'

Eadulf shook his head.

'No. Though I have studied at the medical school of Tuaim Brecain, as I have said, and know much, I am not qualified in all the arts of a physician.'

'I see. Then you will have no objection if we ask the Abbess Hilda to have Étain's body removed to the *mortuarium* and examined by the physician of the abbey in case there are other injuries that we might have missed?'

'I have no objection,' confirmed Eadulf.

Fidelma nodded absently. 'I doubt whether there is anything else we might learn from this pitiful cell—'

She suddenly paused and bent down to the floor, coming more slowly to her feet with something held in her hand. It was a tuft of golden strands of hair.

'What is that?' Eadulf asked.

'The confirmation of your theory,' replied Fidelma flatly. 'You said that the attacker grabbed Étain's hair from behind, to hold her neck back while stabbing her in the throat. Such a grip would tear some of the hair from her scalp. And here we have that hair, which the attacker dropped as he or she left the cell.'

Sister Fidelma stood still and gazed around the small chamber, her eyes moving carefully so that she might not miss anything of importance or meaning. She had a curious pricking at the back of her mind that she was overlooking something. She moved across to the side table and looked through the few toilet articles and personal possessions. A pocket missal lay among them. Étain's crucifix was the only jewellery there. Fidelma had already noted that her ring of office was still on her finger. Why, then, did she feel that something was missing?

'There is little in the way of any sign to suggest who our miscreant might be, sister.' Eadulf interrupted her thoughts. 'We can rule out robbery with greed as the motive,' he added, indicating the crucifix and ring.

'Robbery?' She had to confess that it was the last motive in her thoughts. 'We are in a house of God.'

'Beggars and thieves have been known to break into abbeys and churches before,' Eadulf pointed out. 'But not in this case. There is no sign at all.'

'The scene of a misdeed is like a piece of parchment on which the transgressor must make some mark,' Fidelma replied. 'The mark is there, it is for us to spot it and interpret it.'

Eadulf shot a curious glance at her.

'The only mark here is the body of the abbess,' he said softly.

Fidelma turned a withering glance on him.

'Then, by your own admission, it is still a mark and one to be interpreted.'

Brother Eadulf bit his lip as the rebuke hit home.

He wondered whether the Irish religieuse was always as sharp as this or whether it was some reaction to him.

Curiously, when he had accidentally knocked into her in the cloisters last evening, he could have sworn that some light of understanding, of empathy, had passed between them – some chemical reaction. Yet now it was as if that encounter had never happened and the woman was a hostile stranger.

Well, he ought not to wonder at such hostility. She was a supporter of Columba's rule while he, by his very *corona spinea*, had declared for Rome. And the hostilities of those gathered at the abbey were obvious for even the most insensitive to interpret.

His thoughts were interrupted by a hollow rasping cough from the doorway of the cell. Both Fidelma and Eadulf turned together as an elderly religieuse paused on the portal.

'*Pax vobiscum*,' she greeted. 'Are you Fidelma of Kildare?'

Fidelma acknowledged her identity.

'I am Sister Athelswith, *domina* of the *domus hospitale* of Streoneshalh.' She kept her eyes focused on Fidelma, making an obvious effort not to let them stray to the cot on which the body of Étain lay. 'Abbess Hilda thought that you might wish to talk with me for I am in charge of all the arrangements for the accommodation of our brethren during the synod.'

'Excellent,' chimed in Brother Eadulf, incurring another glance of displeasure from Fidelma. 'You are exactly the person to whom we should speak—'

'But not immediately,' snapped Fidelma irritably. 'First,

Sister Athelswith, we would like the physician of your abbey to examine the body of our poor sister as soon as possible. We would wish to speak with the physician as soon as the examination has been made.'

Sister Athelswith looked nervously from Fidelma to Brother Eadulf and back again.

'Very well,' she said reluctantly. 'I will tell Brother Edgar, our physician, at once.'

'Then we will meet you at the north door of the abbey shortly after we have finished here.'

Again the troubled eyes of the elderly sister roamed from Fidelma's face to that of the young Saxon monk. Fidelma was annoyed by her hesitation.

'Time is of importance, Sister Athelswith,' she said sharply.

The mistress of the guests' quarters bobbed her head uncertainly and hurried off about her errand.

Sister Fidelma turned to face Eadulf. Her features were controlled, but her green eyes sparkled with annoyance.

'I am not used—' she began, but Eadulf disarmed her with a grin.

'—to working with someone else? Yes, I can understand that. No more am I. I think we should devise some plan in order that we might carry out our investigation without conflict. We should decide who is in charge of conducting the investigation.'

Fidelma stared at the Saxon in surprise. She sought for words for a moment or two to express her annoyance but they came so disjointedly into her mind that she did not utter them.

'As we are in the land of the Saxons, maybe I should take charge,' Eadulf went on, ignoring the storm that seemed about to erupt. 'After all, I know the law and customs and language of this country.'

Fidelma's lips had thinned as she controlled herself and found the words she wanted.

'I concede that it is indisputable that you have such knowledge. Nevertheless, Oswy the king, with the support of the Abbess Hilda of this house and Colmán, Bishop of Northumbria, suggested that I undertake this investigation because of my experience in this field. You were appointed as a political expediency so that the investigation might be seen to be even-handed.'

Brother Eadulf apparently refused to take offence and simply chuckled.

'By whatever means I was appointed, sister, I am here.'

'Then, as we are in dispute, I think we should go to the Abbess Hilda and ask her who should stand in preference as being in charge of the investigation.'

The warm brown eyes of Eadulf met the sparkling, fiery green eyes of Fidelma and locked for several long seconds in challenge.

'Perhaps,' Eadulf said slowly, 'perhaps not.' Suddenly his features split into a grin. 'Why cannot we decide between ourselves?'

'It seems that you have already decided that you should take charge,' Fidelma replied frostily.

'I'll compromise. We bring different abilities and talents to this matter. Let no one be in charge.'

Fidelma suddenly realised that the man might have been testing her, exploring her resolve and confidence in herself.

'That would be the logical solution,' she admitted reluctantly. 'But to work together one should have an understanding of one another and know how the other's mind works.'

'And how can that be learnt except by working together

81

and learning? Shall we attempt it?'

Sister Fidelma gazed into the deep brown eyes of the Saxon monk and found herself colouring. Once more she felt that strange chemical sensation she had experienced on the previous evening.

'Very well,' she replied, distantly, 'we shall attempt it. We will share all our ideas and knowledge in this matter. Now let us go to meet Sister Athelswith at the north door of the abbey. I find this building oddly oppressive and would like to walk in the open and feel the sea breeze on my face.'

She turned without another glance around the cell or casting a look at the body of Abbess Étain. By applying her mind to the problem the murder presented she had already begun to deal with her personal grief.

Fidelma and Eadulf stood at the edge of a crowd that had clustered beyond the north gate of the abbey buildings. A market and fair had been set up as the local merchants attempted to make some wealth from the gathering of illustrious churchmen and princes from the kingdoms of the Angles and Saxons.

At the north door of the abbey they had found a good-natured crowd clustered around a beggar, a man from Ireland to judge by his voice and appearance. The crowd were taunting him as he kept shouting a prophecy of death and gloom. Fidelma shook her head as she realised that it was the same man she had seen from the window on the evening before.

Everywhere one went there were prophets and soothsayers these days, proclaiming catastrophe and doom. But then no one really believed in prophecies unless they were ones that could be feared and which foretold ruin and damnation. There was no accounting for the mind of humankind.

Fidelma and Eadulf paused for a while but the fascination of the stalls and tents attracted their attention and, without thinking, they found themselves drawn away from the gates towards the colourful throng. They turned through the tents and fairground booths that had sprung up outside the towering sandstone walls of Streoneshalh.

There was an invigorating salt sea smell to the air. In spite of the growing lateness of the hour, the merchants were still conducting a thriving business. They saw rich-looking groups of people, nobles, thanes, princes and petty kings, moving with stately arrogance around the fair. Beyond, on both sides of the valley, through which a broad river ran into the sea, were dark hills and across the hills numerous tents were pitched, pennants proclaiming the nobility of their inhabitants.

Fidelma remembered that Brother Taran had pointed out that the synod was attracting regal representatives not only from the kingdoms of the Angles and Saxons, but even from the kingdoms of the Britons with whom the Saxons were constantly at war. Eadulf was able to point out pennants belonging to some Frankish nobles, who had crossed the sea from Frankia. She recognised some from Dál Riada and from the lands of the Cruthin, whom the Saxons called Picts. It was truly a debate of importance that attracted so many nations. Oswy was right – the decision of Streoneshalh would chart the course of Christianity not only in Northumbria but in all the Saxon kingdoms for centuries to come.

It seemed to them that the entire settlement of Witebia was endowed with a carnival atmosphere. Wandering minstrels, entertainers of all sorts and merchants and vendors were thronging the town. Brother Eadulf, upon enquiry, pointed out to Fidelma that the prices they were charging were exorbitant and said they should utter a prayer of thanks that they were staying under the patronage of the abbey.

Among the stalls, gold and silver coins were swiftly exchanging hands. A Frisian merchant was taking the opportunity of a rich clientele of thanes and ealdormen, with their retainers, to sell a ship load of slaves. As well as potential buyers, groups of churls, common freemen, gathered round to watch the proceedings with morbid curiosity. So often, in the wake of a war or civil disturbance, could a family find itself taken as prisoners and sold as slaves by the conquerors.

Fidelma viewed the proceedings with open distaste.

'I feel uneasy at seeing human beings sold like beasts.'

For the first time Eadulf found himself in total agreement with her.

'We Christians have long declared how wrong it is for an individual to own another as property. We even set aside funds for buying the emancipation of slaves who are known to be Christians. But many who call themselves Christians do not subscribe to the abolition of slavery and the church has no policy or programme for the ending of slavery.'

Fidelma was pleased to hear his agreement.

'I have even heard that your Saxon Archbishop of Canterbury, Deusdedit, has argued that slaves in good households were better fed and housed than free labourers and churls and that the freedom of a churl was relative rather than absolute. Such views could not be held among the bishops of Ireland, where slavery is forbidden by law.'

'Yet you hold hostages and those you class as non-freemen,' Eadulf replied. He suddenly felt that he had to defend the Saxon system of slavery, even though he disagreed with it, simply because it was Saxon. He disliked the idea that a foreigner should sound so superior and disapproving.

Fidelma flushed in annoyance.

'You have studied in Ireland, Brother Eadulf. You know our system. We have no slaves. Those who trespass against our laws can lose their rights for varying periods, but they are not excluded from our society. They are made to contribute to the welfare of the people until such time as their crime is requited. Some non-freemen can work their own land and pay their taxes. Hostages and prisoners of war remain as contributing to our society until tribute or ransom is paid. But, as well you know, Eadulf, even the lowest of our non-freemen are treated as intelligent beings, as humans with rights and not mere chattels as you Saxons treat your slaves.'

Brother Eadulf opened his mouth angrily to retort in emotional defence of the system, quite forgetting his intellectual condemnation of it.

'Brother Eadulf! Sister Fidelma!'

A breathless voice interrupted them.

They turned. Sister Fidelma felt suddenly guilty as she saw the elderly Sister Athelswith hurrying to catch up with them.

'I thought that you said you would be by the north door,' protested the sister breathlessly.

'I am sorry.' Fidelma was contrite. 'We were carried away by the sights and sounds of the market.' Sister Athelswith grimaced in disgust.

'It would be well to avoid such dens of depravity, sister. But then, as you are a foreigner, our Northumbrian markets may well have a curiosity for you.'

She turned and guided them out of the section of the abbey grounds which had been given over to the stalls and booths of the market, where the fair had been pitched, and turned eastward along the top of the dark cliffs overlooking the harbour of Witebia. The sun was already low in the western sky and their shadows stretched before them as they walked.

'Now, Sister Athelswith—' began Fidelma. But the *domina* of the guests' hostel interrupted breathlessly.

'I have seen Brother Edgar, our physician. He will perform the autopsy within the hour.'

'Good,' Brother Eadulf said approvingly. 'I doubt whether there will be anything new to add to our knowledge but it is best if the body is so examined.'

'As mistress of the hostel,' went on Fidelma, 'how do you assign *cubicula* to the visitors?'

'Many of the guests have pitched their tents around our house. And there are so many attending the debate that our dormitories have become filled to capacity. The *cubicula* are assigned to special guests.'

'The Abbess Étain was allotted her chamber by you?'

'Indeed.'

'On what basis?'

Sister Athelswith frowned.

'I do not understand.'

'Was there any special reason for Étain of Kildare being allotted that particular *cubiculum?*'

'No. The guest chambers are allotted on the order of rank. Bishop Colmán, for example, requested that you be allocated a *cubiculum* because of your rank.'

'I see. So who had the chambers on either side of the abbess?'

Sister Athelswith had no difficulty in replying.

'Why, on one side the Abbess Abbe of Coldingham and on the other Bishop Agilbert, the Frank.'

'One a firm adherent of the church of Columba,' interrupted

Brother Eadulf, 'the other equally firmly for Rome.'

Fidelma raised an eyebrow and gazed quizzically at him. Eadulf replied to her obvious question with an indifferent shrug.

'I point this out, Sister Fidelma, in case you search for pro-Roman culprits in this matter.'

Fidelma bit her lip in irritation.

'I search only for the truth, brother.' Turning to the puzzled Sister Athelswith, she continued: 'Is a check kept on who visits the *cubicula* of your guests? Or is everyone free to wander in and out of the guests' hostel?'

Sister Athelswith raised her shoulders and let them fall expressively.

'Why should such a check be made, sister? People are free to come and go as they please in the house of God.'

'Male and female?'

'We are a mixed house at Streoneshalh. Male and female are free to visit each other's *cubicula* whenever they like.'

'So you would have no way of knowing who visited the Abbess Étain?'

'I know of only seven visitors today,' the elderly religieuse replied complacently.

Sister Fidelma tried to control her exasperation.

'And these were?' she prompted.

'Brother Taran, the Pict, and Sister Gwid, who is secretary to the abbess, visited in the morning. Then Abbess Hilda herself and Bishop Colmán came together towards midday. There came a beggar, one of your countrymen, sister, who demanded to see her. He created such an uproar that he had to be removed. Indeed, this same beggar was whipped yesterday morning by order of the Abbess Hilda for disturbing the quiet of our house.'

She paused.

'You mentioned seven persons,' prompted Sister Fidelma gently.

'Brothers Seaxwulf and Agatho. Seaxwulf is the secretary to Wilfrid of Ripon.'

'And who is this Agatho?'

It was Eadulf who replied.

'Agatho is a priest in the service of the Abbot of Icanho. He was pointed out to me this morning as being of an eccentric character.'

'One of the Roman faction then?' she asked ingenuously.

Eadulf gave a curt nod.

'So? Can you estimate the time when these visitors saw the abbess? For example, who was the last to see her?'

Sister Athelswith stroked her nose as if the action helped in recalling.

'Sister Gwid visited early this morning. I remember that well, for they stood at the door of the *cubiculum* arguing quite heatedly. Then Sister Gwid burst into tears and ran past me along the corridor towards her *dormitorium*. She is a rather emotional young woman. I gather the abbess had cause to rebuke her. Then Brother Taran came to see her. Abbess Hilda and Bishop Colmán came together, as I have said, and they all went in to the refectory together when the bell for the *prandium* sounded. The beggar arrived after lunch. Brother Seaxwulf visited but now I am not sure whether that was after the midday meal or before. The last visitor I remember was the priest Agatho, who came in the early afternoon.'

Fidelma had followed Athelswith's recitation with some amusement. The old woman was clearly something of a busybody, keeping track of every visitor to her guest house as well as their business.

'So? This Agatho, so far as you know, was the last to see the Abbess Étain alive?'

'If he *was* her last visitor of the day,' interrupted Eadulf hurriedly. There was a defensive tone in his voice.

Sister Fidelma smiled softly.

'Just so.'

Sister Athelswith glanced unhappily from one to the other.

'I saw no other visitors after Brother Agatho,' she replied firmly.

'And are you in a position to see all visitors?' demanded Eadulf.

'Only when I am in my *officium*,' she replied, colouring a little. 'I have much to do. Being the *domina* of the guests' quarters is a great responsibility. In normal times we provide for the hospitality of forty pilgrims at one time. I have one brother and three sisters to help me in the discharge of my duties. There is a need to clean the *dormitoria* and the *cubicula*, to prepare beds and assure ourselves that the needs of prominent visitors have been met. So I am often in the hostel area ensuring that our tasks are carried out. But when I am in my *officium* I cannot help but observe who passes to and fro to the guests' quarters.'

Fidelma smiled in mollification. 'And it is good luck for us that you do so.'

'Would you take oath, sister,' pressed Eadulf a little aggressively, 'that no one else visited Abbess Étain before her body was discovered?'

Sister Athelswith brought her chin up stubbornly.

'Of course not. As I said at the beginning, we are free to enter when and how we please. I am only sure that the people that I have named entered the Abbess of Kildare's *cubiculum*.'

'And when was the body discovered and who by?'

'I, myself, discovered the body at half past the hour of five o'clock this afternoon.'

Fidelma was astonished and showed it.

'How can you be so certain of the hour?'

Sister Athelswith swelled with visible pride.

'Among the duties of the *domina* of the *domus hospitale* of Streoneshalh is that of time-keeper. It is my task to ensure that our clepsydra functions accurately.'

Brother Eadulf was bewildered.

'Your . . . what?'

'Clepsydra is a Greek word,' Fidelma explained, allowing a slight patronising tone to enter her voice.

'One of our brethren brought it back from the east,' Sister Athelswith said proudly. 'It is a mechanism by which time is measured by the discharge of water.'

'And exactly how did you note the time of discovery?' pressed Eadulf.

'I had just made my check on the clepsydra when a messenger from the *sacrarium* came to inform me that the assembly had opened but there was no sign of the Abbess of Kildare. I went to her *cubiculum* to summon her. That is when I found her and sent the messenger straight away to Abbess Hilda. By our clepsydra, the time was lacking a half hour to the sounding of the evening Angelus bell, which task I also have to oversee as time-keeper of Streoneshalh.'

'That certainly agrees with the time that the messenger arrived in the assembly hall and informed the Abbess Hilda,' Eadulf confirmed.

'I was there also,' Fidelma agreed. 'And you, Sister Athelswith, you disturbed nothing? All was left exactly as you found it in Étain's cell?'

The *domina* of the *domus hospitale* nodded emphatically.
'I disturbed nothing.'

Sister Fidelma bit her lip thoughtfully.

'Well, the shadows are lengthening. I think we should retrace our footsteps to the abbey,' she said, after a moment's pause. 'We should continue by seeking out this priest, Agatho, and seeing what he has to say.'

A figure was hurrying towards them through the gloom from the direction of the abbey gates. It was one of the brethren, a thick-set, moon-faced young man.

'Ah, brother, sisters. The Abbess Hilda has sent me in great haste to search for you.'

He paused a moment to recover his wheezy breath.

'Well?' demanded Fidelma.

'I have to tell you that the murderer of the Abbess Étain has been discovered and is even now under lock and key within the abbey.'

Chapter Eight

Fidelma entered Abbess Hilda's chamber, closely followed by Eadulf. The abbess was seated while before her stood a tall young man with blond hair and a scar on his face. Fidelma recognized him immediately as the man Brother Taran had identified in the *sacrarium* as Oswy's eldest son, Alhfrith. She had an immediate impression, observing him close up, that the scar suited him well, for his features, though handsome, gave an indefinable impression of cruelty – perhaps because the lips were thin and sneering and the eyes ice-blue, cold and lifeless as if they were the eyes of a corpse.

'This is Alhfrith of Deira,' announced the abbess.

Brother Eadulf immediately bowed low in the manner of the Saxons when greeting their princes, but Fidelma remained upright, merely giving a hint of a nod of respectful acknowledgment. She would do no more than that even when meeting a provincial king of Ireland, for her rank entitled her to speak on a level with kings, even the High King himself.

Alhfrith, son of Oswy, glanced briefly at Sister Fidelma in disinterest and then proceeded to address himself to Brother Eadulf in Saxon. Fidelma had some knowledge of the language, but the delivery was too fast and accented for her to understand a word. She raised a hand and interrupted the heir-apparent of Northumbria.

'It would be better,' she said in Latin, 'if we observed a

language common to all. I have no Saxon. If we do not have a common language then, Eadulf, it behoves you to translate.'

Alhfrith paused in his delivery and made a noise conveying annoyance at being interrupted.

The Abbess Hilda suppressed a smile.

'As Alhfrith speaks no Latin, I suggest we continue to use Irish as a language we can all understand,' she said in that language.

Alhfrith turned to Fidelma, his brows drawn together.

'I have a little Irish, taught by the monks of Columba when they brought Christianity to this land. If you have no Saxon, then I shall speak this language.' The words were slow and thickly accented, but his knowledge was adequate.

Fidelma made a gesture with her hand, inviting him to continue. To her irritation he turned back to Eadulf and continued to address his remarks to him.

'There is little need to continue your investigation. We have the culprit locked away.'

Brother Eadulf was about to reply when Sister Fidelma interrupted.

'Are we to be informed who the culprit is?'

Alhfrith blinked in surprise. Saxon women knew their place. But he had some experience of the boldness of Irish women and had learnt from his step-mother, Fín, something of their arrogance in considering themselves equal to men. He swallowed the sharp reply that rose in his mouth and his eyes narrowed as he gazed at Fidelma.

'Surely. A beggar from Ireland. One called Canna, the son of Canna.'

Fidelma raised a quizzical eyebrow.

'How was he discovered?'

Brother Eadulf felt uncomfortable about the challenging note in his colleague's voice. He was accustomed to the manner and customs of Irish women in their own land but uneasy about such attitudes among his own people.

'The discovery was made easily enough,' replied Alhfrith coldly. 'The man went round foretelling the day and time of the Abbess Étain's death. He is either a great sorcerer or he is the murderer. As a Christian king adhering to Rome,' he said emphatically, 'I do not believe in sorcery. Therefore, the only way the man could foretell the day and time of the abbess's death is if he were the perpetrator of the crime.'

Eadulf was nodding slowly at the logic, but Fidelma smiled sceptically at the Saxon prince.

'Are there witnesses to the fact that he foretold the exact hour and manner of Abbess Étain's death?'

Alhfrith gestured, a trifle dramatically, to Abbess Hilda.

'There is a witness and one beyond reproach.'

Sister Fidelma turned questioningly to the abbess.

Hilda seem caught off guard and a little flustered.

'It is true that yesterday morning this beggar was brought to me and foretold that blood would be spilt on this day.'

'He was precise?'

Alhfrith hissed in irritation as Hilda shook her head.

'In truth, all he told me was that blood would be spilt on the day the sun was blotted from the sky. A learned brother from Iona told me that this event did occur this very afternoon when the moon passed between us and the sun.'

Fidelma's expression grew even more sceptical.

'But did he name the Abbess Étain and the precise hour?' she insisted.

'Not to me—' began Hilda.

'But there are other witnesses who will swear he told them,' interrupted Alhfrith. 'Why do we waste time? Do you question my word?'

Sister Fidelma turned to the Saxon with a disarming smile. Only a close examination would have told how false the smile was.

'Your word is not evidence in the legal sense, Alhfrith of Deira. Even under Saxon law, there must be direct evidence of the wrongdoing and not merely hearsay or conjecture. As I understand it, you are merely reporting what someone else has told you. You have not heard this man's words directly.'

Alhfrith's face reddened in mortification.

Brother Eadulf suddenly spoke for the first time.

'Sister Fidelma is right. Your word is not in question, because you are not a witness and cannot testify to what this man said.'

Fidelma hid her surprise at being supported by the Saxon brother. She turned back to the Abbess Hilda.

'Nothing alters our commission to investigate this matter, Mother Abbess, only that we now have a suspect. Is that correct?'

The Abbess Hilda agreed, though seemingly nervous at being seen to go against her young kinsman.

Alhfrith exhaled in annoyance.

'This is time-wasting. The Irish woman was killed by one of her own countrymen. The sooner that news is announced the better. At least it will stop the rumours and unjust accusations that she was killed to prevent her speaking at the debate by one of the pro-Roman faction.'

'If that is the truth, then it shall be announced,' Fidelma assured him. 'We have yet to discern whether it is the truth.'

'Perhaps,' Brother Eadulf said hurriedly as the Saxon prince's brows furrowed, 'you would tell us who the witnesses are against this man and how he came to be arrested?'

Alhfrith hesitated.

'One of my thanes, Wulfric, overheard the man boasting in the market that he had foretold the death of Étain. He found three people who will swear they heard the beggar announce this before the death of the abbess was discovered. He is guarding the prisoner even now, preparatory to our burning him at the stake for daring to mock the laws of God by claiming omniscient precognition.'

Fidelma stared directly at Alhfrith of Deira.

'You have already condemned the man before he has been heard.'

'I have heard him and I have condemned him to death by fire!' snapped Alhfrith.

Sister Fidelma opened her mouth to protest but Eadulf cut her short.

'This is in accord with our custom and law, Fidelma,' he said hurriedly.

Fidelma's eyes were cold.

'But Wulfric,' she breathed slowly. 'I have already met this Wulfric of Frihop on the road here. Wulfric, the thane of Frihop, who hanged a brother of Columba on a roadside tree for no other reason than that of pleasure. He would make a good witness against any of our nation and faith.'

Alhfrith's eyes rounded and his mouth opened but no sound would come as he struggled with his shock at her audacity.

Abbess Hilda had risen nervously from her chair. Even Brother Eadulf looked astounded.

'Sister Fidelma!' Hilda was the first to recover from the surprise of her implication and spoke sharply. 'I know of your distress at witnessing the dead body of Brother Aelfric of Lindisfarne but, as I informed you, the matter is under investigation.'

'Just so,' Fidelma was abrupt. 'And the investigation bears on the credibility of Wulfric as a witness. The thane of Frihop is hardly a creditable witness in this matter. You mention three others. Are they independent or does this thane hold them under threat or bribe by payment?'

The meaning of the question registered with Alhfrith, whose features tightened in a scowl of anger.

'I shall not remain here to be insulted by a . . . woman, no matter of what rank,' he snapped. 'Were she not under the protection of my father I would have her whipped for such insolence. And so far as I am concerned, the beggar will burn at the stake at dawn tomorrow.'

'Whether guilty or not?' Fidelma replied heatedly.

'He is guilty.'

'Highness,' Brother Eadulf's quiet voice halted the petty king of Deira in mid-stride to the door. 'Highness, it may be as you say – that the beggar is guilty. But we should be allowed to carry on our investigation for much hangs in the balance here. Our commission comes directly from the king, your father. The eyes of Christendom are on this small abbey at Witebia and much is at stake. Guilt must be established beyond any question or it may well be that war will ravage the kingdom and not just Northumbria will be darkened under the raven's bloody wing. We have an oath and duty to obey the king, your father.'

The last sentence was heavy with emphasis.

Alhfrith paused and glanced from Brother Eadulf to the Abbess Hilda, now purposefully ignoring Sister Fidelma.

'You have until tomorrow at dawn to prove the beggar

entirely innocent . . . or he burns at the stake. And have a care of that woman,' he gestured to Fidelma without looking at her. 'There is a limit beyond which I will not be pushed.'

The door slammed behind the tall form of the son of Oswy.

Abbess Hilda looked at Fidelma reproachfully.

'Sister, you seem to forget that you are no longer in your own land and our customs and laws are different.'

Sister Fidelma bowed her head.

'I shall do my best to remember and hope that Brother Eadulf here will advise me when I am wrong. However, my primary aim is to get to the truth of this matter and truth should be served more than princes.'

The abbess sighed deeply.

'I will inform Oswy the king of this development and, in the meantime, you may carry on the investigation. But remember that Alhfrith is king of Deira, the province in which this abbey stands and a king's word is law.'

In the corridor outside Brother Eadulf halted and smiled with some degree of admiration at Fidelma.

'Abbess Hilda is right, sister. You make little headway with our Saxon princes if you do not acknowledge their status. I know it is different in Ireland but you are in Northumbria now. Nevertheless, you have given young Alhfrith something to think over. He seems a vindictive young man, so I would have a care of yourself.'

Fidelma found herself answering his smile.

'You must remind me when I do something wrong, Brother Eadulf. But it is hard to like someone like Alhfrith.'

'Kings and princes are not placed on thrones to be liked,' replied Eadulf. 'What is your next step?'

'To see the beggar,' she replied promptly. 'Do you want to see the physician, Edgar, for his report on the autopsy or to come with me?'

'I think that you may need me.' Eadulf was serious. 'I would not trust Alhfrith.'

In fact they met with Sister Athelswith, who informed them that Brother Edgar had already conducted an examination of the body, found nothing other than the obvious, and that the body had been taken to the catacombs of the abbey for entombment.

It was Sister Athelswith who conducted them down into the abbey's *hypogeum*, which term she used for the vast underground cellars of the buildings. A circular stone stairwell led twenty feet below the main abbey floor into a stone-flagged area with passageways spreading in all directions leading into cavernous chambers with high vaulted roofs. At the top of the stairs she had paused to light an oil lamp and by its light she guided them through a complex of musty passageways until they reached the catacombs, where the dead of the abbey were entombed in rows of stone sarcophagi. The smell had that curious quality of death which is inexplicable.

Sister Athelswith was leading the way through these damp catacombs, somewhat hurriedly, when an echoing wail rooted her to the spot. The hand in which she held up the lamp trembled violently and she genuflected with undue haste.

Sister Fidelma laid a hand on the nervous *domina*'s arm. 'It is only someone sobbing,' she reassured her.

Holding the lamp high, Sister Athelswith continued to lead onwards.

The source of the sobbing was evident almost immediately. Towards the end of the catacombs there was a small alcove in which two candles burned. The body of Abbess Étain had been removed to it for interment. It lay in funeral garb on a stone slab, the candles burning by its head. At the foot of the bier the figure of a sister lay in the *flecto* position, prostrating herself before the corpse. It was Sister Gwid. The girl raised herself, still sobbing, and hit the ground, crying out: '*Domine miserere peccatrice!*'

Sister Athelswith started forward, but Fidelma stayed her.

'Let's leave her alone with her grief for a while.'

The *domina* bowed her head in submission and resumed the path forward.

'The poor sister is distraught. She seems to have had a great attachment to the abbess,' she observed as she continued onward.

'We all have different ways of dealing with our grief,' replied Fidelma.

Beyond the catacombs was a series of storerooms and beyond those was the *apotheca* or wine cellar, in which stood great casks containing wines imported from Frankia, Gaul and Iberia. Here Fidelma paused, sniffing. The scent of the wines was powerful but some other bitter-sweet odour seemed to permeate the underground chambers, a curious aroma which made her face pucker in distaste.

'We are below the abbey kitchens, sister,' Athelswith said, as if in apology. 'Smells permeate along this area.'

Fidelma made no comment but motioned the *domina* to continue onwards. A little way further they came on a series of cells, usually kept for the storing of provisions, so Sister Athelswith told them, but also used in extreme circumstances for the imprisonment of miscreants. Brand torches lit the grey, cold subterranean chambers.

Two men sat playing dice in the gloomy light.

It was Sister Athelswith who announced their presence in sharp authoritative Saxon.

The two men rose grumbling to their feet and one of them took a key from a hook by a stout oak door.

Sister Athelswith, her task fulfilled, turned to vanish back in the gloom.

The man was handing the key to Eadulf when he suddenly glanced at Fidelma. He grinned lewdly and said something which his companion found amusing.

Eadulf spoke to them sharply. The two men shrugged and the first man tossed the key on to the table. Fidelma had enough Saxon to hear Eadulf ask for the names of the witnesses against the condemned man. The first warrior grunted some names including that of Wulfric of Frihop. They then returned to their dice game and took no more notice.

'What did he say?' whispered Fidelma.

'I asked for the names of the witnesses.'

'That I could understand. But what did he say beforehand?'

Eadulf looked embarrassed and shrugged. 'It was just the mouthing of the ignorant,' he replied evasively.

Fidelma did not press him further but watched as he unlocked the door.

There was no light inside the tiny, foul-smelling cell.

On the straw, in a corner, sat a man with an unkempt beard and long hair. He had obviously been roughly treated for his face was bruised and there was blood on the tattered garments he wore.

He raised dark hollow eyes to Fidelma and some noise approaching a chuckle gurgled in his throat.

'A hundred thousand welcomes to this house!' His voice

tried to express confident sarcasm but it croaked nervously.

'Are you Canna?' asked Fidelma.

'Canna, son of Canna of Ard Macha,' agreed the beggar conversationally. 'Am I to be allowed the last rites of the Church?'

'We are not here to perform that service,' replied Brother Eadulf sharply.

The beggar examined him for the first time.

'So? A Saxon brother, and one who adheres to Rome. It is no use asking me to confess. I did not kill Abbess Étain of Kildare.'

Fidelma gazed down at the wreckage of the man.

'Why do you think you stand accused?'

Canna glanced up. His eyes widened as he saw the youthful sister and recognised her as a compatriot.

'Because I excel at my art.'

'Which is?'

'I am an astrologer. I can foretell events by means of the interrogation of the stars.'

Eadulf gave a grunt of disbelief.

'Do you admit that you foretold the death of the abbess?'

The man nodded complacently.

'There is no surprise in that. Our art is ancient in Ireland as the good sister will confirm.'

Fidelma nodded agreement.

'It is true that astrologers have this gift—'

'Not a gift,' corrected the beggar. 'An astrologer studies as in any other science or art. I have studied for many years.'

'Very well,' agreed Fidelma. 'Astrologers have practised their art for many years in Ireland. It was once the prerogative of the druids but still the art continues and many kings and chieftains

103

will not even have their new houses constructed until a horoscope is cast as to the most auspicious time for such an event.'

Eadulf sniffed disparagingly.

'Are you saying that you cast a horoscope and saw the death of Étain?'

'I did.'

'And you named her and the hour of her death?'

'I did.'

'And did people hear you say this before the hour of her death?'

'They did.'

Eadulf stared at the man in disbelief.

'Yet you swear that you did not kill her or have any part in the encompassing of her death?'

Canna shook his head.

'I am innocent of her blood. This I swear.'

Eadulf turned to Fidelma.

'I am a plain man, not given to fanciful notions. I think that Canna must have had prior knowledge of this event. No man can see the future.'

Sister Fidelma shook her head firmly.

'Among our people the science of astrology has been far advanced. Even the simple people are taught to know the sky and make simple astronomical observations in daily life. Most know the hour of the night throughout the year by the position of the stars.'

'But to foretell that the sun will be blotted from the sky to the very minute—' began Eadulf.

'Easy to do,' interrupted Canna, annoyed at the Saxon's tone. 'I have trained long years to be proficient in my art.'

'Among our people, it would not be difficult to foretell such a thing,' agreed Fidelma.

'And to tell that a person will be killed?' pressed Eadulf. 'Is that so simple?'

Fidelma hesitated and bit her lip.

'More difficult. But I know these people have an art and can do so.'

Canna interrupted with a wheezy laugh.

'Do you want to know how it is done?'

Sister Fidelma nodded encouragement at the beggar.

'Tell us how you arrived at your conclusion,' she invited.

Canna sniffed loudly and reached into his tattered clothing, drawing forth a piece of vellum on which lines and computations were drawn, thrusting it forward to their gaze.

'This is simple to relate, brethren. On the first day of this month, which in Ireland is given over to the sacred fires of Bel, the moon stands in the way of the sun at the seventeenth hour of the day, perhaps several minutes after the hour for we are not able to be accurate to the minute or second. Here, in the eighth house, stands Taurus. The eighth house is that which signifies death. Taurus represents the land of Ireland and also is the sign that governs the throat. A death by strangulation or the cutting of the throat or even a hanging is indicated. And from Taurus I deduced such a tragedy would befall a child of Éireann.'

Eadulf looked sceptical but Sister Fidelma, who seemed to follow the logic of the astrologer, merely nodded and indicated that Canna should continue.

'See here, then.' Canna pointed to his calculations. 'We have, at this time, the planet Mercury standing in mutual reception to Venus. Does not Mercury rule the twelfth house, which represents murder, secrecy and deception? And is not Venus

105

the ruler of the eighth house of death, which also represents the female? And Venus sits in the ninth house which is also ruled by Mercury which additionally rules religion in this particular chart. And if all these signs were not enough, by a translation of light, which is practised in our profession, Mercury goes to conjunct the sun which is in eclipse.'

Canna sat back and gazed at them triumphantly.

'Any child could read the astrology.'

Eadulf sneered to hide his ignorance.

'Well, I am no child. Tell me plainly what all this means?'

Canna drew his brows together in anger.

'Plain, then, plain it is to see. The sun went into eclipse just after five o'clock of the afternoon. The planets showed that a death would take place by strangulation or throat cutting; that the victim would be a woman, a woman of Ireland and that she would be a religieuse. The planets also showed that this death would be a murder. Have I not made it plain enough?'

Eadulf stared for a long time at the beggar and then raised his eyes to Fidelma.

'Though I studied long in your country, sister, I did not study this science. Do you know anything of it?'

Fidelma pursed her lips.

'Little enough. But enough to know that Canna is making sense according to the strictures of his art.'

Eadulf shook his head doubtfully.

'But I can see no way of saving him from the fires of Alhfrith tomorrow. Even if what he says is true and he did not kill Étain, my fellow Saxons will be afraid of one who had read portents in the sky in such a manner.'

Sister Fidelma sighed deeply.

106

'I am coming to learn much about your Saxon culture. But my aim must be to discover the murderer not to appease superstition. Canna admits that he foretold the death of Étain. Now we must find those witnesses who heard him give her name and the precise hour. In short, we must find out exactly what he said. I fear he is a vain man.'

Canna spat angrily.

'I have told you what I said and why I said it. I am not afraid of these Saxons and their punishments, for my name will go down to posterity as the greatest seer of my age by reason of this prophecy from the stars.'

Sister Fidelma raised an eyebrow disdainfully.

'Is that what you want, Canna? To be martyred so that you may have your place in history?'

Canna chuckled wheezily.

'I am content to let posterity judge me.'

Sister Fidelma motioned Eadulf towards the cell door and then turned back abruptly.

'Why did you visit the Abbess Étain today?'

Canna started. 'Why . . . to warn her, of course.'

'To warn her against her own murder?'

'No . . .' Canna's chin came up. 'Yes. Why else?'

Outside the cell Eadulf turned to Fidelma.

'It could be that this man killed Étain to fulfil his prophecy?' he suggested. 'He admits going to warn her and Sister Athelswith was a witness to it.'

In fact, Eadulf had forgotten Sister Athelswith's mention of a beggar visiting the abbess before her death. It was clever of Fidelma to spot the connection.

'I doubt it. I have respect for this art which he practises for it is an ancient and honourable profession in my land. No one could so perfectly form the stars to his own bidding. No, I have a feeling that Canna saw what he saw in the stars but the real question is, was he so specific about who was to be killed? Remember that the Abbess Hilda said that he was not specific at all when he warned her that blood would flow at the time of the eclipse?'

'But if Canna did not know who was to be the victim why did he specifically warn Abbess Étain?'

'The hour grows late. But if Alhfrith is intent on burning this man tomorrow at dawn we have little time. Let us seek out and question these witnesses and discover what they have to say about Canna's actual words. You pursue the three Saxons and the thane of Frihop and get their testimony and I will have another word with Sister Athelswith about Canna's visit to Étain. We will meet back in the *domus hospitale* at midnight.'

Sister Fidelma led the way back into the abbey from the *hypogeum*. She was convinced that Canna was presenting himself as a willing victim to the flames of the Saxons. She was sure he was not guilty of the murder of Étain. His guilt lay in his colossal vanity, for she was sure that he sought immortality by one great prediction which would be talked of by the chroniclers for generations to come.

She felt an anger against him for, impressive as his prophecy was, he was delaying them from tracking down the real culprit, the genuine murderer of her friend and mother abbess, Étain of Kildare. He was an unnecessary distraction in her task.

One thing she realised, that there were many at the great assembly who apparently feared the oratorical skills of the Abbess Étain of Kildare. Could they have feared those skills enough to attempt to silence her, silence her permanently?

She had seen enough displays of temper between the Roman and Columban factions to know that the dislikes and hatreds ran deep. Perhaps they ran deep enough to cause Étain's death.

Chapter Nine

When Sister Fidelma reached the cloisters leading to the *domus hospitale*, the bell had started to chime for the midnight prayers. Brother Eadulf was already in Sister Athelswith's *officium*, his head bent over his prayer beads, intoning the Angelus in the Roman fashion.

> *Angelus Domini nuntiavit Mariae.*
> The Angel of the Lord announced unto Mary.
> *Et concepit de Spiritu Sancto.*
> And she conceived of the Holy Ghost.

Sister Fidelma waited quietly until Eadulf had finished his office and replaced his beads.

'Well?' she demanded without preamble.

Brother Eadulf pursed his lips.

'It seems that you were right. Only Wulfric claims he heard Canna pronounce the name of the abbess and the exact manner of her death. Of the other three, one says it was Wulfric who told him what Canna had said. He had not even heard Canna speak. The other two say that Canna spoke only in general terms, as he did to the Abbess Hilda. In other words, we have only Wulfric's testimony against Canna.'

Fidelma sighed softly.

'And Sister Athelswith says that Canna was warning Abbess

111

Abbe and others that there would be a death here. He did not single out Étain at all. This was confirmed by two of the brethren here whom Sister Athelswith called to have Canna ejected from Étain's *cubiculum*. Canna seems hell-bent on sacrificing his life for immortal fame. A stupid, vain man.'

'What should we do?'

'I believe that Canna has committed no crime save that of vanity. The idea of him being killed for that is abhorrent. We must release Canna at once. He should put distance between himself and this place before dawn.'

Eadulf's eyes widened.

'But what of Alhfrith? He is the son of Oswy and ruler of Deira.'

'And I am a *dálaigh* of the Brehon courts,' replied Fidelma spiritedly, 'acting under the commission of Oswy, King of Northumbria. I will assume full responsibility. We have been allowed to waste too much time on the cause of Canna as it is – time when we could have been tracking down Étain's true killer.'

Eadulf bit his lip.

'This is true, but to release Canna . . . ?'

But Fidelma had turned and was already leading the way to the *hypogeum* of the abbey. Her mind was already trying to figure out a way to release Canna in spite of the two guards outside. Hurrying along with her, Eadulf was beginning to realise that Fidelma was a determined woman. He had been misled by her youth and attractive softness at the start. He realised just how decisive she could be.

As it was, luck was with them for the two guards were both fast asleep. The nearness of the abbey's *apotheca* had proved too much of a temptation and they had helped themselves to a liberal quantity of wine. They were snoring in a drunken sleep, sprawled over the table outside the cell, empty flagons by their nerveless hands. Fidelma grinned triumphantly as she removed the key from one of the sleeping guards without any trouble.

She turned to a worried-looking Eadulf.

'If you do not want to be party to what I am about to do, you had best leave now.'

Eadulf shook his head, although with some reluctance.

'We are in this together.'

'The sorcerer, Canna, has gone,' announced Alhfrith. 'He has escaped from custody.'

Sister Fidelma and Brother Eadulf had been summoned yet again to the chambers of the Abbess Hilda following the serving of the *jentaculum*, the morning breaking of the fast. Abbess Hilda was sitting with pinched features, while Alhfrith paced agitatedly by the window. Oswy himself was sprawled in a chair by the smouldering fire. He was frowning moodily into the smoky turf.

Alhfrith had levelled his implied accusation immediately Fidelma and Eadulf had entered.

Sister Fidelma remained outwardly unperturbed.

'He did not escape. I dismissed him. He had committed no crime.'

The petty king of Deira's jaw dropped in astonishment. Whatever response he had been prepared for, it was not this. Even Oswy's eyes widened as his face was drawn from the fire to gaze in astonishment at Sister Fidelma.

'You dared to release him?' Alhfrith's voice was like the rumble of distant thunder before the storm erupts in its true savagery.

'Dared? I am a *dálaigh*, qualified to the level of *anruth*.

If I believe a person innocent then I am entitled to set him at liberty.'

The king of Deira's mouth was working.

Oswy slapped his thigh and suddenly gave forth a laugh, a loud burst of genuine mirth.

'By Christ's wounds, Alhfrith! She is within her rights!'

'Not so!' snapped his son in response. 'She has no right to practise the laws of her own land in our kingdom. No one but I could order the release of the beggar. She shall be punished. Guards!'

As quick as a lightning flash, Oswy's expression changed from amusement to cold anger.

'Alhfrith! You forget, I am your suzerain as well as your father. You are merely ruler of this province under me and by my patronage. Therefore I am the arbiter of law here and I shall decide who is to be punished and who not. Sister Fidelma is acting under my commission in this land.'

The foxy-faced Wulfric had entered at Alhfrith's call for the guard, but Oswy gestured savagely for him to leave. The swarthy thane gave a hurried glance at Alhfrith, as if seeking his permission, but seeing his lord's red, mortified face he departed swiftly.

Alhfrith's face was a study of suppressed anger. Only the livid scar on his cheek made a curious white weal across the blood-infused skin.

Eadulf was easing his weight from one foot to another, looking uncomfortable.

'If there is blame and punishment, sire,' he said, speaking for the first time since they had entered the chamber, 'then it is mine. I take responsibility. I agreed with Sister Fidelma's assessment of the astrologer's lack of guilt in the matter. I supported her decision to release him to save him from a needless and unjust death by fire.'

Fidelma's eyes widened in surprise and she gave the Saxon monk a brief glance of gratitude. She had not expected him to state his support in so strong a fashion.

Alhfrith seemed to choke.

'So you desire punishment?' Oswy chuckled, turning to the Saxon brother.

'No, sire. I merely say that I am also responsible for the release of the beggar.'

Oswy shook his head in amusement before turning back to Fidelma. Fidelma stood watching the Northumbrian king calmly. Eadulf shivered slightly – one word of displeasure from Oswy and they would both be dead.

'It is a lucky thing for you, Fidelma of Kildare, that I am conversant with your ways and customs and able to check the hot-headedness of my son here. But you have nearly over-reached yourself. You do not have the authority in my kingdom to release prisoners unless I specifically order it.'

Fidelma lowered her head.

'Then I am truly sorry, Oswy of Northumbria. It was my error in thinking that when you commissioned me as a *dálaigh* of the Brehon courts, knowing full well what that entailed, you gave me permission to exercise my role exactly as I would in my own land.'

Oswy frowned. Did he detect a slight mocking tone in the girl's voice?

'I think you knew that you acted without authority,' he said, his eyes narrowing. 'I do not think that you are as ignorant of the laws of this land as you are making out.'

Fidelma grimaced with apparent diffidence.

'Do you not?' she asked with an exaggerated air of wide-eyed innocence.

'No, by thunder! I do not.' Oswy paused and then his expression split into a grin. 'In fact, Sister Fidelma, I think you are a very wise and knowing person.'

'For that, I thank you, Oswy.'

Alhfrith interrupted angrily.

'What of the sorcerer? Let me send Wulfric and some warriors out to track him down.'

Oswy silenced him with a gesture without his blue eyes leaving those reflective green eyes of Sister Fidelma.

'You say that this beggar is innocent?'

'Yes,' agreed Fidelma. 'His only guilt was the sin of pride. He is an astrologer. He foresaw some events in the stars. But we have questioned those he spoke to before the event. He was not specific and only after the event did he attempt to boast that he had accurately predicted the death of the abbess, thus incurring suspicion.'

Oswy slowly nodded his head.

'I have seen the Irish astrologers at work. I can believe in the accuracy of their prophecies. But, you say, he did not name Étain as the victim before the event?'

'That is not so. Wulfric heard him!' interrupted Alhfrith sharply.

'And *only* Wulfric,' Eadulf chimed in. 'The only witness who said he named Étain and the manner of her death before the event was Wulfric, a thane who wishes to discredit the Irish in general and any linked with the church of Columba. Wulfric boasts that he hanged Brother Aelfric not two days ago and that he will do the same to any monk of Columba who trespasses in his domain.'

'This is so,' Fidelma agreed. 'We have questioned three witnesses who maintain that Canna was only vague in his prediction. Four witnesses, counting the Abbess Hilda here, will swear to that. Only after the murder did Canna claim that he had accurately made the prediction.'

'Why should the beggar lie?' queried Oswy. 'Surely he knew the suspicion it would bring on him? And that if he were suspected of employing black arts to encompass a death, then death would be his retribution?'

'He lies because he wished to take the credit for a great prophecy, one that would be remembered for generations,' Fidelma answered. 'He twisted the truth in his mind and claimed his prediction was more accurate than it was.'

'But he was accepting death by so doing,' Oswy pointed out again.

'But the Irish have little fear of entering the afterlife,' Eadulf commented. 'They do so joyously. Even before they turned to the word of Christ, it was their teaching that there was an Otherworld, a life of the ever young into which all living things were admitted. Canna sought glory in this world and was happy to start his new life in the Otherworld.'

'A madman then?'

Fidelma shrugged diffidently.

'Who is to say whether he was mad or sane? Fame and immortality. There is a little of that madness in us all. Nevertheless, he should not be punished for what he did not do and so I released him and told him that unless he wished the truth of his vanity to be talked about throughout the feasting halls of Ireland, unless he wanted to be satirised throughout the five kingdoms, he should stick to the accuracy of his prophecy.' She paused and smiled. 'He should be well on his way to the kingdom of Rheged by now.'

'Father!' It was Alhfrith again. 'You cannot let this pass. It is an insult to me—'

'Silence!' thundered Oswy. 'I have decided the matter.'

'The most important thing is to find out who really did slay the Abbess Étain. Why waste time on petty spite?' Fidelma said, giving Alhfrith a cold glance.

Oswy raised a hand to stifle the outburst that hovered on the lips of his son.

'You are right. I, Oswy the king, endorse what you have done, sister. The beggar, Canna, is at liberty. He can stay or go in freedom. But better he did go to Rheged and the lands beyond.' He looked meaningfully at his mortified son. 'And nothing further shall be mentioned or done about the matter. Is that clear, Alhfrith?'

His tall, blond-haired son stood silent, his eyes downcast, his lips compressed.

'Is it clear?' repeated the king ominously.

Alhfrith raised his rebellious eyes and tried to meet his father's gaze and then lowered then again, nodding silently.

'Good,' smiled Oswy, relaxing again in his chair. 'Then we have the synod to attend to while you and the good Brother Eadulf here continue your quest.'

Sister Fidelma bowed her head in acknowledgment.

'Much time has been wasted on this matter,' she remarked quietly. 'Eadulf and I will withdraw and continue our investigation.'

Outside the Abbess Hilda's chamber, Brother Eadulf wiped a hand across his perspiring forehead.

'You have made a bitter enemy in Alhfrith, Sister Fidelma.'

The girl seemed disinterested.

'The conflict was none of my seeking. Alhfrith is a bitter young man by his own nature and is at odds with his world. Making enemies is more easy to him than making friends.'

'Nevertheless,' Eadulf said, 'you had best have a care. Wulfric is his man and does whatever Alhfrith tells him. He probably lied about Canna on Alhfrith's instruction. Could Alhfrith have killed Étain to create a problem in the synod?'

Fidelma had not ruled that possibility out and said so as they turned into the cloisters.

'What next?' asked Eadulf.

'Seven people are known to have visited Étain in her cell before she was found murdered. We have spoken with one of them – Canna the astrologer. Now we must speak with the other six.'

Eadulf agreed.

'Sister Gwid, Brother Taran, Abbess Hilda, Bishop Colmán, Brother Seaxwulf and Agatho the priest from Icanho,' he counted.

Fidelma grinned lightheartedly.

'You have a good memory, brother. That is good. We will learn nothing from Colmán and Hilda other than what we have already. They merely accompanied Étain to the midday meal and talked about the debate.'

'Shall we see Sister Gwid first?' he suggested. 'As she was the abbess's secretary she may well know something which could be of help.'

Sister Fidelma sceptically shook her head.

'I doubt it. I journeyed with her from Iona. She is a gawky but well-meaning girl. I do not think she was a close confidant of the abbess but simply followed her about with a sheep-like devotion. The abbess was once her tutor in Ireland.'

'Even so, we should speak with her. According to Sister Athelswith, the abbess was arguing with her on the morning of her death. What could that have been about?'

Fidelma had forgotten mention of an argument.

They had reached the *officium* of the guest quarters and found Sister Athelswith bending over some ledgers.

'We wish to speak with several brethren in private, sister,' Fidelma told her. 'With your permission, we will use your *officium* as the most convenient place to conduct our questioning. I am sure that you will have no objection?'

From her facial expression, Sister Athelswith had many objections but she knew that Fidelma and Eadulf had the full support of the Abbess Hilda and so she simply exhaled and removed her ledgers.

'And may we ask you to serve us by summoning these people as we want them?' pressed Eadulf with a winning smile.

The elderly sister sniffed, trying to hide her displeasure at this interruption to her routine.

'It will be as you request, brother. I will serve you in whatever way I can.'

'Good,' smiled Fidelma brightly. 'Then bring us Sister Gwid. She should be in her *dormitorium*.'

It was a short time later when the gawky Sister Gwid entered. She was more in control of her emotions now, although her eyes were still red from crying. She looked from Fidelma to Eadulf with an air of a child lost and bewildered.

'How are you feeling this morning, sister?' asked Fidelma, motioning her to take a seat.

Gwid bowed her head and seated herself on a wooden stool before the table that served as Sister Athelswith's desk.

'I apologise for my display of emotion,' she replied. 'Étain was a good friend to me. The news of her death unnerved me for a while.'

'But you will do your best to help us?' Fidelma's tone was almost cajoling.

Sister Gwid shrugged indifferently and Eadulf felt he had to explain their task and their authority.

'There is little I can say,' Sister Gwid became a little more accommodating. 'You will recall that I was in the *sacrarium* with you, Sister Fidelma, waiting for the opening of the debate when news came of the Abbess Étain's death.'

'Indeed,' Fidelma acknowledged. 'Yet you held the office of her secretary and met with her in her *cubiculum* yesterday morning.'

Gwid inclined her head in agreement.

'I did. Can you track down the foul thing that killed her?' she asked, her voice suddenly fierce.

'That is what we are here to discover, Gwid,' Brother Eadulf intervened. 'Firstly, we must ask some questions.'

Gwid made an inviting gesture with her hand. It made her seem even more awkward, drawing attention to her large bony hands.

'Ask away.'

Fidelma glanced at Eadulf and indicated that he should continue. The Saxon leant forward across the table.

'You were seen to be arguing with Étain outside her *cubiculum* yesterday,' he said abruptly.

'Étain was my friend,' Gwid replied abashed.

'Did you argue with her?' Eadulf demanded.

'No!' The reply came immediately. 'Étain was . . . was simply annoyed with me because I had forgotten to collate some facts for her in the preparation of her argument for the debate. That is all.'

It was logical enough that Étain, in preparing to meet with Wilfrid, would be highly strung and quick to temper.

'Are you from the land of the Picts?'

Fidelma frowned at Eadulf's abrupt change of tack.

The dark face of Sister Gwid became bewildered.

'From the land of the Cruthin whom you call "Picts" which is but a corruption of a Latin nickname meaning "painted ones",' she said pedantically. 'It was a custom of our warriors in ancient times to paint themselves when they went into battle – a custom that has long since ceased. I was born when Garnait son of Foth ruled the Cruthin and extended his rule over the kings of Strath-Clòta.'

Fidelma could not help smiling at the fierce pride in the girl's voice.

'But not all Picts are Christian,' Eadulf observed slyly.

'And certainly not all Saxons are Christian,' responded Gwid sharply.

'True. But you were trained in Ireland, weren't you?'

'I studied firstly in the abbey of Iona but then crossed to Ireland to study at Emly before finally returning to Iona. It was at Emly that I studied under Sister Étain, as she then was.'

'So?' Fidelma leant forward now. 'How long did you study with Étain?'

'Only three months. She was teaching philosophy in the faculty of Rodan the Wise. Then she heard from her own mother house of Kildare that the Abbess Ita had died and on hastening back to Kildare she was elected as head of the house. After Étain became Mother Abbess of Kildare, I saw her only once.'

'When was that?' Eadulf asked.

'When I had finished my studies with Rodan and was passing

on my way back to Bangor, to get ship to Iona. I sought hospitality at Kildare.'

'How were you chosen to become secretary to Abbess Étain during this debate?' demanded Eadulf.

'I was chosen because Abbess Étain knew of my skills as an interpreter, for I was a prisoner of the Northumbrians for five years, until Finán of Lindisfarne had me freed and sent back to my homeland. Also I am able to construe the Greek of the writings of the Gospels without difficulty. For these reasons, Étain chose me.'

'I did not ask why, I asked how.'

'I have no idea. I was waiting for the ship at Bangor when a message reached me asking me to attend the assembly here and serve in the capacity of secretary to Étain. This I agreed to do most willingly. I sailed for Iona the day after and there, of course, I met with you, Sister Fidelma. Brother Taran was organising a mission to Northumbria and, as you know, we both found ourselves, with others of the brethren of Columba, journeying to this place together.'

Sister Fidelma inclined her head in agreement at Gwid's interpretation of events.

'And when was the last time you saw the Abbess Étain alive?' she asked.

Sister Gwid frowned thoughtfully as she considered the answer to the question.

'As soon as the brethren had concluded the midday meal, the *prandium*, an hour after the midday Angelus. The abbess, who had eaten with the Abbess Hilda and Bishop Colmán, asked me to accompany her to her *cubiculum*.'

'So that was after you had the quarrel with her?' Fidelma said quickly.

'I said that it was no quarrel,' Gwid snapped defensively. 'And Étain did not keep her temper long. She was a kind woman.'

'For what purpose did she ask you to attend her after the midday meal?' queried Eadulf.

'To discuss the manner of the debate that afternoon,' replied Gwid. 'As you know, Étain was scheduled to open the proceedings on behalf of the church of Columba. She wanted to discuss her speech with me, the way she could use quotations from the apostles to appeal to the Saxons. Her Greek was sometimes not of the best.'

'How long were you with her?' Fidelma asked.

'An hour. No more than an hour. We spoke about the detail of her arguments with respect to the references from the Gospels. I stood ready to translate should there be doubt about the quotations she chose.'

'How did she seem to you when you left her?' Eadulf asked, rubbing the tip of his nose with his forefinger.

Gwid frowned.

'I do not follow.'

'Was she apprehensive? Was she relaxed? How did she seem?'

'She seemed relaxed enough. Obviously she was preoccupied with her work but no more preoccupied than I have seen her when preparing for one of her tutorials at Emly.'

'She expressed no alarm? No one had threatened her since she had been here?'

'Ah, you mean a threat from one of the Roman faction? She told me that once or twice she had been insulted by Roman priests. Athelnoth, for example. But he—'

Gwid suddenly bit her lip.

Fidelma's eyes sparkled immediately.

'You were going to say something, sister?' Her voice was quiet but insistent.

Gwid grimaced awkwardly.

'It is nothing. Something personal and irrelevant.'

Eadulf scowled.

'We will judge what is irrelevant, sister. What were you going to say?'

'Athelnoth was very antagonistic to Étain.'

'Because?' prompted Fidelma, sensing the woman's extreme reluctance to make herself clear.

'It is not seemly that I should speak of the dead abbess in this manner.'

Eadulf gave a bark of exasperation.

'You have not spoken in any manner as yet. What is not seemly?'

'We know that Athelnoth is not only pro-Roman but he views Northumbrians as superior to all people,' Fidelma remarked, remembering what Étain had told her on her first night at Streoneshalh.

Gwid bit her lip again, colouring slightly.

'The antagonism was one of personal anger rather than one of theological conflict.'

Fidelma was perplexed.

'You will have to explain this. What do you mean by "personal anger"?'

'I believe that Athelnoth made advances to the Abbess Étain. Advances of an amorous nature.'

There was a brief silence.

Sister Fidelma's lips puckered into a long, silent whistle. Étain was an attractive woman, Fidelma had long realised that fact, and Étain was no celibate. She was a woman appreciative of manly attraction. Indeed, Fidelma had placed in the dim recess of her memory what Étain had told her when they had met, of her wish to remarry and resign from the abbacy of Kildare.

Eadulf was shaking his head in surprise.

'Are you sure of this, Sister Gwid?'

The Pictish religieuse raised her broad shoulders and let them fall in a gesture that was one of part indecision and part resignation.

'I cannot say that I am sure. All I know is that Étain disliked him intensely and said to me that under some circumstances she could accept some of the new teachings of Rome.'

'What do you think she meant by that?'

'I believe she was referring to the teachings on celibacy, brother,' responded Gwid with some coyness.

'Did you know, then, Abbess Étain was to announce her resignation as abbess of Kildare after this assembly?' Fidelma asked suddenly. 'Did you know she contemplated taking a husband—?'

'When did Étain make this comment about celibacy?' Eadulf interrupted.

Fidelma bit her lip in irritation for Eadulf had cut off the spontaneity that she had hoped for in Gwid's reply. The Pictish sister stirred uneasily.

'We were talking about how she would respond if the Roman faction brought up the arguments on celibacy. Many of them believe that there should be no mixed houses, and that all the religious, from the brethren to the bishops should remain celibate. It was after this that the abbess made her remark. I did not know that Étain contemplated marriage herself or resigning from the abbacy.' Gwid frowned. 'If this is true, it would have been unjust.'

'Unjust?'

'Immoral then, immoral that a woman of the abbess' talent should resign her office to live with a man. Perhaps her death was a form of absolution from an action which would have been vile and sinful.'

Fidelma gazed curiously at her.

'How do you know that she referred to Athelnoth when she made her remarks? How could you interpret that to mean that the Saxon had made advances to her?'

'Because Athelnoth disturbed us when we were talking of this matter, requesting to speak alone with Étain. Étain told him that she was busy and he went away. It happened while we were talking of celibacy. She said, so far as I recall, "When a man like that makes advances, I could accept these new teachings of Rome" – or words to that effect.'

Eadulf returned to the questioning.

'Are you sure she said "when" rather than "if"? Was she implying that Athelnoth had made such advances or was she hypothesising?' he demanded curtly.

Sister Gwid raised a shoulder and let it fall.

'I came away with the distinct impression that Athelnoth had already made licentious suggestions to the abbess.'

There was a silence while Fidelma and Eadulf digested the significance of what Gwid had told them.

Fidelma continued after a moment or two of silence.

'And was there any other person or incident which Étain spoke of in connection with antagonism or dislike from the Roman faction?'

'Only the subject of Athelnoth was spoken of.'

127

'Very well. Thank you, sister. We are sorry to have added to your sorrow.'

The ungainly sister rose and turned for the door.

'Incidentally – '

Fidelma's voice stayed her.

' – you seemed to indicate that marriage among religious is a vile, sinful practice. What do you think of the controversy of celibacy among the religious?'

Sister Gwid's mouth tightened grimly.

'I am in favour of the teaching of the blessed Paul of Tarsus and of Maighnenn, abbot of Kilmainham. Let the sexes not defile each other in the service of the Almighty!'

Eadulf waited until Sister Gwid had left before rounding on Fidelma in annoyance, interrupting her thoughts.

'If we are working together, sister, you really should not keep information from me.'

Fidelma was about to respond angrily but suddenly realised that Eadulf was right to be annoyed. She had not mentioned Étain's decision to resign her office to marry. She had not even thought it important and she was not convinced that it was. She sighed under her breath.

'I am sorry. I was not sure whether Étain's decision to resign her office was a matter of relevance. Étain only mentioned it to me on the night before her death.'

'Who was she to marry?'

'I presume it was someone she met in Ireland. Her intention was to go back to Kildare and resign her office. Then I suppose she would continue to teach in a double house as she did before at Emly.'

'But you don't know whom she was to marry?'

'She did not tell me. What relevance is it here, in Northumbria?'

Eadulf bit his lip and was silent a moment.

'I find this hard to believe,' he said suddenly.

Fidelma raised an eyebrow.

'What in particular?'

'About Athelnoth. It is reported that he is a haughty man; he seems to believe all foreigners are his inferiors and he is an ardent supporter of Roman rule. Why then would he have developed a passion for Abbess Étain?'

Fidelma was cynical.

'Was he not a man?'

Eadulf felt a colour on his cheeks.

'Surely. But even so—'

'Étain was a very attractive woman,' Fidelma amplified. 'Nevertheless, I take your point. But sometimes opposite personalities are attracted to each other.'

'That is so,' Eadulf agreed. 'You have known Sister Gwid for a while. Can we trust her as an accurate observer? Would she have misinterpreted what Étain said or this business with Athelnoth?'

'She is an awkward girl. One who is intent to please her superiors. But her gawky limbs hide an astute brain. Indeed, I found her almost a pedant on matters of detail. I think we may trust her word.'

'Then I think we should see this Athelnoth next,' Eadulf suggested.

Chapter Ten

Sister Athelswith returned with the news that Athelnoth was occupied in the *sacrarium* listening to the debate and that she could not disturb him without interruption to the entire synod. Fidelma and Eadulf decided to fill in the time by going along to the *sacrarium* and listening to the proceedings. Since they had arrived at Streoneshalh they had not heard any of the speeches made during the synod. Apparently, in the place of the Abbess Étain, Bishop Colmán himself had opened for the church of Columba with a short résumé of the teachings of the monks of Iona. It was a crisp, concise speech but without oratorical eloquence or guile. Wilfrid's response was short and sarcastic, scoring points off his opponent's candour.

Fidelma and Eadulf stood at the back of the *sacrarium*, near to a side door behind the Columban benches, trying to avoid the almost breath-taking odours of burning incense.

A tall, angular man, identified to Fidelma by a sister standing close to them as the venerable bishop Cedd, an original disciple of Aidán, was rising to speak as they entered. The sister whispered that Cedd had just arrived from the land of the East Saxons, where he had been on a mission, and had now been appointed to interpret from Saxon to Irish or from Irish to Saxon as the need arose. Cedd was the eldest of four brothers who had been converted by Aidán and who now led the church of Columba in Northumbria. Chad, another brother, was the bishop of Lastingham, while their brothers Caelin and Cynebill were also attending the assembly. Chad, the sister volunteered, had received his education in Ireland.

'There has been much speculation as to the date of our Easter celebration,' Cedd was saying. 'Our gracious queen, Eanflaed, celebrates according to Rome. Our good king, Oswy, follows the teachings of Columba. Who is right and who is wrong? It can happen that the king has finished the fast and is keeping the Easter Sabbath while the queen and her attendants are still in Lent. This is a situation that sane men cannot countenance.'

'True,' called the pugnacious Wilfrid, not bothering to rise from his seat. 'A situation rectified when you admit your error in your computation of Easter.'

'A computation sanctioned by Anatolius, who ranks among the learned men of the church,' replied Cedd, his parchment-like, bony face suffused by two bright spots of pink on the cheek bones.

'Anatolius of Laodicea? Rubbish!' Wilfrid had risen to his feet now, spreading his arms in appeal to his pro-Roman brothers. 'I have no doubt that your calendrical computations were concocted among the Britons scarcely two centuries ago. Rome's computations were carefully worked out by Victorinus of Aquitaine.'

'Victorinus!' A sun-tanned man, scarcely more than thirty years old, sprang up from the Columban benches. He was fair haired and his expression was intense. 'Everyone knows that those computations were in error.'

The informative sister leant close to Fidelma.

'That is Cuthbert of Melrose. He is now prior there since our blessed brother Boisil died. He is one of our best orators.'

'Error?' Wilfrid was sneering. 'Explain the error.'

'We stick firmly to the original computations agreed at the Synod of Arles and to the earliest ritual practices,' replied Cuthbert. 'It is Rome that is in error. Rome has broken away from the original dating of Easter by adopting these new computations arrived at by Victorinus. This Victorinus of Aquitaine simply made a few amendments during the time of Pope Hilary. He did not even make full calculations.'

'Aye,' cried the gaunt Abbess Abbe of Coldingham vehemently, Oswy's sister. 'And were not more amendments proposed by Dionysius Exigius during the pontificate of Felix III? The original rules governing the dating of Easter, which were all agreed at Arles, have been distorted by Rome several times during the last three hundred years. We maintain the original computation agreed at Arles.'

'That is a falsehood before God!' snapped Agilbert, the Frankish bishop, irritably.

There was uproar until the venerable Cedd indicated that he wished to speak again.

'Brethren, we should show charity to one another in this place. Those who argue against the Columban church do so surely from ignorance. Even after the Council of Arles the Christian world agreed that our calendar for the commemorative feast days must be based on the calendar of the land in which the Christ was born and grew to manhood. Thus we agreed that they should be based on the Jewish lunar calendar and thus did the Passover, at which time our Saviour was crucified, fall in the month of Nisan. This was the seventh and Spring month of the Jewish calendar, the period we now designate as March and April.

'Thus do we call our festival the Pasca from the Hebrew *Pesach* or Passover. Did not Paul, in writing to the Corinthians,

133

refer to Christ as their Passover Lamb – their sacrifice – because it was well known that he was executed at that festival, under the old computations that Passover fell on the fourteenth day of Nisan. Using this calculation we celebrate the festival on whatever Sunday falls between the fourteenth and twentieth days after the first full moon following the spring equinox.'

'But Rome has made it unlawful for Christians to celebrate a Christian festival on the same day as a Jewish one,' Wilfrid interrupted.

'Exactly so,' replied Cedd calmly. 'And that was nonsensical when the Council of Nicaea, debating after the Council of Arles, declared such a thing to be unlawful. Christ was, in the flesh, a Jew—'

There was a gasp of horror among the assembly.

Cedd looked round at the assembly complacently.

'Was he not?' he queried cynically. 'Or was he a Nubian? Or a Saxon even? Perhaps he was a Frank? In what land was he born and grew to manhood if it was not the land of the Jews?'

'He was the Son of God!' Wilfrid's voice was enraged.

'And the Son of God chose to be born into the land of Israel, with his earthly parents Jewish, bringing the Word first to those who were Chosen of God. Only in killing their Messiah did the Jews reject the Word leaving it to be taken up by the Gentiles. Is it not odd, then, to reject the fact that Christ was executed during a particular feast of the Jews and then to designate an arbitrary date for the Christian world to commemorate that execution which bears no relationship to the actual date it happened?'

Abbess Abbe was nodding her head in agreement.

'I hear that those who argue for Rome are seeking to change our day of repose as well because it falls on the same day as the

Hebrew sabbath,' she observed bitingly.

Wilfrid pursed his lips in anger.

'Sunday, the first day of the week, is rightly the day of repose for it is symbolic of the Resurrection.'

'Yet Saturday is the traditional day of repose, it being the last day of the week,' argued another brother, whom the sister at Fidelma's side identified as Chad, the abbot of Lastingham.

'These amendments made by Rome take us further and further away from the original dates and render our commemorative ceremonies and anniversaries arbitrary and without meaning,' Abbe called out. 'Why not accept that Rome is in error?'

Wilfrid had to wait for the applause from the Columban benches to die away.

He was clearly flustered by the ageing Cedd's erudition and so resorted to ridicule.

'So Rome is in error?' sneered Wilfrid. 'If Rome is in error then Jerusalem is in error, Alexandria is in error, Antioch is in error, the whole world is in error; only the Irish and the Britons know what is right—'

The young abbot Chad was on his feet immediately.

'I would point out to the noble Wilfrid of Ripon' – the taunting tone of his voice was unmistakable – 'that the churches of the East have already rejected Rome's new computations about Easter. They follow the same computations that we do. They do not jeer at the name Anatolius of Laodicea. Neither the church of the Irish and Britons nor the churches of the East have turned away from the original dates given at Arles. Only Rome seeks to revise its practices.'

'The Roman faction speak as if Rome is the centre of everything.' Bishop Colmán now spoke, sensing his advantage.

'They speak as if we are out of step with the rest of Christendom. Yet the churches of Egypt and Syria and the East refused to accept Roman dictation at their council of Chalcedon by—'

He was forced to stop by the rise of protesting shouting from the Roman benches.

Finally, Oswy rose and held up his hand.

Gradually those gathered in the great hall fell silent.

'Brethren, our debate this morning has been long and arduous and doubtless we have exchanged much food for thought. This is a good time to call a recess, so that we may take nourishment for the flesh as well as for the spirit. We can spend this afternoon in meditation. We shall reconvene here this evening.'

The assembly rose and began gradually to disperse, voices still raised in argument among themselves.

'Which is Athelnoth?' asked Fidelma of her informant.

The sister turned, frowning slightly, as she surveyed the groups of religious.

'That man there, sister, across the far side of the hall. Next to the young man with the corn-coloured hair.'

With a glance at Eadulf, Sister Fidelma turned and pushed her way through the arguing throng towards the figure her informant had indicated, a man who stood slightly behind the small pugnacious figure of Wilfrid of Ripon, as though waiting to speak with him. He stood by a blond-haired monk who stood holding several books and documents at Wilfrid's elbow.

'Brother Athelnoth?' she asked, coming up behind his shoulder.

The man started slightly. She saw the sudden tensing of the muscles in the back of his neck. Then he turned slightly with a frown.

He was not a tall man, perhaps five feet five inches in height, but he seemed to dominate his companions. A man with a broad face, the forehead high and sloping, and with an aquiline nose and dark eyes. Fidelma supposed that many women would find him attractive, but he was too saturnine and brooding for her taste.

'You wanted me, sister?' he asked, his voice low, resonant and pleasant.

She was conscious of Eadulf arriving, slightly breathless at forcing his way through the crowd, at her shoulder.

'We did.'

'It is not a convenient time.' Athelnoth's tone was one of distant superiority and now, observing Eadulf, he addressed his remarks to the Saxon monk. Fidelma found it an irritating mannerism of all Saxons that if a man were present he always took precedence over a woman. 'I am waiting to speak with Abbot Wilfrid here.'

Brother Eadulf spoke before Fidelma could answer. Perhaps he saw the anger boiling in her.

'It will take but a short amount of time, brother. It concerns the death of the Abbess Étain.'

Athelnoth could not quite keep control of his facial features. There was a momentary change in his expression – gone before Sister Fidelma was sure of its meaning.

'What has the matter to do with you?' countered the man a little belligerently.

'We are charged with the investigation of the matter under the authority of Oswy the king, also Colmán, bishop of Northumbria, and Hilda, Abbess of Streoneshalh.'

Sister Fidelma replied quietly but clearly enough for Athelnoth's mouth to set firmly. With such authority he could not argue.

'What do you wish of me?' he demanded. She could accept the tone of defensiveness which now crept into his voice.

'Let us walk where we may hear ourselves speak,' Eadulf said, indicating the side door of the *sacrarium*, away from the still-argumentative religious, many of whom had not yet dispersed to the refectory for the midday meal.

Athelnoth hesitated, glancing at Wilfrid, who was deep in conversation with Agilbert and the rotund figure of Wighard, who was supporting the frail-looking Archbishop of Canterbury, Deusdedit, on his arm. They were too animated by their exchange to notice anyone else and, with a suppressed sigh, Athelnoth turned and walked with Eadulf and Fidelma towards the door. They turned across the *hortus olitorius*, the abbey's extensive kitchen gardens, beyond the *sacrarium*.

The warm May sun was casting a brilliant light on the vegetation and causing the scent of a myriad herbs and plants to lie fragrantly on the air.

'Let us walk awhile and breathe God's fresh air after the closeness of the assembly hall,' suggested Eadulf almost unctuously.

Fidelma took one side of Athelnoth while Eadulf walked upon the other side.

'Did you know the Abbess Étain?' asked Eadulf, almost casually.

Athelnoth cast a quick glance in his direction.

'It depends on what you mean,' he countered.

'Shall I rephrase the question, perhaps?' Eadulf said quickly. '*How well* did you know Étain of Kildare?'

Athelnoth frowned. His face coloured and he hesitated. Then he replied shortly, 'Not well at all.'

'But how well?' pressed Fidelma, pleased with the way the

138

Saxon monk had begun the interrogation.

'I met her only four days ago.'

When neither replied, Athelnoth plunged on hurriedly.

'Bishop Colmán called me to him a week ago and told me that he had heard that the Abbess Étain of Kildare was arriving to take part in the great synod. Her ship had landed at the port of Ravenglass in the kingdom of Rheged. Her route would take her across the high hills to Catraeth. Colmán asked me to take some brothers and go to Catraeth to meet the abbess to escort her safely to Witebia. This I did.'

'This was your first meeting with the abbess?' Fidelma pressed for confirmation.

Athelnoth frowned briefly.

'What makes you ask these questions?' he replied guardedly.

'We wish to have a clear picture of Étain's last days,' explained Eadulf.

'Then, yes. This was my first meeting with her.'

Fidelma and Eadulf exchanged a glance. Both felt sure that Athelnoth was lying. But why?

'And nothing untoward happened on your journey here to Streoneshalh?' Eadulf asked, after a while.

'Nothing.'

'You did not enter into any argument with the abbess or her followers?'

Athelnoth bit his lip.

'I don't know what you mean,' he said sullenly.

'Oh come,' Fidelma said cajolingly. 'You are known to be ardent for Rome and the Abbess Étain was the chief spokesman for Columba's rule. Surely some words were exchanged? After all, you were two or three days on the road with her and her entourage.'

Athelnoth shrugged.

'Oh, that. Of course we had some discussion.'

'*Some* discussion?'

Athelnoth's sigh spoke of ill-concealed irritation.

'We had one argument, that is all. I told her what I thought. No crime in that.'

'Of course not. But did your arguments descend to any physical disagreement?'

Athelnoth flushed. 'One young Columban monk had to be restrained. Being young, he had to be forgiven that he had no knowledge of wisdom to argue in any other form but violence. A foolish young man. It was of no consequence.'

'And when you arrived here, what then?'

'Then I had discharged my duty to my bishop. Having brought the abbess and her party safely to the abbey here, that was all.'

'All?' Fidelma's voice was sharp.

Athelnoth glanced at her and made no reply.

'Did you see her afterwards, after you had brought her to the safety of these walls?' prompted Eadulf.

Athelnoth shook his head, his lips compressed.

'So.' Fidelma let out a long breath. 'You did not call upon her in her cell and wish to speak with her alone?'

Fidelma could almost see the man's mind working furiously; she saw the slight widening of the eyes as he remembered the witness to his indiscretion.

'Ah, yes . . .'

'Yes?'

'I did call upon her once.'

'When and for what purpose?'

The man was clearly on his guard. Fidelma could feel a

140

detached sympathy for the man as he attempted to conjure a suitable excuse.

'Just after the *prandium* was finished, on the first day of the debate. The day of her death. I wanted to return something that belonged to the abbess. Something that she had dropped during our journey from Catraeth.'

'Really?' Eadulf scratched an ear. 'Why was it not returned before?'

'I . . . had only just discovered it.'

'And did you return "it" – whatever it was?'

'A brooch.' Athelnoth sounded confident. 'And I did not return it.'

'Why?'

'When I went to see the abbess she was not alone.'

'So why not leave the brooch?'

'I wished to speak with her.' Athelnoth hesitated again and bit his lip. 'I decided to return later.'

'And did you?'

'I am sorry?'

'Did you return later?'

'Later, the abbess was found dead.'

'So you still have her brooch?'

'Yes.'

Sister Fidelma held out her hand silently.

'I do not have it with me.'

'Very well,' smiled Fidelma. 'We will accompany you to your *cubiculum*. I presume it is there?'

Athelnoth hesitated and nodded slowly.

'Lead on,' Eadulf invited.

Together they turned, Athelnoth moving awkwardly.

'What is so important about the brooch?' he asked hesitantly.

'We cannot tell you until we have seen it,' Fidelma replied calmly. 'At the moment, we have to pursue all matters relating to the abbess.'

Athelnoth sniffed in irritation.

'Well, if it is suspects that you are searching for, I can name one. When I went to see the abbess, to bring her the brooch, that strange-looking sister was with her.'

Fidelma raised an eyebrow sardonically.

'Are you referring to Sister Gwid?'

'Gwid!' Athelnoth nodded. 'The Pictish girl who is so resentful and jealous of petty things. The Picts are always the enemies of our blood. My father was slain in the Pictish wars. She was always with the abbess.'

'Why not?' Eadulf replied. 'She was secretary to the abbess.'

Athelnoth grimaced as if in surprise.

'I did know that the Abbess Étain had appointed the girl her secretary. Out of pity, I presume? The girl followed the abbess about like a dog after a sheep. You would imagine that she thought the abbess was a reincarnation of some great saint.'

'But Étain had sent an invitation to Gwid to come here from Iona to be her secretary,' Fidelma pointed out. 'Why would she do that out of pity?'

Athelnoth shrugged. He turned to lead the way silently through the shadow-strewn cloisters to his *cubiculum*.

It was a small functional cell, like all the other *cubicula* in the abbey but that Athelnoth was assigned a separate chamber rather than merely a bed in the *dormitorium* was indicative of his status in the church of Northumbria. Fidelma quietly registered this fact.

Athelnoth stood hesitating on the threshold, gazing around the bare sandstone room.

'The brooch . . . ?' prompted Fidelma.

Atholnoth nodded, crossing to the wooden pegs from which his clothes hung. He took down a *epera*, a leather satchel in which many travelling brethren carried their possessions.

He thrust his hand in. Then his frown deepened and he proceeded to search carefully.

He turned to them with an expression of bewilderment.

'It is not here. I cannot find it.'

Chapter Eleven

Fidelma raised a quizzical eyebrow as she returned the bewildered gaze of Athelnoth.

'You placed the brooch in your bag?'

'Yes. I placed it in there yesterday afternoon.'

'Who would take it?'

'I have no idea. No one knew I had it.'

Eadulf was about to make a pointed remark when Fidelma stopped him.

'Very well, Athelnoth. Have a careful search and if you find the brooch contact us and let us know.' Outside Athelnoth's cell, Eadulf turned to her with a frown.

'You surely don't believe him?'

Fidelma shrugged.

'Did you think he was speaking the truth?'

'By the living God, no! Of course not!'

'Then Gwid would seem to be right. Athelnoth was visiting Étain for some reason other than the return of a mere brooch.'

'Yes, of course. Athelnoth is lying.'

'But does that prove that Athelnoth killed Étain?'

'No,' admitted Eadulf. 'But it gives us a motive for the killing, doesn't it?'

'This is true, though something is not quite in order. I was sure that Athelnoth invented the story of the brooch until he claimed it was still in his possession in his *cubiculum*. If it was a lie, it would be so easy to discover it.'

'He was under pressure to come up with a story quickly. He thought of it on the spur of the moment, not realising its weakness.'

'That is a good argument. Yet we can afford to leave Athelnoth to his own devices for a while. Would you know anyone among the Saxon clergy who would give you some information on Athelnoth's background? Perhaps someone who accompanied him when he went to meet Étain on the border of Rheged? I'd like to know more of this Athelnoth.'

'A good idea. I will make some enquiries during the evening meal,' agreed Eadulf. 'In the meantime, shall we question the monk Seaxwulf next?'

Fidelma nodded her head.

'Why not? Seaxwulf and Agatho were among the last to see Étain. Let us return to Sister Athelswith's *officium* and have the good sister send for Seaxwulf.' They were walking through the guests' quarters when the sound of distant shouting came to their ears. Eadulf pursed his lips in perplexity.

'What new problem is this?'

'One we shall not identify by standing here,' Fidelma said, turning towards the origin of the sound. They came on a group of brethren peering through the windows of the abbey building at something below. Eadulf made a space for himself and Fidelma at a window. For several moments Fidelma could not identify what was happening. A crowd was gathered around what seemed a bundle of rags on the ground. They were clearly angry, yelling and throwing stones at it, although, curiously, keeping a good distance from it. It was only when she caught sight of a slight movement of the rags that, with horror, she realised that it was a person. The crowd were stoning someone to death.

'What is going on?' she demanded.

Eadulf asked one of the brothers, who replied with an expression of fear.

'A victim of the Yellow Plague,' Eadulf translated, 'the pestilence that is tearing this land apart, destroying men, women and children without deference to race, sex or rank. The person must have wandered here, seeking aid, and wandered too near the market set up by the traders below the abbey walls.'

Fidelma stared aghast.

'You mean they are stoning a sick and dying person to death? Is no one going to put a stop to this outrage?'

Eadulf bit his lip, embarrassed.

'Would you face that hysterical mob?' He pointed down to where the crowd were still screaming their fear at the now still bundle of rags. 'Anyway,' he added, 'it is all over.'

Fidelma compressed her lips. The stillness of the rags confirmed Eadulf's assessment.

'Soon, when the people realise the person is dead, they will disperse and someone will go to drag the body away to be burnt. Too many have died from this plague for us to be able to reason with these churls.'

The Yellow Plague, Fidelma knew, was an extreme form of jaundice, which had swept across Europe for several years and was now devastating both Britain and Ireland. It had reached Ireland, where it was known as the *buidhe chonaill*, eight years before, ushered in, claimed the scholars, by a total eclipse of the sun. It attacked mainly during the height of the summer and had eliminated half of the population of Ireland already. Two High Kings, the provincial kings of Ulster and Munster and many other persons of rank were among its victims. High-ranking churchmen such as Fechin of Fobhar, Ronan, Aileran the Wise, Cronan, Manchan and Ultan of Clonard had succumbed to its fury. So many parents had died leaving young children starving that Ultan of Ardbraccan had been moved to open an orphanage to feed and nurture these youthful victims of the plague.

Fidelma knew well the horrors of the pestilence.

'Are your Saxon churls then animals?' sniffed Fidelma. 'How can they treat their fellow creatures so? And, worse still, how can the brethren of Christ stand by and watch it as if it were some side show at a fair?'

Already the brethren who had lined the windows and witnessed the tragedy were dispersing indifferently back to their tasks. If they understood her outspoken criticism they gave no sign.

'Our ways are not your ways,' Eadulf said patiently. 'That I know. I have seen your sanctuaries for the sick and feeble in Ireland. Maybe one day we will learn from them. But you are in a country where the people fear sickness and death. The Yellow Plague is seen as a great evil, sweeping all before it. What people fear they will attempt to destroy. I have seen sons turning their own dying mothers out into the cold because they have the symptoms of this plague.'

Fidelma was about to argue with Eadulf, but what was the use? Eadulf was right. The ways of Northumbria were not those of her own land.

'Let us find Seaxwulf,' she said, turning from the window.

Below the window the shouting had abated. The people were dropping their stones and turning back to the gaiety of the market which stretched below the walls of the abbey. The bundle of rags huddled immobile in the mud where it had fallen at the first cast of the stone.

When Seaxwulf entered the room, Fidelma recognised him at once as the young monk with corn-coloured hair who had stood at Wilfrid's side in the *sacrarium.*

Seaxwulf was a slender, smooth-faced young man who giggled nervously every now and again when asked a direct question. He had light blue eyes and had a curious habit of fluttering his eyelids and speaking with a hissing lisp in a soprano voice. In all, Fidelma had to keep reminding herself that she was speaking to a male and not a flirtatious young girl. Nature seemed to have played the young man a cruel trick by a moment of sexual indecision. She found his age hard to guess but presumed he was in his early twenties, although there was hardly a sign of a razor touching the soft downy hair on his cheeks.

It was Brother Eadulf who questioned the young man in Saxon while Fidelma struggled hard to follow with her inadequate but growing knowledge of the language.

'You visited the Abbess Étain on the day she died,' Eadulf stated flatly.

Seaxwulf actually tittered slightly and placed a slender hand over his thin lips.

His bright eyes peered at them over the top of his palm, almost coquettishly.

'Did I?'

The voice had an odd sensual quality.

Eadulf snorted disgustedly.

'For what purpose did you visit the Abbess of Kildare in her cell?'

149

The eyelids fluttered again, accompanied by another nervous giggle.

'That is my secret.'

'It is not,' contradicted Eadulf. 'We have the authority of your king, bishop and the abbess of this house to discover the truth. You are oath bound to inform us.'

Eadulf's voice was sharp and incisive.

Seaxwulf blinked and pouted in mock annoyance.

'Oh, very well!' The voice was now petulant, like a child's. 'I went at the behest of Wilfrid of Ripon. I am his secretary, you know, and confidant.'

'For what purpose did you go there?' demanded Eadulf again.

The young man paused and frowned, an almost peevish frown.

'You should speak of this to Abbot Wilfrid.'

'I am asking you,' snapped Eadulf, his voice suddenly harsh. 'And I expect an answer. Now!'

Seaxwulf stuck out his lower lip. Sister Fidelma cast her eyes to the ground to contain her amusement at the actions of the curious young monk.

'I went to negotiate with the abbess on Wilfrid's behalf.'

Here Fidelma broke in, not sure she had heard the word correctly.

'*Negotiate*?' She emphasised the word.

'Yes. As chief counsels for Rome and Columba, Wilfrid and the Abbess Étain were intent on agreeing points before the public assembly started.'

Fidelma's eyes widened.

'The Abbess Étain was making agreements with Wilfrid of Ripon?' She put the question swiftly through Eadulf.

Seaxwulf shrugged his slender shoulders.

'To agree points before the debate saves much time and energy, sister.'

'I am not sure what you mean. Are you saying that points of dissension were to be agreed before the public discussions?'

Again Eadulf had to translate this question into Saxon for the monk and the reply back into Irish.

Seaxwulf raised his eyebrows as if the question need not have been asked.

'Of course.'

'And the Abbess Étain was a willing party to making such agreements?'

Fidelma was astonished at the revelation that negotiations were being carried out away from the public debate. It did not seem honest that the two factions could decide points without bringing them into the open before the synod.

Seaxwulf shrugged languorously.

'I have been to Rome. It happens all the time. Why waste time squabbling in public when a private agreement will get you what you want?'

'How far had these agreements gone?' demanded Fidelma through Eadulf.

'Not far,' replied Seaxwulf confidently. 'We had reached some agreement on the tonsure. As you know, Rome regards the tonsure of your church of Columba as barbaric. We adhere to the tonsure of the saintly Peter which he cut in commemoration of Christ's crown of thorns. The Abbess Étain was considering accepting that the Columban church had been misled as to the nature of the tonsure.'

Fidelma swallowed hard.

'But that is impossible,' she whispered.

Seaxwulf smiled, as if pleased at her reaction.

151

'Oh yes. Oh yes, the abbess could concede that point in return for the concession of the blessing, whereby we of Rome hold up the thumb and the first and second fingers to represent the Trinity when giving the blessing whereas you of the Columban church hold up the first, third and fourth fingers. Wilfrid was ready to concede that either form was valid.'

Fidelma pursed her lips in controlled surprise.

'How long had such bargaining been going on?'

'Oh, since as soon as the Abbess Étain arrived here. Two or three days. I forget exactly.' The young man stared down at his extended hands in distaste as if observing his fingernails for the first time and disapproving of their manicure.

Fidelma glanced at Eadulf.

'I think a new dimension has been cast on this matter,' she said quietly, resorting to Irish, knowing that Seaxwulf did not understand.

Eadulf pulled a long face.

'How so?'

'What would be the reaction of many of the brethren if they knew that such negotiations were going on behind the scenes without their knowledge or approval? That, in return for a concession on this point, a concession on another point would be given by one or other of the two factions? Wouldn't that inflame the enmity already felt by the brethren? If so, would someone not feel so enraged that they might attempt to put a stop to such negotiations?'

'True – though the knowledge doesn't help us.'

'Why so?'

'Because it means that we still have hundreds of suspects, both of the Columban and Roman factions.'

'Then we have to find a way to narrow them down.'

Eadulf nodded slightly, turning back to the young blond monk.

'Who knew of your negotiations with the abbess?'

Seaxwulf pouted again like a little child keeping a mystery.

'They were secret.'

'So only you and Wilfrid of Ripon knew?'

'And Abbess Étain.'

'What of her secretary, Gwid?' interposed Fidelma through Eadulf.

Seaxwulf chuckled scornfully.

'Gwid? The abbess did not regard her as being in her confidence. In fact, she told me to have no dealings with her over these secret matters, least of all to mention her communications with Wilfrid of Ripon.'

Fidelma hid her surprise.

'What makes you say that Étain did not regard Sister Gwid as being in her confidence?'

'If she did, then she would have been a party to the negotiations. The only time I saw her with Gwid, they were shouting at each other. I had no idea of what they were saying for they spoke in your own language of Ireland.'

'So?' Eadulf said. 'Did no one else know of the negotiations then?'

Seaxwulf grimaced awkwardly.

'I don't think so – except, Abbess Abbe came upon me when I was leaving the *cubiculum* of Abbess Étain. She had the chamber next to Étain. She stared suspiciously at me. I did not say anything but went about my business. I saw that she had gone to speak with the Abbess Étain in her chamber. I heard voices raised in argument. I do not know whether she had guessed the purpose of my visit or not. I suspect that

Abbe realised that Étain and Wilfrid were making agreements.'

Fidelma decided to press the point.

'You say Abbe argued with Étain as you were leaving?'

'So far as I know. I heard their voices raised that is all.'

'And did you see the Abbess Étain again?'

Seaxwulf shook his head.

'I went to report to Wilfrid about the abbess's willingness to concede the greater authority of Peter on the matter of the tonsure. Then the call came for the assembly in the *sacrarium* and I went in with Wilfrid. It was shortly after that we heard that the abbess had been murdered.'

Fidelma sighed, a long-drawn-out breath. Finally she looked at Seaxwulf and gestured.

'Very well. You may go.'

When the door shut on Seaxwulf, Eadulf turned to Fidelma, his brown eyes shining in excitement.

'The Abbess Abbe! The sister of Oswy himself! She is one visitor to Étain's *cubiculum* that Sister Athelswith's perceptive eye missed. A natural mistake because her chamber was next to Étain's.'

Sister Fidelma did not look satisfied.

'We will have to speak with her. Certainly there is a motive here. Abbe is a powerful supporter of the Columban order. If she felt that Étain was making concessions without the prior knowledge of those supporting the rule of Columba then that could be a cause for anger and anger can beget a motive for murder.'

Eadulf nodded eagerly.

'Then perhaps our original thought that this was a murder motivated by the anger of the debate is right. Except that Étain of Kildare was killed by her fellow churchmen and not by the pro-Roman faction.'

Fidelma pulled a face.

'We are not here to get the Roman faction absolved of blame but to discover the truth.'

'The truth is what I am after,' Eadulf felt stung to reply. 'But Abbe seems a likely suspect—'

'So far we have only Brother Seaxwulf's word for her presence in Étain's cell after he had left. And you may remember that Sister Athelswith named the priest Agatho as having visited Étain after Seaxwulf? If this is so, then Abbe left Étain alive. For if she visited Étain directly Seaxwulf left, then Agatho must have visited after Abbe left.'

The bell began tolling for the commencement of *cena*, the chief meal of the day.

Eadulf's face had fallen.

'I had forgotten about Agatho,' he muttered contritely.

'I had not,' replied Fidelma firmly. 'We will talk with Abbe after the evening meal.'

Fidelma had not been hungry. Her mind was too full of thoughts. She had merely eaten some fruit and a piece of *paximatium*, the heavy bread, and then gone immediately to her *cubiculum* to rest for a while. With the main body of the brethren in the refectory, it was quiet in the *domus hospitale* and therefore a place conducive to being alone with one's thoughts. She tried to explore what information she had to work some order and sense into it. Yet the thoughts would not make sense. Her instructor, the Brehon Morann of Tara, had always used to impress on his pupils that one should wait until one had heard all the evidence before attempting a solution. Yet Fidelma felt

155

an impatience that was hard to control.

Finally she rose from her cot, deciding to take a walk along the cliff tops in the hope that the fresh early-evening air would clear her mind.

She left the *domus hospitale* and crossed a quadrangle towards the *monasteriolum*, the abbey buildings in which the brethren laboured in their studies and teaching. Someone had scratched a piece of graffiti on the wall: '*docendo discimus*'. Fidelma smiled. It was apt. People did learn by teaching.

Within the *monasteriolum* was the *librarium* of the abbey to which Fidelma had already paid a visit when she had delivered the book that Abbot Cummène of Iona had sent as a gift. It was an impressive collection, for Hilda had made it her task to develop the library and collect as many books as possible in her determination to spread literacy among her people.

The sun was very low behind the hills now and long shadows cast dark fingers among the buildings. The structure would soon be shrouded in gloom. Time enough, though, to take a walk and be back in Sister Athelswith's *officium* to meet with the Abbess Abbe.

She turned through the outer cloisters which led to the side gate of the abbey wall from which a path led to the cliff tops.

She became aware of a monk walking before her, head enshrouded in his *cucullus*, or cowl.

Some instinct made Fidelma pause in her stride. It struck her as curious that a brother was wearing his cowl within the confines of the abbey. And now a second figure appeared by the gate ahead. Fidelma drew back into the shadows of the arched cloisters, her heart beating a little faster for no logical reason except that she recognised the second figure as the foxy-faced thane of Frihop, Wulfric.

A greeting was called in Saxon.

She strained forward, wishing her Saxon consisted of a greater vocabulary than it did.

The brother halted. The two men appeared to be laughing. Why not? What was so sinister about a Saxon thane and a Saxon monk exchanging pleasantries? It was only some sixth sense that caused Fidelma disquiet. Her eyes narrowed. Both men, during their conversation, were casting glances about them as if wary of eavesdroppers. Their voices lowered conspiratorially. Then they grasped each other's hands and Wulfric turned out of the gate while the becowled brother turned back.

Fidelma pressed further into the shadow of the cloisters, behind a pillared arch.

The brother strode purposefully at right angles to where Fidelma stood, crossing the quadrangle towards the *monasteriolum.* As he did so he threw back his cowl, presumably as it had served its purpose and wearing it in the confines of the abbey would seem strange. Fidelma could not restrain the sharp breath of astonishment that came as she recognised the man with his Columban tonsure.

It was Brother Taran.

Abbe was a stocky woman, looking very much like her brother Oswy. She was in her mid-fifties, the lines etched deep on her face, the blue eyes bright but rather watery. Together with her three brothers, she had been taken into exile in Iona when her father, the king of Bernicia, had been killed by his rival Edwin of Deira who had then united the two kingdoms into the single kingdom 'by the north of the River Humber', Northumbria. When her brothers Eanfrith, Oswald and Oswy had returned to reclaim their kingdom on Edwin's death, Abbe had come with them as a religieuse, baptised in the Columban church. She had established a monastery at Coldingham, a double house for men and women on a headland, and was confirmed as its abbess by her brother Oswald, who had become king on the death of their eldest brother Eanfrith.

Fidelma had heard much of Coldingham, for it had required a dubious reputation as being given over to the pursuit of hedonistic pleasures. It was said that the Abbess Abbe believed too literally in a God of Love. She had heard that the *cubicula* that were built for prayer and contemplation had been turned into rooms of feasting, drinking and the enjoyment of the flesh.

The abbess sat regarding Fidelma with an amused but approving stare.

'My brother, Oswy, the king, has told me of your purpose.' She spoke fluent and idiomatic Irish, that being the only language she had known during her childhood on Iona. She turned to Eadulf. 'You, I believe, were trained in Ireland?'

Eadulf smiled briefly and nodded.

'You may speak in Irish for I understand.'

'Good,' the abbess sighed. She gazed at Fidelma, again with a look of approval. 'You are attractive, child. There is always a place in Coldingham for such as yourself.'

Fidelma felt herself colouring.

Abbe tilted her head to one side and chuckled.

'You disapprove?'

'I take no offence,' replied Fidelma.

'Neither should you, sister. Do not believe all you hear of our house. Our rule is *dum vivimus, vivamus* – while we live let us live. We are a house of men and women dedicated to life, which is the gift of God. God has made men and women to love one another. What better form of worship than to enact His

158

Great Design, living, working and worshipping together. Does not the Gospel of the Blessed John say, "There is no fear in love; but perfect love casts out fear"?'

Fidelma shifted uneasily.

'Mother Abbess, it is not my place to call into question how your house is governed and by what rule. I am here to enquire into the death of Étain of Kildare.'

Abbe sighed.

'Étain! There was a woman. A woman who knew how to live.'

'Yet she is now dead, Mother Abbess,' interposed Eadulf.

'I know.' The eyes were kept on Fidelma. 'And I await to know what this has to do with me?'

'You quarrelled with Étain,' Fidelma said simply.

The abbess blinked but showed no other sign of the barb going home. She made no reply.

'Perhaps you will tell us why you argued with the abbess of Kildare?' prompted Eadulf.

'If you have learnt that I argued with Étain, you will doubtless have discovered the reason why,' replied Abbe, her voice stiff and uncompromising. 'I grew up in the shadow of the walls of the abbey of Colmcille on Iona. I was educated there among the brethren of Christ from Ireland. It was at my instigation, rather than that of my brother Oswald, that this kingdom first entreated Ségéne, the abbot of Iona, to send missionaries to convert our pagan subjects and reveal to them the path of Christ. Even when the first missionary from Iona, another named Colmán, returned to Iona saying our kingdom was beyond Christ's redemption, I pleaded again with Ségéne and so the saintly Aidán came here and began to preach.

'I have witnessed the conversion of the land and the gradual spread of the word of God, first under Aidán and then under Finán and lastly under Colmán. Now all that work stands in jeopardy because of the likes of Wilfrid and others. I adhere to the true church of Columba and will continue to do so whatever prevails here at Streoneshalh.'

'So what was the reason for the conflict with Étain of Kildare?' prompted Eadulf, returning to the question.

'That slimy man Seaxwulf, a man who is no man at all, has probably told you that I realised that Étain was striking a bargain with Wilfrid of Ripon. Bargains! Devices *ad captandum vulgus*!'

'Seaxwulf has told us that he was being used as an intermediary between Étain and Wilfrid and that they were attempting to come to some agreement before the main debate.'

Abbe grunted in disgust.

'Seaxwulf! That contemptible little thief and gossip!'

'Thief?' Eadulf's voice was sharp. 'Isn't that a harsh word to describe a brother?'

Abbe shrugged.

'A correct word. Two days ago, when we were gathering here, two of our brothers caught Seaxwulf going through the personal belongings of some cenobites in the *dormitorium*. They took him to Wilfrid, who is his abbot as well as his secretary. He admitted the breaking of the eighth commandment and so Wilfrid had him punished. They took him out and beat his back with a birch rod until it was red raw and bloody. Only the fact that he was Wilfrid's secretary saved him from having his hand severed. Even then, Wilfrid refused to dismiss him as his secretary.'

Fidelma shivered slightly at the cruelty of the Saxon punishments.

Abbess Abbe went on without noticing Fidelma's look of distaste.

'There is gossip that Seaxwulf is like a magpie. He is tempted by the desire for bright and exotic objects that are not his own.'

Fidelma exchanged a glance with Eadulf.

'So are you saying that Seaxwulf is not to be trusted? That he could be lying?'

'Not so in this case of his being the go-between with Wilfrid and Étain. Wilfrid trusts Seaxwulf as he trusts no other; I presume because Wilfrid could have Seaxwulf killed or mutilated whenever he wanted. Fear makes for a sound contract of trust.

'But Étain of Kildare had no authority to make such agreements on behalf of the Columban faction. When I saw that conniving worm Seaxwulf sneaking from Étain's chamber, I realised what might be afoot. I went in to see Étain and demand that she be honest. She was betraying us.'

'And how did Étain respond to your admonishment?'

'She was angry. But candidly admitted what she was doing. She justified herself by saying that it was better to agree on unimportant matters in order to lull her opponents into a false sense of security than to be like cows with horns locked from the first moment.'

Abbess Abbe's eyes suddenly narrowed.

'I suddenly realise, do you think that this argument was a reason for murder? That, perhaps, I—?'

Fidelma found herself under her bright-eyed scrutiny as the abbess suddenly chuckled at the thought.

'Murders often happen when a person loses control in argument,' replied Fidelma quietly.

Abbess Abbe gave a low laugh. It sounded a genuine expression of mirth.

'*Deus avertat*! God forbid! It is ridiculous. Life is too precious for me to waste it on trivialities.'

'But, according to you, the defeat of the Columban church in Northumbria was no triviality,' pressed Eadulf. 'It was something intense and personal. In fact, you believed that Étain was betraying her church, indeed, all you have come to believe in.'

The glance Abbe cast at Eadulf was unguarded for a moment. A look of venomous hate. The features froze in a Medusa-like graven image. Then the look was gone and the abbess forced a cold smile.

'It was not a matter to kill her over. Her punishment would be to see her church destroyed.'

'At what time did you leave Étain?' Fidelma demanded.

'What?'

'When, after this quarrel, did you leave Étain's *cubiculum*?'

Abbe was quiet as she considered the question in order to make an accurate answer.

'I can't remember. I was with her only ten minutes or a little more.'

'Did anyone see you leave? Sister Athelswith, for example?'

'I don't believe so.'

Fidelma glanced with a silent question at Eadulf. Her companion nodded agreement.

'Very well, Mother Abbess.' Fidelma stood up, causing Abbe to follow suit. 'We may wish to ask you a few more questions later.'

Abbe smiled at them.

'I shall be here. Have no fear. Indeed, sister, you really should visit my house at Coldingham and see for yourself how much life can be enjoyed. You are far too beautiful, too youthful and exuberant to accept this Roman concept of celibacy all your life. Indeed, didn't Augustine of Hippo write in his *Confessiones*: "Give me chastity and continence, but not just now"?'

Abbess Abbe gave a throaty laugh and left the room, leaving Fidelma blushing fiercely.

She turned to meet Eadulf's amused gaze and her outraged virtue gave way to anger.

'Well?' she snapped.

The smile came off Eadulf's face.

'I do not think Abbe would have killed Étain,' he said hurriedly.

'Why not?' she rejoined curtly.

'She is a woman, for one thing.'

'And a woman is incapable of committing a crime?' sneered Fidelma.

Eadulf shook his head.

'No; but as I said when we first saw the body of Étain, I do not think a woman had the strength to have held the abbess and cut her throat in the manner that it happened.'

Fidelma bit her lip and calmed down. After all, she thought to herself, why was she growing angry? Abbe was surely complimenting her and stating a fact. Yet it was not Abbe's attitude that annoyed her. It was something deep within her that she was unable to fathom. She stared at Eadulf for a moment.

The Saxon monk returned her gaze bemused.

Fidelma found that she dropped her eyes first.

'What would you say if I told you that I saw Brother Taran, a Columban monk, meeting with Wulfric by the side gate of the abbey this evening and engaging in what looked like a conspiratorial conversation?'

Eadulf raised an eyebrow.

163

'And are you telling me this as fact?'

Fidelma confirmed it with a nod.

'There could be many reasons for such a meeting, I suppose.'

'There could,' agreed Fidelma, 'but none that I am content with.'

'Brother Taran was one of Abbess Étain's visitors, wasn't he?'

'One we have not questioned yet.'

'It was not a priority,' Eadulf pointed out. 'Taran was seen to have gone to Étain's *cubiculum* early in the morning. She was seen alive long after his visit. It was Agatho who was the last known visitor.'

Fidelma hesitated a moment.

'I think we should have a word with Taran next,' she said.

'And I think now we should first ask Agatho to come and speak with us,' he replied. 'He is by far the more important suspect.'

No one was more surprised than Eadulf when Fidelma acquiesced without argument.

Chapter Twelve

Agatho was a lean, wiry man with a thin, narrow face. His skin was swarthy and his face was not smooth-shaven. His black eyes matched the blackness of his thatch of hair. The lips were thin but red, almost as if he had enhanced their redness by the application of berry juice. Fidelma was fascinated by the way his eyelids were prominent, half closed like the hooded lids of a bird of prey.

The priest scowled as he entered the room.

'I am here under protest,' he said, speaking in the *lingua franca* of Latin.

'I shall note your protest, Agatho,' Fidelma replied in the same language. 'With whom shall I raise the matter? With the king, Bishop Colmán or the Abbess Hilda?'

Agatho raised his face in a disdainful gesture as if it were beneath him to reply and proceeded to seat himself.

'You wish to question me?'

'You would seem to be the last person to see the Abbess Étain alive in her *cubiculum*,' Eadulf bluntly pointed out.

Agatho chuckled mirthlessly.

'Not so.'

Fidelma frowned.

'Oh?' she prompted eagerly.

'The last person to see the abbess would be the person who killed her.'

Fidelma stared at his hooded eyes. They were cold and expressionless. She could not tell whether he was challenging her or making fun of her.

'That is true,' Eadulf was saying. 'And we are here to discover just who did kill her. At what time did you go to her cell?'

'At four o'clock precisely.'

'Precisely?'

Again the mirthless smile on the thin red lips.

'So the clepsydra of the redoubtable Sister Athelswith had informed me.'

'Just so,' conceded Eadulf. 'Why did you go there?'

'To see the abbess, naturally.'

'Naturally. But for what purpose did you wish to see her?'

'I create no deception. I am of the Roman faction. It was my belief that the Abbess Étain was being misled in allowing herself to speak for the heresies of the Columban church. I went with her to plead my case.'

Fidelma stared at the man.

'That is all?'

'That is all.'

'How would you achieve this rapid change of mind in the abbess?'

Agatho looked round conspiratorially and then smiled.

'I showed her this . . .' He reached into the *crumena*, a leather pouch carried on a strap around his neck, and spilt the contents into his hand.

Eadulf leant forward, frowning.

'It is just a splinter of wood.'

Agatho looked at him contemptuously.

'It is the *lignum Sanctae Crucis*,' he pronounced, his voice hushed in awe and genuflecting as he did so.

'Truly, this is the wood of the true cross?' whispered Eadulf, reverence overcoming him.

'I have said as much,' replied Agatho distantly.

Fidelma's eyes brightened and for a moment or two there was a trembling around her lips.

'How would the presentation of this, supposing you are right, have convinced the abbess to support Rome rather than Iona?' she asked solemnly.

'That is obvious. By recognising the true cross in my hands she would realise that I was the chosen one, that Christ spoke through me, as he spoke through Paul of Tarsus.'

The voice was quiet and complacent.

Eadulf shot a bewildered glance at Fidelma.

'Christ chose you? How do you mean?' he asked.

Agatho sniffed as if the monk were a fool.

'I speak only what is true. Have faith. I was instructed to go to the woods beyond Witebia and in a clearing a voice told me to pick up a splinter from the ground for it was the *lignum Sanctae Crucis*. Then the voice told me to go and preach to those misled and confused. Have faith and all will be revealed!'

'Did Étain have faith?' queried Fidelma gently.

Agatho turned towards her, his eyes still hooded.

'Alas, she did not. She was still bound for she could not see the truth.'

'Bound?' Eadulf sounded more than confused.

'Did not the blessed apostle John say "the truth shall make you free"? She was confined. She had not the faith. The great Augustine wrote that faith is to believe what you do not yet see; the reward for that faith is to see what you believe.'

'What did you do when the Abbess Étain rejected your

argument?' Eadulf said hurriedly.

Agatho drew himself up in outraged dignity.

'I withdrew, what else should I do? I did not want to contaminate myself with an unbeliever.'

'How long were you with Étain of Kildare?'

The man shrugged.

'No more than ten minutes or less. I showed her the true cross and told her that Christ spoke through me and that she must accept Rome. When she treated me as a child, I withdrew. I knew she was beyond all hope of salvation. That is all.'

Eadulf exchanged another glance with Fidelma and smiled at Agatho.

'Very well. We have no more questions. You may go now.'

Agatho slipped the sliver of wood back into his *crumena*.

'You both believe now – now that you have seen the true cross?'

Eadulf kept his smile fixed, perhaps a little too fixed.

'Of course. We will speak with you about this later, Agatho.'

When the priest left the room, Eadulf turned with a worried glance to Fidelma.

'Mad! The man is absolutely mad.'

'If we remember that we are all born mad,' replied Fidelma phlegmatically, 'then many of the mysteries of the world are explained.'

'But with such attitudes this Agatho might well have killed the abbess when she refused to accept his faith.'

'Perhaps. Somehow I am not convinced. But out of all this there is one firm conclusion we can make.'

Eadulf stared at her.

'It is obvious.' Fidelma smiled. 'Sister Athelswith, in observing all the visitors to Étain's *cubiculum*, did not see every visitor. And I doubt whether she saw the visitor who killed Étain.'

There was a soft knock at the door and Sister Athelswith put her head into the chamber.

'Oswy the king asks that you join him in Mother Hilda's chambers immediately,' she said apprehensively.

Sister Fidelma and Brother Eadulf stood silently before the king. Oswy was alone in the room and turned from the window, where he had been gazing down at the harbour below. The frown of anxiety that he wore lightened a little.

'I sent to ask you whether you have any news for me yet? Are you any closer to discovering the culprit?'

Fidelma heard the stress in his voice.

'We have nothing concrete to report as yet, Oswy of Northumbria,' she replied.

The king bit his lip. The lines on his face deepened.

'Have you nothing to tell me at all?' There was almost a pleading tone in his voice.

'Nothing of use.' Fidelma remained calm. 'We must proceed cautiously. Is time suddenly pressing that you wish the matter to be resolved more quickly than you did before?'

The king heaved his great shoulders in an indeterminable gesture.

'You are ever perceptive, Fidelma. Yes. Tensions are growing.' Oswy hesitated with a sigh. 'There is civil war in the air. My son Alhfrith now plots against me. There are rumours that he is gathering warriors to drive out the Irish religious by force while my daughter Aelflaed is rumoured to be gathering those who support the church of Columba to defend the abbeys against Alhfrith. All it needs now is but a single spark and this whole kingdom will erupt in flames. Both sides accuse the other of the death of Étain of Kildare. What am I to tell them?'

There was a desperation in the king's voice. Fidelma felt almost sorry for him.

'We can still tell you nothing, my lord,' Eadulf insisted.

'But you have questioned everyone who saw her just before her death.'

Fidelma parted her lips in a mirthless smile.

'Doubtless this has been reported to you from a good source. Perhaps Sister Athelswith?'

Oswy made an uncomfortable gesture of affirmation.

'Is it a secret then?'

'No secret, Oswy,' replied Fidelma. 'But Sister Athelswith ought to be more cautious than to report our activities lest they come to the wrong ears. There is still one person whom we have not yet questioned.'

'I asked Sister Athelswith specifically to let me know when you had finished your questioning,' Oswy said defensively.

'You said just now that your son Alhfrith plots against you,' Fidelma said. 'Did you mean that seriously?'

Oswy raised his arms and let them fall in a motion indicating indecision.

'A king has no friends in ambitious sons,' he said heavily. 'What ambition does a king's son have but to be king?'

'Alhfrith wishes to be king?'

'I made him petty king of Deira to contain his ambition but he wishes the throne of the entire kingdom of Northumbria. I know it. He knows I know it. We play a game of dutiful son and father. But the day may well come . . .'

He shrugged with eloquence.

'An investigation like this takes time,' Fidelma said soothingly. 'There are many considerations to be taken into account.'

Oswy stared at her for a moment and then grimaced.

'You are correct, of course, sister. I have no right to put pressure on you. Your search is for truth. But mine is to keep a kingdom from being divided and destroying itself.'

'Do you really think that the people are so firmly convinced by one faction or the other as to fight each other?' queried Eadulf.

Oswy shook his head.

'It is the people manipulating religion not the religion itself that threatens to break the peace of this land. And Alhfrith is not above using religion to motivate people to help him in his search for power. The longer people speculate on who killed Étain of Kildare, the longer they will have to formulate preposterous theories to fuel their prejudices.'

'All we can say, Oswy, is that as soon as we are near the solution, you will be the first to know,' Fidelma said.

'Very well. I will remain content with that assurance. But remember what I say – there are many rumours being voiced abroad. Much depends on this assembly and the decisions we reach here.'

As they walked back through the cloisters from the Abbess Hilda's chambers to the *domus hospitale* Eadulf suddenly said:

'I think your suspicions are right, Fidelma. We should speak with this Taran.'

Fidelma raised her brows with a mocking smile.

'And you know what my suspicions are, Eadulf?'

'You believe that there is a plot afoot, hatched by Alhfrith of Deira, to overthrow Oswy and use the tensions of this synod as the means to create civil war.'

'I do believe that,' Fidelma confirmed.

'I think you believe that Alhfrith, working through Wulfric and perhaps Taran, had Étain of Kildare killed to create this tension.'

'It is a possibility. And we must endeavour to discover if it is true or not.'

Fidelma and Eadulf were entering the *officium* of Sister Athelswith, which they had made their centre, when the solemn toll of the midnight Angelus bell began to sound.

Fidelma heaved a sigh as Eadulf immediately took out his prayer beads.

'It is late now. Tomorrow we will meet with Taran,' she announced. 'But don't forget that you are to make enquiries about Athelnoth's background. At the moment, I still have suspicions about Athelnoth.'

Brother Eadulf nodded his head in agreement while he began to recite the Hail Mary:

> *Ora pro nobis, sancta Dei Genetrix*
> Pray for us, O Holy Mother of God.

The bell announcing the serving of the first meal of the day, the *jentaculum*, had ceased to toll, and the grace had already been said, when Sister Fidelma slid into her place at the long wooden refectory tables. The sister chosen as the reciter of the day was a member of the Roman faction and had taken her place at the lectern at the head of the table, frowning disapprovingly as Fidelma joined them.

'*Benedicamus, Domino,*' she greeted frostily.

'*Deo gratias,*' responded Fidelma with the others.

The sister then intoned the *Beati immaculati* which preceded the reading and they began to eat.

Fidelma mentally shut her ears to the scratchy voice of the woman, and ate mechanically of the cereal and fruit placed before her. She raised her eyes from time to time to study those gathered in the refectory but she saw no sign of Eadulf. She did see Brother Taran seated at a table nearby. The Pictish monk's dark features seemed animated. She was surprised when she saw that he was engaged in conversation with the young monk with corn-coloured hair, Seaxwulf. The young man was seated with his back to her but his hair, his slender shoulders and his effeminate gestures were unmistakable. Curiously, she watched the expression on Taran's face as he spoke. It was intense, angry and insistent. She abruptly found the black eyes of Taran staring directly back at her. Their eyes held for a moment and then an unctuous smile slid across the swarthy features of the Pict and he nodded his head in her direction. Fidelma forced herself to incline her head in response before turning back to her meal.

As she left the rectory, she caught sight of Eadulf seated with a group of Saxon clerics in a far corner. They appeared in earnest conversation and so she made no effort to approach him, deciding to leave the abbey and take a walk down to the sea shore. It seemed a long time since she had breathed in the fresh air of the sea. Her attempt yesterday evening had been interrupted by Taran and his apparently clandestine meeting with Wulfric. She felt as if she had been enclosed in the abbey for ages. Yet that was not so, the tension merely made it seem like it.

What puzzled her was that Taran had suddenly become very friendly with Wulfric and now Seaxwulf. Did this mean something significant and linked to the death of Étain ?

She felt unsure of herself. She was in a strange, foreign country and the fact that it was her own friend, Étain, whose death she was investigating caused her uneasiness and depression.

She walked down the pathway to the harbour entrance and turned along the rocky shoreline. There were a few people about but none seemed to cast a second glance at her as she walked, head bowed, as if she were meditating.

She tried to cast her mind over the facts as she knew them.

The curious thing was that she now found herself thinking about the Saxon monk, Eadulf.

She had never worked with anyone else since she had qualified as a *dálaigh* of the Brehon courts. She had always been the sole arbiter of the truth. Never had she had to rely on a second judgment, much less have to work with a foreigner. Yet the intriguing part was that she did not feel that Eadulf was entirely a stranger, as her people referred to a foreigner. She put this down to the fact that he had spent so many years studying at Durrow and Tuaim Brecain. But that could not be the full answer to the odd feeling of companionship she was beginning to feel with Eadulf.

This land of Northumbria was a strange land, full of strange customs and attitudes so totally unlike the straightforward order of Ireland. She suddenly caught herself and laughed inwardly. She presumed that a Saxon would consider the system here straightforward compared to the laws and attitudes of Ireland. She found herself recalling the line from Homer's *Odyssey*: 'I, for one, know of no sweeter sight for a man or woman's eyes than that of their own country.'

She had only come to this land because Étain of Kildare had asked her to. Now Étain was dead. She found herself disliking the land and its people, its pride and its arrogance, it martial attitudes and the savagery of its punishment for wrongdoers.

Here was a land where punishment was all and the transgressor was given no hope of redeeming himself or compensating the victims. She wanted to return home, to her home of Kildare. She disliked all Saxons. But then Eadulf was a Saxon.

She found her mind racing forward again and caught herself with an angry muttered exclamation.

But was Eadulf typical of his breed? He had good qualities. She found herself liking him, amused by him, admiring his analytical mind. Yet she disliked Saxons.

But then she disliked many of her own nation. Pride and arrogance was not a sin particular to one group.

She heaved a deep sigh. Fidelma prided herself on the logic and method of her thinking. She was disturbed how this disorganised and jumbled series of thoughts could enter her mind when she was supposed to be analysing the murder of Étain. And every path her mind took, it seemed to end with the image of Eadulf. Why Eadulf? Perhaps because she had to work with him that he kept entering her thoughts? Somehow, at the back of her mind, Fidelma felt that there was some other reason.

By the time Fidelma returned to the abbey she could find no sign of Eadulf. She went to Sister Athelswith's *officium* and waited for a while. She wondered whether she should ask Sister Athelswith to find Brother Taran and start questioning him herself. She was just coming to this decision when the door of the *officium* opened with a crash and Sister Athelswith burst in, her voice raised in distress.

'Sister Fidelma! Sister Fidelna!'

Fidelma rose in surprise from her seat at the *domina*'s agitation.

Sister Athelswith looked anxious, her face was flushed and she seemed to have been running.

'Why, sister, what does this mean?'

Sister Athelswith gazed at Fidelma with wide, staring eyes. Her face became as white as a winter's snow shower. It took a time before she could collect herself and articulate.

'It is the Archbishop of Canterbury, Deusdedit. He lies dead in his *cubiculum*.'

Chapter Thirteen

'What did you say?' Fidelma asked in astonishment, unsure that she had heard correctly.

'Deusdedit, the Archbishop of Canterbury, is dead in his *cubiculum*. Please come at once, Sister Fidelma.'

Fidelma swallowed hard.

Another murder? The archbishop himself? This was surely madness? She stared hard at Sister Athelswith's panic-stricken face and reached forward to seize her arm.

'Pull yourself together, sister. Have you told anyone else of this?'

'No, no. I am so distracted that I only thought of you because . . . because . . .'

Sister Athelswith was obviously confused.

'Have you sent for the physician?' cut in Fidelma.

Sister Athelswith shook her head negatively.

'Brother Edgar, our physician, has left for Witebia on an errand of mercy to the son of the thane. We have no other physician here.'

'Then send for Brother Eadulf at once. He has some knowledge of physic. After that, find the Abbess Hilda and tell her what has happened. Tell them both to come to Deusdedit's *cubiculum* immediately.'

Sister Athelswith nodded automatically and hurried off.

Sister Fidelma hurried through the *domus hospitale* to where she knew Deusdedit's room was situated. It had been pointed out to her by Sister Athelswith when she was explaining the layout of the guests' quarters.

She paused at the door, which Sister Athelswith, in her haste, had left ajar. Reaching forward she pushed it open and glanced in.

Deusdedit lay on his bed. At first glance, she saw the bedclothes were undisturbed. His hands were folded peacefully, the eyes shut, as if in sleep. The skin was a curious parchment texture, almost yellowing. She recalled that the archbishop had not looked very well during the times she had seen him in the *sacrarium*.

She made to step forward into the room but a heavy hand seized her by the shoulder. She started, letting out an exclamation, and turned.

The round cherubic features of the archbishop's secretary, Wighard, were staring at her.

'Do not enter, sister.' His voice was sibilant. 'Not for your life.'

Fidelma stared at him in incomprehension.

'What do you mean?'

'Deusdedit is dead, of the Yellow Plague!'

Fidelma's lips parted in surprise.

'The Yellow Plague? How do you know this?'

Wighard sniffed, reached forward and drew the door closed.

'I have suspected that Deusdedit was suffering from the scourge for some days now. The yellowing of the eyes, the texture of the skin. He was constantly complaining of weakness, of lack of appetite and of constipation. I have seen too many victims this year not to know these symptoms.'

Fidelma felt suddenly cold as she began to realise the

implication of what the man was saying.

'How long have you known?' Fidelma demanded of the lugubrious Wighard.

The secretary to the archbishop grimaced unhappily.

'Several days. I think I first knew on our voyage here.'

'And you allowed Deusdedit to come here and remain among the brethren?' demanded Fidelma, outraged. 'What of the risk of contagion? Why was he not placed somewhere to be treated and nursed?'

'It was necessary that Deusdedit, as the heir of the Blessed Augustine of Rome, who came to bring our people into Rome's fold, should attend this synod,' replied Wighard stubbornly.

'At whatever cost?' Fidelma snapped.

'The most important thing was the synod, not whether a man was ill or not.'

Abbess Hilda came hurrying up.

'Another death?' she greeted, her eyes going wonderingly from Fidelma to Wighard. 'What terrible news is this that Sister Athelswith has brought me?'

'Yes, another death; but not from murder,' Fidelma said. 'It seems that Deusdedit was suffering from the Yellow Plague.'

Hilda stared at her a moment, a look caught between incredulity and panic.

'The Yellow Plague brought here to Streoneshalh?'

Hilda genuflected swiftly.

'God preserve us. Is this true, Wighard?'

'I wish it were not, Mother Abbess.' Wighard was uncomfortable. 'Yes, it is true.'

'It seems that our Roman brethren felt it more important to have their spiritual head at the synod than to consider the risk of contagion,' Fidelma remarked bitterly. 'Who knows how this disease will spread now?'

Wighard was opening his mouth to reply when Sister Athelswith came hurrying up.

'Where is Brother Eadulf?' demanded Fidelma.

'He will be here in a moment,' panted Sister Athelswith. 'He has gone to collect some things to help him make an examination of the body.'

'There is no need for that,' Wighard said, frowning. 'I speak truly.'

'Even so, we must be sure of the cause of death and we must find a way to save any contagion from spreading,' Fidelma replied.

Almost as she ceased speaking Eadulf came hurrying along the corridor.

'What is it?' he asked anxiously. 'Sister Athelswith says someone else is dead? The throat cut?'

Wighard began to speak but Fidelma cut him short.

'Deusdedit is dead.' As Eadulf's eyes widened, she went on quickly, 'Wighard believes the cause to be the Yellow Plague. There is no physician in the abbey at the moment. Can you confirm the manner of his death?'

Eadulf hesitated, apprehension growing in his eyes. Then he compressed his lips firmly and nodded, although somewhat reluctantly. He seemed to brace himself before he pushed open the door of the *cubiculum* and disappeared inside.

After a few moments, he re-emerged.

'The Yellow Plague,' he confirmed flatly. 'The symptoms are well known to me.'

'What do you advise?' demanded Abbess Hilda at once, her anxiety obvious. 'We have hundreds crowded into this place. How can we stop the contagion?'

'The body should be removed at once and burnt on the sea shore. The *cubiculum* must be disinfected and not used for a while until the contagion is dispersed. Several days at least.'

Wighard was eager to make amends now.

'The news of this should not be spread beyond us four people. It would create too much alarm before the synod is ended. Let us say Deusdedit had a heart attack. We can tell the truth after the decision of the synod. I will find slaves to perform the necessary tasks. Better that they, rather than we of the brethren, should be contaminated.'

'I doubt it matters now,' replied Eadulf flatly. 'If anyone is to suffer contagion then they will have suffered it already. Why, if you suspected that Deusdedit was suffering such illness, did you not warn us?'

Wighard lowered his head but did not reply.

'It is a bad omen, Wighard,' Hilda observed fearfully.

'Not so,' replied the rotund cleric. 'I have no use for omens. I will get the slaves to take out the body of the archbishop.'

He turned and left to fulfil his task.

Eadulf turned to the abbess.

'Let no one else in this *cubiculum* until it has been cleansed, as I have said. And make sure that anyone who has had dealings with the archbishop drinks of herbal teas made from borage or sorrel or tansy and continues to drink them thrice daily for a week or more. Do you have such preparations in your abbey?'

Hilda confirmed that they did.

Eadulf took Fidelma by the arm and hurried her along the corridor.

'The trouble is,' he whispered, 'that the plants that best counter this dreadful disease grow only in the months of June and July or through the summer. I have taken to travelling with some preparations in my *pera* and I have a mixture of golden rod and toadflax which mixed with hot water, cooled and taken as a drink will help to keep this Yellow Plague at bay. Also, I advise you to eat as much parsley as you can, raw if you can take it.'

Fidelma stared at him a moment and suddenly smiled at his apparent anxiousness.

'You seem greatly concerned for my health, Eadulf.'

The Saxon frowned for a moment.

'Of course. We have much work to do,' he replied shortly. He halted at the *dormitorium* he shared with other brothers of no particular status, disappearing for a moment before re-emerging with a small leather bag, his *pera* or satchel.

Fidelma found herself being led by Eadulf into the large kitchens, where thirty of the brethren laboured over steaming cooking pots to supply the wants of the great abbey and its guests. Fidelma screwed up her face as the stench of rancid food mingled with innumerable other smells that were impossible to describe. She choked a little as she picked out the stink of rotting cabbage. Eadulf asked for the use of an iron kettle from the dour-faced chief cook, who said she would send an assistant to them.

To their surprise Sister Gwid came forward with a kettle.

'What are you doing here, Gwid?' asked Fidelma.

The gawky Pictish sister smiled sadly.

'As my Greek no longer has a role to play, I have sought occupation in the kitchens until I have decided what I am to do. I think, when the synod is ended, I shall join any group that goes back to Dál Riada, perhaps back to Iona.' She handed the kettle to Eadulf. 'Is there anything else?'

Eadulf shook his head.

The tall girl returned to some task on the further side of the kitchen.

'A poor girl,' Fidelma said softly. 'I feel sorry for her. She took Étain's death badly.'

'You may be sorry later,' reproved Eadulf. 'At this moment we must do what we can to prevent any danger of contagion from the plague.' He set to work simmering water and preparing his herbs while Fidelma looked on with interest.

'Are you serious about this herbal protection from the Yellow Plague?' she asked as he stirred the herbs into his concoction.

Eadulf was irritated at her question.

'It does work.'

She waited in silence while Eadulf prepared the mixture and poured it into a large earthenware jar. From the jar he poured two pottery mugs and handed one to Fidelma, raising his own in silent toast.

Fidelma smiled and raised the drink to her lips. The taste was foul and her expression showed it.

'It is an ancient cure.' Eadulf grinned disarmingly.

Fidelma found herself returning his smile ruefully.

'So long as it does work,' she observed. 'Now let us leave here and walk among the fragrance of the cloisters. The kitchen smells cause my head to ache violently.'

'Very well, but we will take the jug of this mixture to your *cubiculum* first.

'You must drink a glass every evening before retiring,' Eadulf told her solemnly as they deposited the jug at her *cubiculum* and then went out into the quietness of the cloisters. 'There is enough there for a week.'

'Was it something you learnt at the medical school of Tuaim Brecain?' she enquired.

Eadulf inclined his head.

'I learnt many things in your country, Fidelma. At Tuaim Brecain I saw many things I thought impossible. I saw doctors cut into the skulls of men and women and remove growths and those men and women have lived.'

Fidelma grimaced indifferently.

'The school of Tuaim Brecain is renowned throughout the world. The great Bracan Mac Findloga, the physician who established the school two centuries ago, is still spoken of with awe. Did you have an ambition to become a physician?'

'No.' Eadulf shook his head. 'I wished for knowledge, any knowledge. In my own land I was the son of the hereditary *gerefa*, the local arbiter of the law, but I wanted to know more. I wanted to know everything. I tried to devour knowledge like the bee devours nectar, flitting from one flower to another but never staying long. I am no specialist but have a little knowledge of many things. It comes in useful from time to time.'

'Sometimes that is good thing,' agreed Fidelma. 'Especially in the pursuit of truth, knowledge in a single subject can blind one as much as having no knowledge at all.'

Eadulf grinned, that brief boyish grin of his.

'You have a specialised knowledge of law, Sister Fidelma. The law of your own land.'

'But in our ecclesiastical schools a general knowledge is also demanded of students before they can be qualified.'

'You are an *anruth*. I know it translates as "noble stream" and is one step below the highest educational qualification in your land. But what does it mean?'

Fidelma smiled. 'It means that the *anruth* has studied for at least eight years, often nine years, and become a master of the subject but with a knowledge also of poetry, literature, historical topography and many other things.'

Eadulf sighed.

'Alas, our people here have no such establishments of learning as you do. Only since the coming of Christian teaching, the foundation of the abbeys, have we begun even to learn to read and write.'

'It is better to start late than never to start at all.'

Eadulf chuckled.

'Truly said, Fidelma. That is why I have this insatiable thirst for knowledge.'

He paused. They sat for a few moments in silence. Oddly, so Fidelma felt, it was not an uncomfortable silence. It was a companionable silence. Companionable. She suddenly identified the feeling she had. They were companions in adversity. She smiled, happy in the conclusion of the chaos of her thinking.

'We should get back to our investigation,' she ventured. 'Deusdedit's death brings us no closer to solving Étain's murder.'

Eadulf suddenly snapped his fingers, causing her to start.

'I am a fool!' he snarled. 'Here am I pondering on my own ego when I should be about the business in hand.'

Fidelma frowned in surprise at his sudden anger with himself.

Eadulf continued: 'You asked me to make enquiries about Brother Athelnoth.'

It took her a moment to dredge her mind back to their suspicions of Athelnoth.

'And you discovered something?'

'Athelnoth was lying to us.'

'That we already know,' affirmed Fidelma. 'But you have

discovered something specific about his lies?'

'As we agreed, I made some enquiries among the other brothers about Athelnoth. Do you remember that he said he first met Étain when he was sent by Colmán to meet her at the border of Rheged and escort her here to Streoneshalh?'

Fidelma nodded.

'You told me that Étain was an Eoghanacht princess whose husband was killed and she then entered the religious order.'

'Yes.'

'And she taught in the abbey of the Blessed Ailbe of Emly before she became abbess at Kildare?'

Again, Fidelma inclined her head patiently.

'And she was elected abbess at Kildare . . . ?'

'Only two months ago,' supplied Fidelma. 'What are you driving at, Eadulf?'

Eadulf smiled almost complacently.

'Only that last year Athelnoth spent six months at the abbey of Emly. I found a brother who was a student with him. They both went to Emly together and returned to Northumbria together.'

Fidelma's eyes widened.

'Athelnoth studied at Emly? Then he must have met Étain there and must have a knowledge of Irish, both of which matters he denied.'

'So Sister Gwid was right, after all,' confirmed Eadulf. 'Athelnoth knew Étain and doubtless desired her.' His voice was tinged with self-satisfaction. 'When Étain rejected Athelnoth, he was so mortified that he killed her.'

'It does not necessarily follow,' Fidelma pointed out, 'although, I grant you, it is a feasible deduction.'

Eadulf spread his hands.

186

'Well I still think the story of the brooch was false. Athelnoth was lying all the time.'

Fidelma grimaced suddenly.

'One other thing we have overlooked – if Athelnoth was at Emly last year then he must have known Gwid there. She was studying under Étain.'

Eadulf gave a confident smirk.

'No; that did occur to me. Athelnoth was at Emly before Gwid. He left Emly the month before Gwid arrived. I asked Gwid when she attended Emly and then checked the time that Athelnoth was there. Athelnoth's fellow student was most obliging with the information.'

Fidelma rose, unable to suppress a tinge of excitement.

'We will send for Athelnoth immediately to explain this mystery.'

Sister Athelswith put her head through the door of the *officium*.

'I have been unable to locate Brother Athelnoth, Sister Fidelma,' she said. 'He is not in the *domus hospitale* nor is he in the *sacrarium*.'

Fidelma was exasperated.

'He must be somewhere in the abbey,' she protested.

'I will send a sister to look.' Sister Athelswith turned and hurried off.

'We might as well examine the *sacrarium* ourselves,' Eadulf suggested, 'in case the good sister has missed him. It would be easy to do so among so many people gathered there.'

'At least we might find Brother Taran and take the opportunity to have a word with him,' Fidelma agreed, rising.

They could hear the shouting before they opened the doors to the *sacrarium* and slipped inside. The debate was in full angry flood. Wilfrid was on his feet, banging his hand in agitation on the wooden lectern before him.

'I say it is a scandal! An invention of Cass Mac Glais, the swineherd of your pagan Irish king Loegaire!'

'That is not so!' Cuthbert was also on his feet, his face red with anger.

Old Jacobus, the ageing James who had arrived in the kingdom of Kent with the Roman missionary Paulinus fifty years before, was rising to his feet as well, helped by his neighbours. He balanced insecurely, both hands placed in front of him on a stick over which he bent. The benches fell silent at the sight of the old man. Even the supporters of the Columban order grew quiet. There was no denying that Jacobus had authority for he was the link with the blessed Augustine sent by Gregory the Great to preach to the pagans of the Saxon kingdoms.

Only when the great chapel was silent did he commence to speak in a sharp, cracked voice.

'I apologise for my young friend, Wilfrid of Ripon.'

There was a murmur of surprise and Wilfrid's head snapped up, irritation on his features.

'Yes,' went on Jacobus, undeterred, 'Wilfrid is in error about the origin of the tonsure affected by the Irish and the Britons.'

He held their attention now.

'Our brethren have been misled. This tonsure they affect was that worn by Simon Magus of Samara who thought he could buy the power of the Holy Spirit and was duly rebuked by Peter. When I was a young man, I came to this island with Paulinus. We wore the same tonsure as that worn by our Holy Father, Gregory the Great; the same tonsure as worn by Augustine and his companions. Such was our outrage when we saw the Britons and our brethren of Ireland affecting a symbol which is contradictory to the faith.

'Let me ask you, Brother Cuthbert, you who aspire to the everlasting crown of life, why do you persist in bearing on your head the semblance of an imperfect crown in contradiction to that faith?'

Cuthbert sprang up angrily.

'By your permission, venerable Jacobus, this is the tonsure ascribed to the blessed apostle John and no other and you will see that it has the appearance of a crown or circle.'

Jacobus shook his head.

'If I stand facing you directly, brother. But if you would bow your head towards me or stand in any other position you like . . .'

Frowning, Cuthbert did so.

There was a roar of laughter from the Roman benches.

'See, an imperfect crown, a semicircle: *decurtatam eam, quam tu videre putabas, invenies coronam!*' cried the old man.

Cuthbert sat down abruptly, his face reddening.

Jacobus pointed to his own small circle shaved on the crown of his head.

'Here is the true circle, the symbol of the crown of thorns, blessed of Peter, the rock on which our church is built. Even some churches of the Britons now accept the truth of it. Those Britons who fled this land to settle in distant Iberia, in the land of Galicia, have now accepted the *corona spinea*. Thirty years ago the Synod of Toleda demanded the suppression of this barbaric tonsure among the clergy of the Britons of Galicia.'

Jacobus resumed his seat, smiling in self-satisfaction.

Fidelma felt a stirring of anger that there was silence on the Columban benches. Why did no one come forward to explain the tonsure of Columba and its deep mystical meaning? The warriors of Ireland and Britain considered it dishonourable to be deprived of that part of their hair, making them less than men. In the ancient times of the druids, the tonsure – the *airbacc giunnae* – was similarly cut. For the people of Ireland, the tonsure had a long and mystical association. Fidelma took a step forward and was opening her mouth to speak when Eadulf's hand closed on her arm.

She gave a startled jump and turned.

Eadulf gestured with his head across the *sacrarium*.

Brother Taran was leaving through a side door.

Fidelma bit her lip, half turning back to the debating chamber but another speaker was on his feet, his voice raised in querulous argument.

Fidelma realised that it was impossible to cross the *sacrarium* to follow Taran, therefore it was best to leave by the door through which they had entered and then try to intercept him.

She motioned Eadulf to follow her.

By the time they had circumvented the walls of the *sacrarium* there was no sign of Taran.

'He cannot have gone far,' Eadulf commented, his voice full of annoyance.

'Let us try in that direction.' Fidelma pointed to the route by the *monasteriolum*.

They hurried along a cloistered area and emerged into the quadrangle before the *monasteriolum*.

'Wait!' hissed Fidelma as she suddenly pulled Eadulf back into the shadows.

In the middle of the quadrangle the figures of Wulfric and Brother Seaxwulf stood, as if waiting for Taran as the Pictish monk hurried towards them.

Seaxwulf said something and immediately turned away towards the *monasteriolum*. Fidelma noticed for the first time that Seaxwulf walked curiously, his back bent, and obviously in discomfort. She remembered what Abbess Abbe had said about Abbot Wilfrid's punishment for his thieving secretary. A beating with a birch. She shivered slightly at the thought of the wounds such an assault could make.

Wulfric and Taran were now standing looking after the Saxon brother until he disappeared inside the building of the *monasteriolum*. Then Taran reached inside his habit and took out something which he handed to Wulfric. Wulfric glanced at it, slid it into his tunic, said something in a low voice and chuckled. He turned and hurried away towards the side gate.

Brother Taran paused for a few moments gazing after him, his hands on his hips. Then he turned slowly and began to walk back across the quadrangle towards the place where Fidelma and Eadulf stood.

Fidelma drew Eadulf out of the shadows.

Taran started as he saw them, giving a quick glance over his shoulder, obviously to see if Wulfric had disappeared. Wulfric had already gone through the side gate and so Taran turned back with a confident smile of greeting.

'A bright day, Sister Fidelma,' he called. 'And Brother Eadulf, is it not? I have heard of your investigation. Indeed, the entire abbey speaks of it. It is almost as controversial a debating point as the matters before the synod.'

Fidelma did not respond to his attempt at being gregarious and amiable.

'We were having a walk away from the dull dustiness of our chambers. As you say, it is a bright day. But it is good that we encountered you.'

191

'Oh? How so?' queried the Pictish monk, suddenly on his guard.

'You visited Étain in her *cubiculum* on the day of her death, did you not?'

For a passing moment Taran looked surprised.

'I . . . I did,' he admitted. 'Why do you ask?' Then he smiled. 'Of course, I am stupid. Yes, I went to see her but early in the morning.'

'Why?' asked Eadulf.

'It was a personal matter.'

'Personal?' Fidelma's voice had a biting edge to it.

'I know . . . I *knew* Abbess Étain and thought it only right that I should make my presence at Streoneshalh known to her and wish her well in the debate.'

'When did you know her?' asked Fidelma. 'You did not mention this to me on our journey from Iona.'

'You did not ask,' replied Taran with aplomb. 'You knew I studied in Ireland. I studied philosophy at Emly and Sister Étain, as she was then, was my tutor for a while.'

'You also studied at Emly?' asked Fidelma with raised brows. 'Emly is famed for its learning but it seems many people have studied there. Did you meet Sister Gwid at Emly?'

Taran blinked, recovered from his surprise and shook his head.

'No. I did not even know that she had studied there. Why did she not tell me?'

'Perhaps because you did not ask her.' Fidelma could not help the riposte.

'Did you know Athelnoth at Emly?' Eadulf asked.

'Him I did know. I was just completing my studies when Athelnoth arrived to study there. I knew him for perhaps a month or so before I left. But did you say Sister Gwid was at Emly?'

'For a while,' Fidelma said. 'Had you seen Étain since you left Emly?'

'No. But I always had respect for her. She was an excellent tutor and when I heard she was here I made it my business to seek her out. You see, I did not know she had become Abbess of Kildare. That was why I did not connect Étain with yourself, Sister Fidelma.'

'How long were you together with Étain on the day of her death?' Eadulf queried.

Taran pursed his lips as he thought for a moment or two.

'A short while, I think. We agreed to meet later that day for she was busy preparing her opening address for the debate and had no time to talk.'

'I see,' said Fidelma. Then she smiled. 'Well, we must detain you no longer.'

Taran inclined his head to each of them and turned away. He had taken a few paces when Fidelma called softly.

'By the way, have you seen Wulfric recently?'

Taran swung round, brows drawn together. For a moment Fidelma thought she saw a look of panic on his face. Then he re-formed his features into a mask, frowning as if he did not understand.

'You remember the obnoxious thane we encountered on our journey here? The one who boasted of his hanging the monk from Lindisfarne.'

Taran's eyes half closed as if he were attempting to see behind what Fidelma was implying. Fidelma retained a smile as she gazed on him.

'I . . . I believe I have seen him about.'

193

'One of Alhfrith's guards, I think,' offered Eadulf as if to help him identify Wulfric.

'Really?' Taran tried to make himself sound only distantly interested. 'No, I have not seen him recently.'

Sister Fidelma began to turn away towards the *monasteriolum*.

'An evil man. One to watch out for,' she called over her shoulder as she began to walk off.

Eadulf hurried after her, aware that Taran continued to stand, his mouth slightly open, his brows still drawn together, staring anxiously after them.

'Was it wise to put him on his guard?' Eadulf whispered, even though they were out of earshot.

Fidelma sighed patiently.

'He will not tell us the truth. Let him think we know more than we do. Sometimes this method may alarm people and push them to do things that they might otherwise have a care of doing. Now let us see what Seaxwulf is up to.'

They found Seaxwulf in the *librarium* poring over a book. He looked up flustered as they entered.

'Improving your mind, brother?' inquired Eadulf with cheerful irony.

Seaxwulf slammed the book shut and stood up. But there was something hesitant in his manner as if he wished to say something but was too embarrassed to do so. His desire for knowledge won over.

'I wish to know something about Ireland, Sister Fidelma. Is it customary for lovers to exchange gifts?' he asked brusquely.

Fidelma and Eadulf exchanged a look of surprise.

'That I believe is the custom,' replied Fidelma gravely. 'Do you have someone in mind as the recipient of such a gift?'

Seaxwulf's face was red and he muttered something and hurried out of the gloomy library room.

Inquisitively, Fidelma bent over the desk and opened the book Seaxwulf had been reading. Her lips broadened into a smile.

'Hellenistic love poetry. What is young Seaxwulf about, I wonder?' she mused.

Eadulf cleared his throat gruffly.

'I think this is an appropriate time for us to go in search of Athelnoth.'

Fidelma replaced the book as an anxious *librarius* descended on them to retrieve the volume.

'Perhaps you are right, Eadulf,' she said.

However Athelnoth was nowhere to be found in the abbey. Eadulf asked the gate-keeper if he had seen the brother leave and the man was immediately forthcoming. He said that Brother Athelnoth had left the abbey just after the morning Angelus bell, but was expected to return later that evening. What was more, the gate-keeper confided conspiratorially, Athelnoth had taken a horse from the royal stable but no one had complained of its disappearance.

By the time the bell announcing the *cena*, the main meal of the day, sounded, Athelnoth had not returned.

Finally Fidelma decided they would have to wait until the following morning to question Athelnoth, provided that the missing monk fulfilled his promise to return to the abbey.

Chapter Fourteen

Sister Fidelma was swimming in crystal-clear water, feeling the warmth of the wavelets on her body as she languorously pulled herself along. Above her was an azure sky in which the gold disc of the sun hung high and bright. The water was warmed by its rays. She could hear the birds chirping along the green, tree-lined bank. She felt at peace, content with the world. Then, suddenly, something was clutching at her leg, some weed, she thought, encircling her ankle. She tried to kick free, but her leg became more ensnared, dragging her downwards. Her vision began to blacken. She was being pulled down to the bottom, pulled relentlessly downward. She fought and struggled for breath, fought . . .

She came awake, sweating. Someone was pulling at her and she was fighting against the insistent tugging.

Sister Athelswith was standing over Fidelma holding a lighted candle in a holder. Fidelma blinked. She took a moment to get her bearings and then raised a hand to wipe the sweat from her face.

'You were having a nightmare, sister,' said the elderly *domina* of the *domus hospitale* in a reproving tone.

Sister Fidelma found herself yawning, observing that her breath took visual form against the flickering light. It was still dark and she shivered in the early morning frosty atmosphere.

'Was I disturbing the guests with my dream?' she asked.

Then, realising that the anxious *domina* could not have entered her *cubiculum* to wake her merely because she was dreaming, she added: 'What is it?'

It was hard to discern Sister Athelswith's expression in the gloomy light.

'You must come with me immediately, sister.'

The *domina* spoke in a whisper. Her voice was tight as if there was some stricture in her throat.

Frowning, Fidelma threw back the blanket, feeling the icy cold of the early morning strike against her body.

'Do I have time to dress?' she asked, drawing her clothes towards her.

'Better that you come as quickly as possible. Abbess Hilda awaits you and I have already sent for Brother Eadulf.'

Fidelma's mind worked rapidly now.

'Has there been another death from the Yellow Plague?'

'Not from the Yellow Plague, sister,' the *domina* replied.

Intrigued, Fidelma decided to draw her dress and veil hurriedly over her night attire before following the agitated figure of Sister Athelswith, who led the way holding her candle aloft.

To her surprise, the sister did not lead the way to the abbess's chamber but hurried towards the male *dormitorium*, pausing before the door of another *cubiculum* before pushing it open, eyes curiously averted, and motioning Fidelma inside. Even as she entered, Fidelma realised that she had been to this *cubiculum* before. The cell was lit by two candles.

The first person Fidelma saw was a dishevelled-looking Eadulf, his hair tousled and a look of sleepy surprise on his face. Beyond him stood the gaunt figure of the Abbess Hilda, hands folded in her clothing, head downcast.

'What is it?' demanded Fidelma, stepping forward into the *cubiculum*.

Eadulf said nothing but nudged the door closed with the toe of his sandal.

He nodded silently towards the back of the door.

Fidelma turned and her mouth opened involuntarily.

The body of Athelnoth was hanging from the wall behind the door from the pegs on which his clothes and *pera* usually hung. Of course, the *cubiculum* had been familiar. This was Athelnoth's chamber.

Fidelma stepped back, her eyes narrowing as she mastered her surprise. Athelnoth was in his night attire. The strong cord of his habit was twisted around his neck and attached to one of the wooden pegs in the wall which was inserted at a height of six feet above the floor. Athelnoth's shoeless feet just brushed the floor at the point of the toes but scarcely made contact with it. A footstool lay upturned nearby. Athelnoth's face was blackened and the tongue protruded.

'A suicide, here in Streoneshalh.'

It was the Abbess Hilda who broke the silence. Her tone was shocked and disapproving.

'When was this discovered?' asked Fidelma, her voice calm.

'Within the last half hour,' Eadulf replied. 'Apparently Athelnoth returned to the abbey after nightfall. You may have noticed that the clepsydra, the water clock which the good *domina* is so fond of, stands at the end of the corridor in which this chamber is situated. Sister Athelswith was on her way to adjust the clock when she heard a noise from this *cubiculum*. Doubtless it was the sound of the overturning footstool as Athelnoth kicked it away. She heard some strange sounds, no doubt the sound of the poor devil choking to death.

She knocked on the door of the *cubiculum* to enquire what was the matter. There was no response. Finally she opened it and saw Athelnoth hanging there. She went directly for Abbess Hilda and the abbess thought we should be immediately informed.'

Abbess Hilda nodded slowly in confirmation.

'You questioned Athelnoth about Abbess Étain's murder, I believe? Brother Eadulf tells me that you were waiting to question him again for you both have great suspicion of him. Brother Eadulf says that Athelnoth had lied to you.'

Sister Fidelma nodded absently, turning back to the hanging figure. She took a candle from a table and held it up so that she might see the figure more clearly. Her bright green eyes examined the body closely, moving to the upturned three-legged stool. Then she moved forward, picked up the stool and placed it near the body, climbing carefully on to it. From this position she stared at the back of the dead man's head. She dismounted and pursed her lips in silent contemplation for a moment before turning to the abbess.

'Mother Abbess, may we report to you later this morning? I believe that this death of Brother Athelnoth does, indeed, have something to do with the murder of the Abbess Étain. How much so is a question that we still have to determine.'

Abbess Hilda hesitated, frowned at Eadulf and then nodded.

'Very well. But you must now be quick in arriving at an answer to this mystery. There is much at stake here.'

Fidelma said nothing until the abbess had passed from the room.

She found Eadulf's puzzled glance on her.

'Surely it is obvious, sister?' he ventured. 'We were right that Athelnoth killed Étain because she had rejected his licentious advances. Once he realised that he was discovered, after we had questioned him, he was overcome by remorse and decided to take his own life.'

Fidelma viewed the hanging body with compressed lips.

'It would seem obvious,' she replied after a moment or two. Then she took a step to the cell door and opened it.

Sister Athelswith was waiting outside.

'Tell me, sister, when you heard the noise from this cell, where exactly were you?'

The elderly *domina* bobbed her head.

'I was at the end of the corridor, adjusting the mechanism of the clepsydra.'

'From the time you heard the noise until the time you saw the body, did you lose sight of the door of this *cubiculum*?'

The *domina* frowned, trying to understand the question.

'I heard the noise and stood still, trying to locate whence it came. It took me a few moments to locate the *cubiculum*. I walked along the corridor at a slow pace and it was as I was approaching that I heard a further noise. Then I knocked and called out: "Is anything the matter?" There was no reply. So I entered the cell.'

Fidelma looked thoughtful.

'I see. So the door was in full view the whole time?'

'Yes.'

'Thank you. You may go about your duties now. I'll find you when I need you.'

Sister Athelswith bobbed her head again and hurried off.

Eadulf was still standing in the same position with his brows drawn together in perplexity.

Fidelma ignored him.

She stood behind the closed door and surveyed the

201

cubiculum. It was like all the other accommodation, a tiny narrow cell furnished with a small wooden cot, the pillow indented and blankets askew where Athelnoth had obviously slept. There was also a table and the stool. She let her eyes wander over the chamber. The window was a small barred affair some six feet above the floor level.

To Eadulf's bewilderment, Fidelma abruptly went down on her knees and peered under the wooden cot. There was a space of a foot or so there. She reached up and took one of the candles and brought it down to the floor.

She saw the dust beneath the cot but it had been disturbed. In one spot there were some blood spots.

She glanced up with a grin of triumph.

'It is good that there is some slovenliness in Athelswith's hostel. We must be thankful that our sisters have a habit of not sweeping under the cots.'

'I don't understand,' Eadulf responded. 'Dust? Why is that lucky for us?'

But Fidelma was already examining something else – a splinter of wood on one of the legs of the cot. From it she was detaching some strands of coarse woollen fibre.

She gave a sigh and rose to her feet.

'Well?' prompted Eadulf.

Fidelma smiled at him.

'How do you read this scene?'

Eadulf shrugged.

'As I have said. Athelnoth took his own life in remorse once he knew that he had been discovered.'

Fidelma shook her head in disagreement.

'Does it not strike you as odd that Athelnoth showed no signs of remorse when he spoke to us the day before yesterday?'

'No. Remorse can be long in the gestation.'

'True. But does it not strike you as odd that Athelnoth then left the abbey yesterday morning and did not return until after dark? Where did he go? On what mission? Then, having gone on this mysterious mission, he returns to the abbey. He prepares for bed and goes to sleep. You have observed the cot has been slept in. He wakes before dawn and then, and only then, does the remorse strike at him so that he decides to take his own life?'

Eadulf grimaced defensively.

'I agree there is some strangeness. I would certainly like to know where he went. But everything else fits. Remorse is a strange controller of fate.'

'Remorse does not allow a person to knock himself on the back of the head before hanging himself.'

Eadulf's eyes widened in astonishment.

Fidelma calmly handed him the candle.

'See for yourself.'

The Saxon monk turned and climbed on to the stool, which Fidelma had left in place. He raised the candle and saw the dark stain on the back of the hanging man's head. Blood was matting the hair.

'That doesn't prove anything,' grunted Eadulf reluctantly. 'In his death throes he might have smashed his head against the wall.'

'If so, there will be blood on the wall where the abrasion was made. Show me it.'

Eadulf turned and looked over the wall. He could find no such mark.

He turned with an expression of perplexity.

'Are you saying that he was hit on the back of the head by

someone and then placed in that position so that he strangled to death?'

'Hit with a cudgel or something similar,' she agreed.

'Are you saying that whoever hit him then hanged him to make it seem like suicide?'

'Yes, that is precisely what I am saying.'

'How?'

'Our murderer entered the cell, hit Athelnoth on the head and contrived to hang him while unconscious from that peg.'

'And then he left?'

'He or she,' corrected Fidelma.

Eadulf climbed down and grimaced without mirth.

'You have forgotten one thing, sister. There is nowhere to hide and Sister Athelswith was in the corridor when she heard Athelnoth being hanged. She saw the door the whole time and no one exited from this *cubiculum*.'

Fidelma sniffed at his sarcastic tone.

'On the contrary, I did not forget that fact. Sister Athelswith did hear the deed being done. She called out asking what the matter was. That warned the murderer. The killer, taking the cudgel, hid in the only possible place, under the bed. Some fibres from the murderer's garment caught on the splintered leg of the cot and some blood spots dropped from the cudgel. You may examine them yourself. When Sister Athelswith entered, she had eyes only for the body of Athelnoth. Then she ran to find Abbess Hilda, allowing the murderer to depart at leisure.'

Eadulf felt the colour on his cheeks. Fidelma made it seem all so easy to deduce.

'I apologise,' he said slowly. 'I thought my eyes were trained against such subterfuge.'

'No matter.' Fidelma almost felt sorry at his woebegone

expression. 'The main thing is that the truth be seen.'

'What do the fibres tell us?' Eadulf went on hurriedly.

'Unfortunately little enough. They are of a common enough weave. They could come from anyone's clothing. But perhaps we may see someone with a tear in their clothing or dust on them which might help us identify them.'

Eadulf rubbed the bridge of his nose.

'The question is, why would the murderer want to kill Athelnoth?'

'I can only assume that Athelnoth knew something that would incriminate the real killer, or that the murderer thought that he knew something. He was killed to prevent him from telling that something to us.' She hesitated and then said firmly, 'We'd best go and inform the Mother Abbess that we are far from finished with this matter yet.'

Abbess Hilda greeted them with an uncharacteristic smile of satisfaction.

'Oswy the king will be pleased at your work,' she began as she indicated seats before the smouldering turf fire.

Sister Fidelma cast a meaningful glance at Eadulf.

'Our work?'

'Of course,' went on Hilda with satisfaction. 'The mystery is solved. The wretched Athelnoth slew Abbess Étain and then in remorse killed himself. And the motive was one of carnal ambition. Nothing to do with the politics of the church. Brother Eadulf explained it to me.'

Eadulf reddened in embarrassment.

'When I told you that, Mother Abbess, there were factors that I had overlooked.'

Fidelma decided not to help the Saxon monk out of the

predicament that he himself had created.

Hilda's brow lowered in annoyance.

'Are you trying to tell me that you made a mistake when you told me that the matter was closed?'

Eadulf nodded unhappily.

Hilda's jaws snapped so that Fidelma winced as she heard the teeth grind.

'Are you making a mistake now?' she demanded.

Eadulf was looking desperately at Fidelma. She took pity on him.

'Mother Abbess, Brother Eadulf was not in full possession of the facts. Athelnoth's death was yet another murder. The murderer remains at large in the abbey.'

Abbess Hilda closed her eyes and was unable to suppress a soft moan escaping her compressed lips.

'What am I to tell Oswy? The debate enters its third day and there is now bad blood between the factions. There have been no less than three brawls between brothers of Columba and those of Rome. Outside the abbey there are rumours rushing like forest fires, hither and thither. We could all be consumed in them. Do you not realise just how important this debate is?'

'That I do, Mother Abbess,' Fidelma said firmly. 'But it is no good inventing a conclusion that is at odds with the truth.'

'Heaven give me patience!' snapped the Abbess Hilda. 'I am talking of civil war ripping this country apart.' Her face was drawn.

'I am well aware of the situation,' Fidelma assured her, feeling sorry for the burden that must be on her shoulders. 'But truth must take precedence over such considerations.'

'And what shall I tell Oswy?' Hilda's voice was almost pleading.

'Tell him that the investigation continues,' Fidelma replied. 'And as soon as there is word then you and Oswy shall have it.'

Chapter Fifteen

The bell announcing the serving of the *jentaculum* was sounding as Fidelma and Eadulf walked away from the chamber of the abbess. Fidelma realised that she was dry-mouthed and hungry. She turned towards the refectory but Eadulf stayed her with a hand on her arm.

'I have no wish to eat,' he said. 'I want to examine the body of Athelnoth more closely.'

'The physician, Brother Edgar, can take care of that matter.'

Eadulf firmly shook his head.

'There is something I have in mind. But do not let me prevent you from eating.'

'That you will not,' Fidelma assured him. 'I will meet you in Athelnoth's *cubiculum* later. We can talk over the facts as we know them.'

She turned and followed the line of brethren hurrying into the refectory. She took her place, absently nodding a greeting to one or two of the sisters with whom she sat.

A sister was intoning the *Beati immaculati* prior to the daily reading.

Jugs of cool milk, jars of honey and *paximatium*, the twice-baked bread, were being distributed to each table.

There was hardly a sound except the monotonous voice of the reciter intoning from the Gospels.

Fidelma had almost finished her food when she became

aware of a monk with corn-coloured hair making his way through the tables towards the door of the refectory. It was Seaxwulf. Fidelma was about to ignore him when she noticed a strange look in the young man's eyes as they fell on her. It was as if he wanted to speak but did not want her to acknowledge him.

As Seaxwulf reached the place where Fidelma sat, he halted and stared down at his sandal. Then he bent down and began to adjust his strap as if it had become loosened.

'Sister!'

He spoke in a sibilant whisper and, to her surprise, in Greek.

'Sister, I hope you understand this language. I know you have little Saxon and I have even less Irish. I wish no one to overhear us.'

She was about to turn to say she understood when Seaxwulf's voice became a hiss.

'Don't look at me! I think I am watched. I have news of Étain's death. Meet me in the *apotheca* by the casks where the wine is stored within fifteen minutes.'

Seaxwulf rose, as if he had re-tied his sandal strap, and resumed his path out of the refectory.

Fidelma continued finishing her meal, forcing herself to eat leisurely.

Finally she bent her head over her empty bowl, rose, genuflected and made her way out of the hall.

She strolled out of the gate of the abbey and through the grounds. She kept her head down, but her eyes were darting hither and thither as she sought any who might be watching or following her. Only after she had circumvented the buildings and was assured that no one was observing her did she hurry her pace, slipping back into the abbey building and moving to the entrance to the *hypogeum*, the vaults that ran beneath the abbey building.

She paused at the top of the flight of circular stone steps that led down into the dark catacombs below. There was a wooden shelf just within the door on which several candles had been placed together with an oil lamp from which they could be lit. She took one and lit it, and began to descend into the darkness. It was the route by which Sister Athelswith had conducted her with Brother Eadulf. Fidelma realised that there was probably an easier route to the *apotheca* but she did not wish to ask anyone the way to her rendezvous with Seaxwulf.

The vaults beneath the abbey had been tunnelled in the first place to accommodate the members of the house who died. The great chambers were lined in sandstone blocks and built with arches to support the floors above. They formed a labyrinth in which many things were stored. Fidelma tried to remember the way to the *apotheca* where the series of great wooden casks containing wines imported from Frankia, Rome and Iberia were stored.

Fidelma paused at the foot of the stairway and looked about her.

It was cold and dank in the vaults. She shivered, half wishing that she had waited to tell Eadulf where she was going.

She moved quietly down the central way, passing a line of stone shelves on which were several wooden coffins containing the bodies of the brethren of Streoneshalh who had died over the years. The musty smell of death hung over the place. Fidelma bit her lip. She passed by the small chamber in which the body of Abbess Étain lay. That of Deusdedit, the archbishop, she knew, had been carried out of the abbey for cremation, as was the custom with all victims of the Yellow Plague.

She was sure that the kitchen servants did not have to come this way every time they wanted to fill the wine flagons. There would obviously be a shorter way from the kitchens to the wine store.

She frowned, trying to remember the way by which the elderly *domina*, Sister Athelswith, had conducted her.

She decided to go straight on.

It was oddly draughty in the vaults. A cold breath caused her candle to flicker every now and again, which indicated that there were entrances that allowed a breeze to enter the catacombs. The only way that could possibly be was if the entrances led directly to the outside of the abbey buildings.

She had gone some way before the scent of wine, mixed with the bitter-sweet stench of stale cooking from the great abbey kitchens above, told her that she was nearing the section of the *hypogeum* reserved for the storage of wine. She halted and peered around. The light of her candle was limited and she could see nothing beyond its immediate ring of light.

'Seaxwulf!' she called softly. 'Are you down here?'

The echoes came back like the rumble of thunder.

She held up her candle, causing grotesque shadows to dance madly in all directions.

'Seaxwulf!'

She moved around the barrels, peering here and there in case he was sheltering.

Then she halted, head to one side.

There came to her ears a hollow thumping sound. Frowning, she tried to identify the noise. It was like someone knocking gently on wood.

'Is that you, Seaxwulf?' she called softly.

There was no answer, yet the knocking continued.

Puzzled, she edged around the great wooden barrels. But there was no sign of Wighard's effeminate secretary.

Then she located the sound. It was coming from the inside of one of the barrels. She stopped, perplexed.

'Seaxwulf? Are you in there?'

It seemed an odd place for the monk to be hiding.

The knocking was distinct now. She reached out a hand and felt the vibration on the wood of the great cask. Thud. Thud. Thud. There was no other answer. She turned and saw a small wooden stool. She manoeuvred it against the side of the wooden cask, which was six feet in height. The stool gave her the extra height so that she could peer over the rim of the cask.

Holding her candle high in one hand, she carefully climbed on to the stool and peered down into the cask.

Seaxwulf lay face down in the vat, floating on the red surface of the wine. There was a ripple in the liquid which was causing the body to move in a regular rhythm, the head knocking against the side of the wooden cask and sending out a hollow thud. Thud. Thud. Thud.

Startled, Fidelma took a step backwards, missed her footing and toppled from the stool. The candle went flying out of her hand. She flailed out wildly, trying to catch something to prevent the inevitable fall. Then she went backwards. She knew that she had hit the ground by the sudden cascade of lights that exploded before her eyes a split second before everything went dark.

At the end of a long, dark tunnel, Fidelma could hear someone moaning softly. She blinked and tried to focus. The tunnel receded and it became more light. She realised that the moaning was coming from her.

213

Brother Eadulf's face swam into her vision. He looked drawn and anxious.

'Fidelma? Are you all right?'

She blinked again and everything came into sharper focus. She realised that she was lying on the cot in her own *cubiculum*. Behind Eadulf's shoulder the anxious grey face of the elderly *domina* was peering at her with concern.

'I think so,' she said ruefully, feeling a thickness in her mouth. 'I would like some water.'

Sister Athelswith reached forward and pressed a pottery mug into her hand.

The water was cold and refreshing.

'I fell,' Fidelma said as she handed it back, realising at once, it seemed a silly thing to say.

Eadulf grinned in relief.

'You did. You seemed to have toppled off a stool in the *apotheca*. What on earth were you up to down there?'

Remembrance came back at once. Fidelma struggled to sit up. She had been placed fully clothed on her own cot. The back of her head was sore.

'Seaxwulf!'

Eadulf frowned uncertainly.

'What has he to do with it?' he demanded. 'Did he attack you?'

Fidelma stared at Eadulf with incomprehension for a moment or two.

'Didn't you see?'

Eadulf shook his head, frowning.

'Perhaps the good sister is distraught,' muttered Sister Athelswith.

Fidelma reached forward and grabbed the young monk's hand.

'Seaxwulf has been killed. Did you not see him?' she demanded urgently.

Eadulf again shook his head, staring at her. Sister Athelswith gave a gasp and placed a hand over her mouth.

Fidelma struggled to get off the cot, but Eadulf held her back.

'Careful, you might well have injured yourself.'

'I am all right,' snapped Fidelma irritably. 'How did you find me?'

It was Sister Athelswith who answered.

'One of the kitchen staff heard a cry from the vaults beneath the kitchen and went down. She found you lying on your back beside a wine cask. She sent for me and I sent for Brother Eadulf who carried you back into your room.'

Fidelma turned back to Eadulf.

'Did you look into the cask? The one I fell from?'

'No. I don't understand.'

'Then go and do so. Someone has killed Seaxwulf. He was dumped in the cask.'

Without another word, Eadulf rose and left. Fidelma irritably waved the fussing Sister Athelswith away. She rose and went to the table on which a bowl and jug of water stood. She splashed it on her face. Her head was throbbing.

'You need not wait, sister,' she said, on finding that Sister Athelswith still stood silently by the door. 'No word of this must be mentioned until we say so. I will give you further news later.'

With a sniff of hurt pride, Sister Athelswith departed.

Fidelma stood a moment, feeling everything swimming out of focus. She sat down again abruptly and began to massage her temples with her fingertips.

215

Eadulf returned a moment later. He was breathless from hurrying.

'Well?' asked Fidelma before he could speak. 'Did you see the body?'

'No.' Eadulf shook his head. 'There was no body in the cask.'

Fidelma jerked her head up and stared at the monk.

'What?'

'I looked in all the casks. There was no body in any of them.'

Fidelma came to her feet, her mouth tight and her dizziness gone.

'I saw it there. I think Seaxwulf had been drowned in the wine. I saw it!'

Eadulf smiled reassuringly.

'I believe you, sister. And since we brought you here someone must have removed it.'

Fidelma sighed. 'Yes. That must be it.'

'You had best tell me exactly what happened.'

Fidelma sat back on the bed, rubbing her pulsating forehead with her hands as the ache came back.

'I told you to take things easy,' reproved Eadulf. 'Does your head ache?'

'Yes,' she groaned irritably. 'What do you think, after receiving a crack like that?'

He smiled sympathetically.

'Don't worry. I'll go and have the kitchen prepare a drink that will help you.'

'A drink? Another of the poisons you claim to have learnt in Tuaim Brecain?' she moaned.

'A herbal remedy,' Eadulf assured her with a grin. 'A mixture of sage and red clover. Drink it and it will ease the ache in your head. Though I doubt your condition is so serious if you can protest as you do.' He disappeared but was back almost before she realised it.

'The remedy will be along shortly. Now tell me what happened,' he invited.

She told him, simply and without embroidering the story.

'You should have told me about this assignation before you went off gallivanting in those vaults,' he admonished.

There was a tap on the door and a sister entered with a steaming pottery mug.

'Ah, the infusion,' grinned Eadulf. 'It may not taste sweetly, sister, but it will cure your head. I guarantee it.'

Fidelma sipped at the noxious brew, screwing her face up.

'Best to swallow it as fast as possible,' advised Eadulf.

Fidelma pulled a face at him but took his advice, shutting her eyes and swallowing the warm drink as fast as possible.

'That was truly horrible,' she said, as she put down the mug. 'You seem to be constantly making me imbibe your noxious concoctions. I think you take a pleasure in it.'

'There is a saying in your language, Fidelma, that the bitterer the medicine the better the cure,' replied Eadulf complacently. 'Now where were we . . . ?'

'Seaxwulf. You say his body has gone? But why? And why kill Seaxwulf and then go to such pains to hide the body?'

'He was killed to prevent him from speaking with you. That much is obvious.'

'But what had Seaxwulf to tell me? What was so important that he had to make a secret rendezvous and then get killed for it?'

'Perhaps Seaxwulf had learnt the identity of our murderer?'

Fidelma sat down on the cot and clenched her teeth angrily.

'Three murders, three and we are not even close to a discovery yet.'

Eadulf shook his head.

'I disagree. We are too close, sister,' he said with emphasis.

Fidelma glanced up in surprise.

'What do you mean?'

'I mean that if we were not close then there would have been only one murder committed. The other two were committed to prevent us gaining the knowledge that those murdered had. We came too close and the murderer was forced to act before we realised that fact.'

Fidelma thought for a moment.

'You are right. I am not thinking straight. You are absolutely right, Eadulf.'

Eadulf smiled ruefully.

'I have also discovered that Athelnoth was not entirely lying to us about the brooch.'

'How?'

Eadulf held out his hand. In his palm was a small silver brooch. Its workmanship was exquisite and its whorls and circular patterns were emphasised by enamel work and semi-precious stones.

Fidelma took it and held it up, turning it over in her fingers.

'There is little doubt that this is of Irish workmanship,' she said. 'Where did you find it?'

'When Brother Edgar, the physician, stripped the body of Athelnoth for the post-mortem examination we found that he had a small purse tied against the flesh of his body on a leather thong. There was nothing in the purse save this brooch. Oh, and a small scrap of vellum with some Greek writing.'

'Show me.'

Eadulf handed it to her a little uncomfortably.

'My Greek is not good enough to understand it fully.'

Fidelma's eyes were sparkling. 'A love poem. "Love shook my heart, like a mountain wind that falls upon oak trees." Short and simple.' She sighed softly. 'Each time we think we have solved a mystery, the mystery only deepens.'

'I don't understand. Surely this is an easy riddle? This must be the brooch that Étain dropped and that Athelnoth said he was going to return – the brooch he mislaid when he took us to his *cubiculum* to show us? And it was obvious that he was writing some love poem to Étain, an attempt to win her favour just as Sister Gwid indicated.'

Fidelma turned worried eyes on Eadulf.

'If this was the brooch Étain dropped, and Athelnoth were going to return it, why would he keep it in a small purse next to his skin? And with a love poem? Surely the brooch was there at the very time he was pretending to search for it in front of us? If so, Athelnoth was lying again. But for what purpose?'

Eadulf smiled: 'Because he did have an infatuation for Étain. He wrote the love poem to her. Perhaps he wanted the brooch as a keepsake. People do become enamoured of objects belonging to people they have a passion for. They sometime vent their passion on the object.'

Fidelma's eyes brightened.

'A keepsake! What a fool I am. I think you have taken us a step nearer to the truth.'

Eadulf cast her a bewildered glance, not sure whether she was being sarcastic or not.

'Seaxwulf was reading Greek love poems in the *librarium* the other evening. And he asked us if lovers exchanged gifts. Don't you see?'

Eadulf looked totally bemused.

'I don't see how this helps us. Are you saying that Seaxwulf killed Athelnoth?'

'And then drowned himself in a cask of wine? Think again, Eadulf!'

With an exclamation of exasperation she stood up abruptly, swaying a little. Eadulf caught her arm anxiously and they stood for a moment as she recovered from the fit of giddiness. Then she broke away in agitation.

'Let us go down to the *apotheca* again and examine the cask from which our third corpse has gone missing. There is something I think Seaxwulf had which we must find.'

'Are you fit enough?' he demanded anxiously.

'Of course,' snapped Fidelma. Then she paused and a smile passed over her features. 'Yes, I am,' she said more softly. 'You were right. It was a bitter medicine but my headache has gone. You have a talent there, Eadulf. You would make a fine apothecary.'

Chapter Sixteen

Eadulf led the way by the quicker route to the wine cellar through a small passageway and stair from the abbey kitchens. Had Fidelma known this short route it would have saved her much time in finding her way through the gloomy catacombs. Fidelma caught her breath as they traversed the kitchens, which were still full of strong odours, with the inevitable reek of stale boiled cabbage and herbs dominating. The stench followed them down a circular stone stair into the *apotheca*.

Fidelma went straight to the cask and sought the stool by which she had climbed to its rim. It took her a moment to mount carefully, watched anxiously by Eadulf, who held an oil lamp aloft to give a better light than the single candle she had previously used.

The cask held nothing more ominous than the dark liquid of the wine.

Fidelma leant over, peering into it. There was nothing in its crimson black murkiness that she could see. She turned and observed a long pole nearby, presumably for measuring the liquid in the casks for it had a series of measures carved into it. She took it and lowered it into the cask, feeling about with it in case the body had somehow sunk to the bottom.

There was no contact. There was nothing in the cask except what there was meant to be. She felt a little light-headed from the perfume of the wine.

Fidelma dismounted and walked around the cask. Then she paused, reaching out and feeling the oak wood. It was damp on one side. She sniffed at her fingertips. The scent of the wine was unmistakable.

'Shine the light on the floor,' she commanded.

Eadulf held the lamp obligingly.

The floor was wet and there were some scuff marks on its surface.

'Our friend pulled the body out of the cask on this side and started to drag it . . . that way. Come on.'

She moved decisively, following the tell-tale line across the stone-flagged floor.

Eadulf followed her.

There were two parallel marks scuffed into the dust of the sandstone surface of the floor, with occasional damp patches. It seemed that someone had dragged the missing body by the arms so that the ankles left the marks across the floor.

The trail led into a passageway off the main *hypogeum* that was cut into the natural sandstone rock and which narrowed so that only two people could walk abreast. Fidelma went to move into it but, to her surprise, she found that Eadulf had laid a restraining hand on her arm.

'What is it?' she demanded.

'I have been told that this leads to one of the more popular of the male *defectora*, sister,' Eadulf replied. Even by the unnatural light of the lamp she could see that he was blushing.

'A lavatory?'

Eadulf nodded.

Fidelma sniffed and turned back into the tunnel.

'Alas, I cannot spare their modesty nor mine. This is the way our murderer dragged the body of Seaxwulf.'

With a sigh of resignation, Eadulf followed her as she moved quickly onward along the narrow defile through the rock.

The tunnel seemed endless.

After a while Fidelma halted, ears straining to catch a discordant sound that had impinged upon her senses.

'What's that?'

Eadulf was frowning as he listened.

'Thunder?'

The faint noise echoing along the passageway did, indeed, sound like the far-off rumble of distant thunder.

'Thunder is not so consistent and remorseless,' commented Fidelma.

She began to move forward again.

The faint breeze that they had felt throughout the abbey cellars and along the tunnel began to grow colder and sharper.

They turned a corner of the man-made tunnel and a sudden blast of cold, damp air hit them, causing the light of the oil lamp to waver and flicker out.

There came the overpowering scent of the sea, not just salt spray but the scent of seaweed.

'We must be near the sea,' Fidelma called, having to raise her voice so that Eadulf could hear. 'Can you relight the lamp?'

'No,' Eadulf's voice came forlornly. 'I have nothing to light it with.'

They were standing in a darkness which, initially, they had thought as black as pitch. But gradually their eyes grew used to the gloom and a faint grey light spread itself along the tunnel.

'There must be an opening up ahead,' yelled Eadulf.

'Let us continue,' Fidelma replied.

Eadulf could just see her dark sharp moving forward.

'Have a care,' he called. 'Stick close by the wall lest you slip.'

223

She made no acknowledgement to his cautious warning but moved firmly on, almost having to feel her way forward.

The roar grew louder.

She realised then that it was the sea. The tunnel entrance was coming out close to the edge of the sea. She could hear its breathless rasping over the shingle, and the angry crash as the waves came in and smashed against the rocks.

She pressed forward. She realised why Seaxwulf's body had been dragged along this passageway towards the sea. The murderer had thrown the body into the waves. The light was growing brighter and the sound was now deafening.

She turned a corner and found herself unable to see as salt sea spray cascaded over her. Involuntarily she closed her eyes and took a step forward. Her foot was not connecting with the rocky floor; she seemed to hang suspended in the air. Then a strong hand caught her arm and she found herself being pulled backwards. She was back on *terra firma* with Eadulf at her side.

The tunnel had twisted and ended abruptly in the mouth of a small cavern from which was a fall of one hundred or more feet to the rocks and sea below.

Fidelma found herself shivering slightly at the nearness of the catastrophe.

'I told you to have a care, sister,' reproached Eadulf, his hand still on her arm.

'I'm all right now.'

Eadulf shrugged and let go her arm.

'That was a dangerous turn. You were blinded by the sudden light and spray.'

'I'm all right now,' she repeated, annoyed with her own awkwardness. 'And I can see why the brethren choose this place to perform their defecations. It is continually washed by the sea. An excellent place.'

She turned, without embarrassment, and examined the cave entrance. She guessed it was situated in the cliffs below the abbey that fronted on to the grey, brooding northern seas.

'At least we know now where Seaxwulf's body has gone,' she said, gesturing at the white froth crashing around the rocks below. She had to raise her voice to be heard above the restless waves.

'But not where the person who transported his body here went,' Eadulf pointed out. 'There were tracks leading into the tunnel but none coming out. There would have been tracks obliterating the first ones had the murderer returned the same way.'

Fidelma looked at Eadulf appreciatively.

'I think that we were only minutes behind the murderer, who perhaps heard us coming along the tunnel and so was prevented from returning that way. Which means' – she peered around in the gloom – 'that there is another exit.' She suddenly grunted in satisfaction and pointed.

To one side a small series of stone steps, carved in the rock, led upwards.

She moved forward, stumbling slightly, for the rock was wet and slippery from the salt sea spray.

She balanced herself and began the ascent, assuming that Eadulf would follow.

It took a while, but she found herself emerging among some brambles on the windy grass atop the cliffs.

The abbey buildings were further up the rise from the spot where she had emerged.

'Sister Fidelma!' She jumped at the sound of a voice nearby.

'Where on earth have you sprung from?'

She turned and found herself gazing into the astonished dark eyes of Abbess Abbe. By the abbess's side Brother Taran stood, mouth agape.

Fidelma could not repress a soft chuckle at the question.

'Not on earth, sister,' she replied.

Abbe showed she did not understand. Then she jumped as Eadulf also emerged from the stairwell among the bramble bushes that covered it and on to the grass.

'From under the earth,' Eadulf explained, dusting himself down.

Abbess Abbe's eyes were wide in her perplexity.

'Where does that hole lead to? What were you doing down there?'

'A long story,' Fidelma said. 'Have you been here long?'

The abbess smiled sadly.

'A little while. I was walking with Brother Taran along the cliffs here to get some fresh air before the afternoon's debate. I was wishing that Étain could be here. She had a way of calming tempers. And tempers are flaring and each exchange gets more heated. I fear that we shall have another Nicaean Council on our hands.'

Eadulf seemed bewildered. The abbess explained for him.

'At the Council of Nicaea, when Arius of Alexandria rose to speak, one Nicholas of Myra was so outraged that he struck him in the face. There was uproar and pandemonium, with the delegates running out of the debating chamber lest they be beaten by either Arius's followers or those that opposed him. In the panic that followed, I believe several of the brethren were killed. I feel that soon we shall have Wilfrid physically assaulting Colmán.'

Fidelma was examining her closely.

'Have you seen anyone else walking near here?'

Abbe shook her head and turned to her companion.

'How about you, Brother Taran? You were here when I arrived.'

Taran raised the fingers of his right hand and pressed the bridge of his nose as if the action might help his recollection.

'I saw Sister Gwid walking nearby and Wighard, Deusdedit's secretary.'

'Were Wighard and Gwid walking together or separately?' Eadulf demanded.

'Sister Gwid was on her own. She seemed to be in a hurry, heading to the harbour. Wighard was heading to the abbey, through the kitchen gardens yonder. Why do you ask?'

'No matter,' said Fidelma hurriedly. 'We should be getting back to the abbey ourselves—'

She paused, frowning.

Sister Athelswith was hurrying in their direction. She was holding her skirts and trotting, in something as near to a run as she could manage without losing dignity.

'Ah, Sister Fidelma! Brother Eadulf!' She paused, gasping for breath.

'What is it, sister?' asked Fidelma, allowing her to regain her breath.

'The king himself . . . the king requests your presence immediately.'

Abbess Abbe sighed.

'I wonder what my brother can want? Let us all go back to the abbey and find out what ails him.'

Brother Taran gave a deprecating cough.

'You'll forgive me. I need to make a visit to the harbour

227

first. I will join you in the *sacrarium* later.'

He left them, turning quickly down the path to the harbour.

Chapter Seventeen

On reaching Abbess Hilda's chamber, Fidelma and Eadulf were told that the king had been waiting for them but had been summoned into the *sacrarium*. A sister who greeted them at the door told Abbess Abbe that her presence was also required immediately, for the synod was in its closing stages and the final arguments were about to be made. But, she informed them breathlessly, the king required the presence of Fidelma and Eadulf immediately after the ending of the session.

It was Eadulf who suggested that they go to the *sacrarium* to hear the closing stages of the debate and wait for Oswy there.

There was a curious look on Fidelma's face, an expression that Eadulf had come to recognise as one denoting deep thought. He had to make the suggestion several times before she acknowledged him.

'I suppose everyone knows about that male *defectorum* that opens to the sea?' she asked. The question was directed at the *domina*. Athelswith spread her hands with a slightly flustered look.

'Everyone in the abbey, I would imagine. It is not a secret.'

'Everyone belonging to this abbey, but what of the visitors?' insisted Fidelma. 'For example, I did not know about it.'

'That is true,' agreed Sister Athelswith. 'But only our male guests are told of it. It is for males only. Our brothers find it more modest to go there rather than use the *defectorum* across the quadrangle from the *monasteriolum*.'

'I see. So what if a female wanders along the tunnel and into it by accident? There is no sign on the entrance.'

'Most of the sisters use the building by the other side of the *monasteriolum*. They have no need to be in the *hypogeum* at all unless they work in the kitchens. And those working in the kitchens know of its existence. There is no need to fix a sign on the tunnel.'

Sister Fidelma was thoughtful as she turned to follow Eadulf to the *sacrarium*.

The atmosphere was tense in the *sacrarium* and the Abbess Hilda was on her feet addressing the packed benches of clerics.

'Brothers and sisters in Christ,' she was saying as Fidelma and Eadulf entered quietly through the side door behind the benches now packed with representatives of the Columban church, 'let the final submissions be made.'

Colmán rose to his feet, blunt as ever. He had elected to speak first – a choice that Fidelma thought unwise, for the man who speaks last is always the one who is listened to.

'Brethren, over these last few days you have heard why we of the church of Columba follow our customs concerning the dating of Easter. Our church claims its authority from the Divine John, son of Zebedee, who forsook the sea of Galilee to follow the Messiah. He was the disciple most beloved of Christ, who rested on his master's breast at the Last Supper. And Jesus did not forsake him. When the Son of the Living God was expiring on the Cross, He had strength enough to confide the care of His mother, the Blessed Mary, to John.

'This same John ran before Peter to the tomb on the morning of the blessed resurrection and seeing it empty was the first to believe and thence was the first to see the risen Lord by the Sea of Tiberias. John was the blessed of Christ.

'When Jesus confided the care of His mother and family into the arms of John, He confided His Church to that care. That is why we accept the ways of John. John is our path to Christ.'

Colmán resumed his seat amid murmured applause from the Columban benches.

Wilfrid rose. There was a smile on his lips. He looked complacent.

'We have heard that the representatives of Columba cite the apostle John as the supreme authority by which their customs stand and fall. I therefore say to you that they must fall.'

There was a ripple of anger from the Columban benches.

Abbess Hilda gestured with her hand for silence.

'We must accord Wilfrid of Ripon the same courtesy as we accorded Colmán, bishop of Northumbria,' she rebuked softly.

Wilfrid was smiling, like a hunter who knows his prey is within his sight.

'The Easter we of Rome observe is the one that is celebrated by all at Rome, the city where the blessed apostles Peter and Paul lived, taught, suffered and were buried. It is a usage that is universal in Italy, in Gaul, Frankia and Iberia, through which I have travelled for the purpose of study and prayer. In every part of the world, by different nations speaking different tongues, this practice is followed by all at one and the same time. The only exception is this people!' He pointed derisively to the Columban benches. 'I mean the Irish, the Picts and the Britons and those of our people who have chosen to follow their erroneous teachings. The only excuse they have for this ignorance is that they come from the two remotest islands in

231

the Western Ocean and then from only parts of them. Because of this remoteness they stand isolated from true knowledge and they pursue a foolish struggle against the whole world. They may be holy but they are few – too few to have precedence over the universal Church of Christ.'

Colmán was on his feet, his face working with anger.

'You are prevaricating, Wilfrid of Ripon. I have stated the authority of our church, John the Divine Apostle. State your authority or remain silent.'

There was a murmur of applause.

'Very well. Rome demands obedience from all parts of Christendom because it was to Rome that Christ's disciple Simon Bar-Jonah went to found His Church. This Simon was he whom we call Peter whom Christ nicknamed "the rock". In Rome did Peter teach, in Rome did Peter suffer and in Rome did he die a martyr's death. Peter is our authority and I shall read from the Gospel of Matthew to give power to my case.'

He turned and was handed a book by Wighard, opened at a page. Wilfrid began to read immediately.

' "And Jesus answered and said unto him, Blessed art thou Simon Bar-Jonah for flesh and blood hath not revealed it unto thee but my Father which is in heaven. And I say also unto thee, that thou art Peter, and upon this rock I will build my church; and the gates of hell shall not prevail against it. And I will give unto thee the keys of the kingdom of heaven . . ." '

Wilfrid paused and gazed round.

'Our authority comes from Peter who thus holds the keys to the gates of the kingdom of heaven itself!' Wilfrid sat down amidst rapturous applause from his supporters.

There was a silence when the applause died away. Eadulf suddenly nudged Fidelma and gestured to the dais. The Abbess

Abbe had risen and was making her way hurriedly out of the *sacrarium.*

Their attention was immediately drawn back to the Abbess Hilda, who had risen to her feet once again.

'Brethren of Christ, the final submissions have been made. It is now up to our sovereign lord, the king, Oswy, by the grace of God, *Bretwalda* of all the kingdoms, to deliver his judgment; the decision as to which church, Columban or Roman, has precedence in our kingdom. The judgment is now yours to make.'

She turned to Oswy, her features expectant as were those of all the participants of the synod.

Fidelma saw that the tall fair-haired king of Northumbria remained seated. He looked nervous and preoccupied. For several long moments he hesitated, biting at his lip as he stared around at the expectant faces in the *sacrarium.* Then he slowly rose. His voice was unnaturally sharp, hiding his anxiety.

'I shall give my judgment tomorrow at noon,' he said abruptly.

Against a chorus of protests, the king turned and left the *sacrarium* hurriedly. Alhfrith, the king's son, was on his feet, his face a mask of barely controlled anger. He turned and rushed from the chapel. Eanflaed, Oswy's wife, seemed better able to control her feelings, but her smile was bitter as she turned to her chaplain, Romanus, and engaged him in conversation. Ecgfrith, Oswy's other son, was also smiling as he gathered his retinue and left the *sacrarium.*

The benches of both factions erupted into argument, voices raised against one another.

Fidelma exchanged a swift glance with Eadulf and motioned towards the doors.

Outside, Eadulf muttered: 'Well, our brethren seemed to have been expecting an immediate decision. Did you notice that the Abbess Abbe left before the decision and that Brother Taran was not in attendance at all?'

Fidelma made little comment as she led the way back to the Abbess Hilda's chamber.

Oswy was already there. His face was white and his features taut.

'There you are!' he snapped. 'I was waiting most of the morning to see you. Where have you been? No matter. I wanted to speak with you before the final session of the synod.'

Fidelma was unabashed at his irritation.

'Have you been told that there has been another murder?'

Oswy frowned.

'Another? Do you mean Athelnoth?'

'No – Seaxwulf, the secretary of Wilfrid of Ripon.'

Oswy shook his head slowly.

'I do not understand. Last night Athelnoth was killed. Now, you tell me, Seaxwulf. For what purpose? Hilda says that you had at first thought Athelnoth had taken his own life in remorse at killing Étain.'

Eadulf coloured a little.

'I leapt to a wrong conclusion. I soon realised I was in error,' he said.

Oswy sniffed in annoyance.

'I could have told you that you were in error,' he said flatly. 'Athelnoth was a man to be trusted.'

'How so?' demanded Fidelma sharply.

'Because Athelnoth was my confidant. I have told you that these are dangerous times, that certain factions wish to oust me as king and are using this synod to create civil war in the kingdom.'

Oswy paused, as if seeking confirmation, but Fidelma motioned him to continue.

'I have had to have eyes in the back of my head. Athelnoth was one of my best informants and advisers. Yesterday I sent him to my army, which waits encamped at Ecga's Tun.'

Eadulf's eyes lightened.

'So that was where Athelnoth was all day yesterday and why he did not return until late last night.'

Oswy compressed his lips a moment, frowning at Eadulf's aside.

'He returned with important news for me, news of a plot to assassinate me and seize control of the kingdom. My army has had to march to counter an attack by the rebel army.'

Fidelma's eyes were sparkling.

'Some things now become clearer.'

'Even clearer than you think, sister.' Oswy was grim. 'This morning my guards killed the thane Wulfric along with twenty of his warriors. They were attempting to enter the abbey secretly from the tunnel on the cliff top. As you know, at midnight all the gates are locked until the morning Angelus, which is rung at six o'clock. During that time all warriors bearing arms are excluded from the abbey. Athelnoth was sure that Wulfric had an accomplice among the brethren, waiting to assist him and his assassins and conduct them to my chambers.'

'Indeed, it does become clear,' Fidelma said.

Eadulf was frowning as he tried to reason what Fidelma was thinking.

'I do not understand.'

'Simple,' Fidelma replied. 'I think you will find that the person willing to let your assassins into the abbey this morning, Oswy of Northumbria, was the Pictish monk Taran.'

235

'What makes you say this?' demanded Oswy. 'Why would a Pict concern himself with the ambitions of Northumbrian rebels to overthrow their king?'

'Firstly because I know that Taran was friendly with Wulfric and that Taran lied about that friendship. Even on the journey here when I first met Wulfric, after he had killed Brother Aelfric, I had the impression that Wulfric recognised Taran, which indicates this plot was long in the hatching. And later I saw Taran meeting Wulfric in friendship. Taran denied this. I believe that Taran was willing to see Northumbria destroyed or at the best divided and at war with itself.'

'Why would he do that?' asked Oswy curiously.

'Because the Picts, as you call the Cruthin, are a people who nurse old grudges and their hate is as long as it is fierce. Taran once told me that his father, a chieftain of the Gododdin, and his mother were both killed by your brother Oswald. Taran believed in an eye for an eye and a tooth for a tooth. That was why he was prepared to help those who would assassinate you.'

'Where is this Brother Taran now?'

'We last saw him hurrying down to the harbour,' interposed Eadulf. 'Do you think that he was seeking a ship, Fidelma? He did not attend the final session of the synod.'

'Should I send warriors after Taran?' asked Oswy. 'Will they be able to catch up with him?'

'He is harmless now,' Fidelma assured him. 'He is, indeed, on the high sea and doubtless fleeing back to the land of the Cruthin. I doubt that Taran will ever trouble your kingdom again. All that can be gained by pursuit and punishment is revenge.'

'So,' Eadulf mused slowly, 'are we saying that all this was some plot to overthrow Oswy and that Étain was killed as part of the plot? But why? I don't see how.'

'One question, Oswy.' Fidelma ignored Eadulf for the moment. 'Your sister, the Abbess Abbe, did not stay for your pronouncement. Do you know why?'

Oswy shrugged.

'She knew that I would not make my decision immediately. I told her.'

'But your sons, Alhfrith, for example, and your wife, did not know.'

'No. I did not have time to explain to them.'

'What of this plot?' demanded Eadulf again. 'How does Étain's murder fit in?'

'The reason—' Fidelma was halted in mid-sentence as the door burst open and Alhfrith entered, followed by an anxious-faced Hilda and a grim-looking Colmán. It was clear that Alhfrith was in a resentful and hostile mood.

'What is this delay, Father?' demanded Alhfrith without preamble. 'All Northumbria waits for your decision.'

Oswy smiled sourly.

'And you were sure that I would decide for Columba so that you could raise the country against me in the name of Rome.'

Alhfrith started in surprise and then his face hardened.

'So you prevaricate and delay?' he sneered. 'But you cannot put off a decision forever. You are weak, but even you have to declare yourself!'

Oswy's face reddened in anger, but he kept his voice even.

'Don't you wonder why I am still alive?' he demanded coldly.

Alhfrith hesitated and a cautious look came into his eye.

'I don't know what you mean.' His voice was filled with bluster.

'Don't look for Wulfric again, he is dead and his assassins

with him. And your army of rebels now marching from Helm's Leah will not appear outside the walls of this abbey. They will be met by my army instead.'

Alhfrith's face was a grey mask.

'You are still weak, old man,' he said bitterly. Abbess Hilda cried out in protest, but Oswy motioned her to silence.

'Even though you are my son, flesh of my flesh, you forget that I am your king,' he said, eyes coldly on his son.

The petty king of Deira thrust out his jaw pugnaciously. He had little to lose now.

'I fought by your side at Winwaed stream ten years ago. You were strong then, Father. But you have weakened since. I know you would rather bow to Iona than to Rome. And Wilfrid and others know it.'

'They'll know my strength soon enough,' returned Oswy quietly. 'And they will also know your treachery to your father and your king.'

Anger was bubbling up in Alhfrith as he realised that his carefully laid plans had been thwarted. Fidelma saw that he could no longer give check to his feelings. She gave a warning cry to Eadulf, who was standing near him.

The knife was in Alhfrith's hand before anyone realised it and the young man had launched himself at his father in a murderous attack.

Eadulf sprang for the knife arm but even as he did so Oswy drew his sword to defend himself. Alhfrith in his forward momentum dragged Eadulf with him and, in so doing, he fell forward with Eadulf's weight on his back.

Alhfrith gave a strangled cry, something like a sob, and the knife dropped from his hand.

There was a silence in the room. Everyone seemed frozen.

Oswy stood staring at the bloodied tip of his sword as if not believing it was there.

Slowly the giant frame of Alhfrith, petty ruler of Deira, crumpled to the floor. Blood was staining his tunic just above the heart.

It was Eadulf who moved first, bending and reaching for the young man's neck, feeling for the pulse. He looked up at Oswy, who had not moved, and then to the Abbess Hilda before shaking his head.

Abbess Hilda crossed to Oswy and laid a hand on his arm. Her voice was now quiet.

'There is no blame in this. He brought his death on himself.'

Oswy moved slowly, shaking himself like a man awakening from a dream.

'Yet he was my son,' he said softly.

Colmán shook his head.

'He was Wilfrid's man. When Wilfrid hears of this he will seek to arm the Roman faction.'

At that Oswy sheathed his bloody sword and turned to Colmán, his old assertiveness re-established.

'I had no choice. He has been waiting to kill me for some time to seize the throne. I have long known that he has conspired to oust me. He had no allegiance for Rome or Iona but was just using the factions to weaken me. However, his temper got the better of him.'

'Even so,' Colmán replied, 'it is now Wilfrid and Ecgfrith that you must have a care of.'

Oswy shook his head.

'My army will deal with Alhfrith's rebels before this day is out and then will march back here.' He paused and then turned with sorrowing eyes on his bishop. 'My heart is with Columba,

Colmán, but if I declare for Columba, Wilfrid and Ecgfrith will attempt to raise Northumbria against me. They will claim that I am selling out the kingdom to the Irish, Picts and Britons and turning my back on my own race. What am I to do?'

Colmán sighed sadly.

'Alas, that is the one decision that you must make on your own, Oswy. None can make it for you.'

Oswy laughed bitterly.

'I was manoeuvred into this synod. Now I am bound to it as it turns like a wheel propelled by water. I may drown as the wheel turns.'

Fidelma suddenly gave a gasp.

'Drowning. We have forgotten Seaxwulf. Before we know whose hand lay behind the slaughter of Étain, Athelnoth and Seaxwulf we still have some work to do.'

She turned, motioning Eadulf to follow her, and leaving the rest of the room astonished at her abrupt departure.

Outside the abbess's chamber she turned quickly to Eadulf.

'I want you to find a local fisherman among the people of Witebia. Ask them how long it usually takes for a corpse to be washed down the coast from the spot where Seaxwulf was thrown in to a point from where it might be recovered. It is essential that we examine that corpse. And let us pray that it is retrieved within hours rather than days.'

'But why?' protested Eadulf. 'I am confused. Were not Alhfrith, Taran and Wulfric behind the murder?'

Fidelma smiled briefly.

'I am hoping that the final piece of this riddle will be on Seaxwulf's body.'

Chapter Eighteen

The grey light of dawn was touching the window of Fidelma's *cubiculum*. Fidelma was already dressed. This was to be the final day of the great synod, the day when Oswy would have to make his final choice. Unless she could resolve the mystery of the slaughter of Étain, Athelnoth and Seaxwulf, the rumour-mongers would take over and a war that might go beyond the borders of Northumbria might commence. She had risen with tension stiffening her body, her mind aching as she tried to resolve the mystery.

The sound of someone hurrying along the corridor caused her heart to beat faster. Some sixth sense recognised the hurried footfalls and she opened the door of the *cubiculum*, almost colliding with a breathless Eadulf.

'There is no time to apologise for my manners,' he said brusquely. 'The fisherman was right. The body of our late lamented friend, Seaxwulf, has been found. The body has been brought ashore in the harbour.'

Without a word, Fidelma followed the Saxon brother as he hastily led the way from the *domus hospitale* through the cloisters and out of the abbey gates to the winding path beyond. They traversed the precipitous cliff path to the sea shore, where the river entered into the bay around which the harbour of Witebia had been constructed.

There was no need to ask the way to where the body of the

Saxon monk had been brought ashore.

In spite of the early hour, a group of people were gathered inquisitively on the foreshore around something that resembled a sodden sack. They parted to let the two religious through, enquiring eyes particularly following Sister Fidelma.

The body of Seaxwulf lay on its back, eyes glazed and staring upwards. Fidelma flinched. The body had received a battering from the rocks and sea since she had last seen it in the wine cask. The clothes of the monk were almost shredded and weed clung to them.

Brother Eadulf was having a swift exchange with several of the bystanders who, by their looks, appeared to be fishermen.

'One of them saw the body floating some way out to sea while he was coming in after fishing in his boat. He pulled it alongside and dragged it ashore.'

Fidelma nodded slowly in satisfaction.

'Well, the fisherman you asked last night said it could come from that spot within six to twelve hours. He was right. And you can see that Seaxwulf did not drown in the sea but in the wine cask of the abbey, look at his mouth.'

She leant over and forced open the mouth of the corpse.

Eadulf let out a sharp exhalation.

'It is stained reddish – only faintly, but you can see the colour around the lips and in the mouth itself. But then I never doubted your word.'

'Red wine,' Fidelma said, ignoring his compliment. 'He was drowned in red wine, as I said.'

She began to remove the clothing around Seaxwulf's neck. Then she paused.

'Look at this. What do you make of it?' she asked.

Eadulf's eyes narrowed as he bent forward.

'Abrasions, some faint bruising fading rapidly, probably due to the immersion in the water. Powerful fingers. A strong man held him down by the shoulders.'

'Strong hands, indeed. He was held down in the wine cask until he drowned in the wine. I must have come along at that moment. Not until I slipped from the stool and was unconscious, or perhaps until you removed me to my *cubiculum*, did the murderer drag the body from the cask and then pull it along the tunnel and cast him into the sea. The poor devil.'

'If only we knew what it was that he had wanted to tell you,' muttered Eadulf.

'I think I know,' Fidelma said softly. 'Look to see if he has a purse.'

Eadulf was fumbling with the monk's clothing, which was a mangled mess of sea-sodden wool. There was no sign of the traditional *pera* or *crumena* that monks usually carried. But Eadulf gave a grunt of astonishment. Inside the clothing he found a small linen *sacculus* which was sewn to the inner side of the garment. In old times the religious of both sexes would carry only a *crumena*, a small sack or purse which hung over their shoulders in which they carried coin or personal items. Some, like Athelnoth, carried a *pera*. But a new fashion was emerging and that was for religious to have a *sacculus* of linen sewn into the folds of their garments as a means of greater protection for their private belongings. The fashion originated in Frankia where they called it a little pouch or pocket.

'What do you make of this, Fidelma?' asked Eadulf wonderingly.

Pinned in a fold of the cloth was a piece of torn vellum, fixed by a small round brooch, worked in bronze with red enamel and curious designs.

She stared at it for a moment and uttered an exclamation of elation.

'That was exactly what I was seeking.'

Eadulf shrugged. 'I don't see how it helps us. Seaxwulf was a Saxon. And I can tell you that the work is Saxon. The motif is ancient, pre-Christian, a symbol representing the ancient goddess Frig—'

Fidelma interrupted. 'I think it helps a great deal. And I mean the vellum as well as the brooch.'

Eadulf stared in disgust.

'Another piece of Greek.'

Fidelma nodded contentedly.

'It reads: "Love the loosener of limbs shakes me again, an inescapable bittersweet creature".'

Eadulf pursed his lips in annoyance.

'Did Athelnoth write this as well?' The monk suddenly snapped his fingers. 'You have implied that Étain's death had nothing to do with the plot to overthrow Oswy. That Taran and Wulfric had nothing to do with her death. I have it! Athelnoth killed Étain after all. But he was caught up in the matter of the king's assassination, revealing it to Oswy, and was killed by Wulfric or Alhfrith. His slaughter was merely a matter of coincidence.'

Fidelma smiled softly, shaking her head.

'A good explanation, Eadulf, but not the correct one.'

'Who else had opportunity and motive?' demanded Eadulf.

'Well, you forget Abbe for one.'

Eadulf groaned, touching his forehead with the palm of his hand.

'I had forgotten her.' Then his face lightened. 'But she would not have the necessary strength to kill any of the victims, would she?'

'I am not saying it is her. But the person we are dealing with is of cunning disposition, a mind whose thinking is like a path through a labyrinth that one tries to follow at one's peril.'

Fidelma was quiet for a few minutes as she knelt by the body of Seaxwulf. Finally she stood up.

'Order these men to remove the body to the abbey,' she instructed. 'Tell them to take it to Brother Edgar.'

She turned and began to walk slowly up the path towards the abbey buildings, hands folded in front of her, clasping the brooch and the vellum, her head slightly bent.

Eadulf quickly issued the orders and followed after her. He waited patiently, watching as she walked deep in thought. Suddenly she turned towards him and he had never seen such a smile of triumph on her face before.

'I think it all fits together now. But first I must visit the *librarium* and find that copy of the lyric poems of the Hellenistic world that Seaxwulf was reading.'

Eadulf exhaled helplessly.

'You have lost me. What has the *librarium* to do with it? What do you mean?'

Sister Fidelma gave a triumphant laugh.

'I know who our murderer is, that is what I mean.'

Chapter Nineteen

Sister Fidelma paused before the door of Abbess Hilda's chambers, glanced at Brother Eadulf and pulled a face.

'Are you nervous, Fidelma?' Eadulf whispered in concern.

'Who would not be nervous in such circumstances?' she replied quietly. 'We are dealing with someone strong and cunning. And the evidence I have is somewhat circumstantial. There is only one point of weakness, as I have mentioned, by which I hope to draw a response from the killer. If that fails . . .' She shrugged. 'Our murderer may well escape us.'

'I am there to back you.'

Eadulf's reassurance was no boast, just a simple and comforting statement.

For a moment she regarded him with a genuine smile of affection and reached out a hand to touch his. Eadulf placed his hand over Fidelma's as their gaze held. Then Fidelma lowered her eyes before knocking sharply on the door.

They were all there as she had requested – Abbess Hilda, Bishop Colmán, Oswy the king, Abbess Abbe, Sister Athelswith, Agatho the priest, Sister Gwid and Wighard, secretary to the now dead Archbishop of Canterbury. Oswy was sprawled moodily in the chair before the fire usually reserved for Colmán. The bishop himself had taken Hilda's chair behind her table. The rest of the company were standing around the room.

They turned with inquisitive looks as Fidelma and Eadulf entered.

Fidelma inclined her head to the king and looked towards the Abbess Hilda.

'With your permission, Mother Abbess?'

'You may proceed at once, sister. We are anxious enough to hear you and I am sure we will all be relieved when this is over.'

'Very well.' Fidelma coughed nervously, glanced to Eadulf for support and then began.

'What has dominated our investigation into the death of the Abbess Étain was the thought, which has become a conviction in the minds of many, that the killing was political.'

Colmán grimaced irritably.

'That was the obvious conclusion.'

Fidelma was unperturbed.

'You have all assumed that Étain, as chief counsel for the church of Columba, was killed to silence her voice; that the Roman faction realised that she was their most implacable enemy. Is that not so?'

There was a murmur of assent from those who supported the Columban ranks, but Wighard was shaking his head.

'It is a scurrilous suggestion.'

Fidelma let her cool gaze fall on the Kentish cenobite.

'But surely an easy mistake to make given the circumstances?' she parried.

'You admit that it was a mistake?' Wighard seized eagerly on her phraseology.

'Yes. Abbess Étain was slain for a reason other than that of the religious belief she held.'

Colmán's eyes narrowed.

'Are you saying that Athelnoth was the killer after all? That he made improper advances to Étain, was rejected and so slew her? That when he knew he was discovered, he killed himself in remorse?'

Fidelma smiled softly.

'You race ahead of me, bishop.'

'That was the rumour whispered in the cloisters of this abbey. Started, I suspect, by the Roman faction.' Colmán's voice was full of anger.

The dark-eyed priest Agatho, who had been quiet so far, suddenly broke his silence. He began to sing in a shrill voice:

'Rumour goes forth at once, Rumour and
No other speedier evil thing exists.'

He dropped his head and was silent as abruptly as he had begun.

All eyes were on him in bewilderment.

Fidelma's eyes flickered to Eadulf, giving him a warning. Soon now. She would have to display her hand soon. She drew herself up and continued, ignoring Agatho's interruption.

'You have the right reason, Bishop of Lindisfarne, but the wrong person.'

Colmán snorted in disgust.

'A crime of passion? Pah! I have always argued that male and female should be separated. In Job it is written: "I made a covenant with mine eyes: how then should I look upon a maid?" We should forbid these double houses as did the blessed Finnian of Clonard who refused to look upon any woman.'

Abbess Abbe was red with indignation.

'If it were left to you, Colmán of Lindisfarne, we would live a joyless life. You would probably applaud Enda who, having taken his vows, refused to speak even with his own sister, Faenche, except when a sheet was hung between them!'

'Better a joyless life than a life of debauchery and hedonism,' responded the bishop hotly.

Abbe's colour increased and she seemed to be choking, for she opened her mouth to speak but no words would come. Fidelma interrupted sharply.

'Sisters, brothers, are we not forgetting the purpose of this meeting?'

Oswy had been smiling bitterly at the arguing of his clerics.

'Yes, Fidelma of Kildare,' he added in agreement. 'This begins to sound like the assembly in the *sacrarium*. Tell us, if you can, why we have seen the death of your abbess, why the death of the Archbishop of Canterbury, why the death of Athelnoth, of Seaxwulf and, indeed, the death of even my own first-born son, Alhfrith. Death hangs around Streoneshalh like a plague. Can this be some ill-omened place?'

'There is nothing ill omened about this matter. And you already have the answer for the death of Alhfrith, Oswy. I know a part of you grieves for a son while a part of you recognises that you have come unscathed from the clutches of a traitorous conspiracy,' replied Fidelma. 'And God can answer for the death of Deusdedit of Canterbury, for he died of a plague. But another and a single hand is responsible for the deaths of Étain, of Athelnoth and Seaxwulf.'

There was an expectant silence in the room.

Fidelma gazed at them, each in turn. They stood glaring back defiantly.

'Then speak. Tell us whose hand?'

Fidelma turned back to Oswy, who had spoken sharply.

'I will speak, but it will be at my own pace and without interruption.'

Agatho lifted his head and smiled, raising his hand in the sign of the Cross.

'Amen. The truth will out, *Deo volente*!'

Abbess Hilda bit her lip.

'Should Sister Athelswith take Brother Agatho to his *cubiculum*, sister? I fear the strain of recent weeks has made him unwell.'

'Unwell? When a man is unwell his very goodness is ill!' cried Agatho, suddenly smiling. 'But the sleep of a sick man has keen eyes.'

Fidelma hesitated and then shook her head.

'It is best if Agatho hears what we have to say.'

Abbess Hilda sniffed her disapproval. Fidelma paused a moment and continued.

'Étain told me that she intended to resign from being abbess of Kildare as soon as she returned to Ireland following the end of this synod. Étain was a woman of enormous gifts, as you all know for you invited her here to be chief spokesperson of the church of Colmcille, whom you call Columba. Had she not been of the family of Brigit, she might have attained high position on her own merits. She married young but was widowed and followed her family tradition of becoming a religieuse.

'She excelled in learning and the time came when she was chosen as abbess of Kildare, the abbey founded by her illustrious kinswomen Brigit, the daughter of Dubhtach.'

'We all know of Étain's reputation and authority,' snapped Abbess Hilda impatiently.

Fidelma threw her a withering look. A silence fell.

'I had scarcely arrived at Streoneshalh,' went on Fidelma

251

after a few seconds, 'when I met and spoke with Étain and she told me that she had found a man whom she wanted to be with, to be with so strongly that she had decided that she would give up the position of abbess and go with her love into a double house where men and women and their children can dedicate themselves to God's work.

'At first I stupidly and wrongly assumed that Étain's new love was in Ireland.'

'It was a natural assumption.' Eadulf suddenly intervened for the first time. 'You see, Étain had never left the shores of Ireland.'

Fidelma cast an appreciative look at Eadulf.

'Brother Eadulf comforts me in my shortcomings,' she murmured. 'But one should assume nothing. In fact, Étain had fallen in love with a Saxon and he with her.'

She had their attention now.

'You see, Étain had met Brother Athelnoth at the abbey of Emly where she instructed in philosophy until last year.'

'Athelnoth had spent six months in the abbey of Emly in the kingdom of Munster in Ireland,' explained Eadulf.

Colmán was nodding his head.

'Indeed. That was why I chose Brother Athelnoth to go to Catraeth to meet the abbess and escort her here to Streoneshalh. He knew Étain.'

'Of course he did,' agreed Fidelma. 'A fact that he denied after Étain's murder. Why? Simply because he was aggressively in favour of the rule of Rome and his association with Étain would be counted against him? I think not.'

'Of course, many of the Roman faction were themselves educated or trained in Ireland,' Oswy pointed out. 'There are even some Irish brethren here, like Tuda, who side with Rome.

No, that is no reason to deny friends among the Columban faction.'

'Athelnoth denied his relationship because he was the man whom Étain was going to marry,' Fidelma said quietly.

Abbess Abbe snorted indignantly.

'How could Étain contemplate a relationship with such a man?' she enquired indignantly.

Fidelma smiled thinly.

'You who preach that love is God's greatest gift to humankind ought to be able to answer that, abbess of Coldingham.'

Abbe brought her chin up, a flush coming to her cheeks.

'Thinking back over Étain's conversation with me,' Fidelma went on, 'I realise now that she had given me all the answers to her subsequent murder. She told me that she loved a stranger. At least, I interpreted her word as "stranger" and took it for a relative term, meaning a man she had not long known, when I should have taken it to be "foreigner", for we in Ireland use that same word in both meanings. She told me that she had exchanged betrothal gifts with her lover and he with her. I should have remembered before that there is an Eoghanacht custom of exchanging brooches. Eadulf later found Étain's brooch in a *sacculus* on the body of Athelnoth.'

Eadulf nodded eagerly.

'And Athelnoth's brooch was found with the body of Seaxwulf,' he added. 'And on both bodies there were pages of vellum copied from a book of Greek love poems.'

Oswy was bewildered.

'Are you now saying that Seaxwulf was the culprit?'

Fidelma shook her head.

'No. The brooch that Athelnoth had was of Irish craftsmanship. Clearly, this was the betrothal gift Abbess Étain had given him. Now Seaxwulf had a brooch of Saxon work-manship. This was the brooch given in reciprocation by Athelnoth. The murderer had taken Athelnoth's brooch from Abbess Étain's body together with the poem found subsequently on Seaxwulf.

'Seaxwulf had found it after it had been removed and was going to show it to me when he was murdered. He might have named the killer to me but the killer discovered that he had taken these incriminating things and killed him instead. I came too quickly to the rendezvous with Seaxwulf to allow the killer to recover the brooch and the incriminating piece of vellum with the poem on it.'

'Incriminating?' demanded Hilda. 'To whom?'

Eadulf was looking nervous. So far, the person whom Fidelma had confided to him that she suspected was behaving with nerves of steel. There was no panic on the suspect's placid but watchful features.

'Let us get this clear,' interposed Wighard sharply. 'You are saying that Étain was killed by a jealous lover? Yet you say Athelnoth, who was her real lover, did not kill her. He was killed by the same man who killed Étain? And Seaxwulf was also killed by this same man? Why?'

Eadulf felt he should make some contribution.

'Athelnoth was killed not only because he was the man whom Étain loved but also because he could point the finger of accusation in the right direction. Seaxwulf learnt who the killer was by discovering the brooch and Greek poem in the murderer's *sacculus*. He took them before he realised what they were. When he realised, he asked Fidelma to meet him. That was why he was killed.'

Oswy sighed in exasperation.

'This seems too complicated. So now you must tell us. Who is the jealous lover of Étain? Name the man!'

Sister Fidelma smiled wistfully.

'Did I say it was a man?'

She turned slowly to where Sister Gwid stood silently, her face grey, almost stony. The dark eyes stared back at Fidelma with hatred, the teeth clenched. 'Sister Gwid, would you like to explain how you came by that tear in your *tunica* which you have sought to mend? Was it when you hid under Athelnoth's cot to avoid detection by Sister Athelswith?'

Before anyone realised what she was doing, Gwid had seized a knife from her robes and thrown it with all her force at Fidelma.

Everything seemed to happen in slow motion. Fidelma was so surprised by Gwid's unexpected reaction that she was frozen to the spot. She was aware of a hoarse cry of alarm and then the breath was knocked from her as she was borne to the ground by the weight of a body knocking into her.

There came a shrill scream.

The force of the fall caused her to wince in pain on landing on the stone floor and she found herself entangled with a breathless Eadulf, who had flung himself at her to knock her out of the path of the murderous missile. Fidelma peered up, trying to identify the source of the scream.

It was Agatho, who had been standing just behind her. Gwid's knife was now embedded in his shoulder with blood pouring across his tunic. He stood staring at the haft in disbelief. Then he began to moan and sob.

Gwid was running for the door but the giant Oswy was there before her. He seized the struggling woman in his arms. Gwid was powerful, so strong that Oswy was beaten back and forced to use his drawn sword to keep the snarling Fury at bay while he called loudly for his guards. It took two of Oswy's warriors to drag the screaming woman from the room with Oswy's orders to lock her in a cell and guard it well.

The king stood for a moment gazing ruefully at the red scratches on his forearms where Gwid had rent his flesh. Then Oswy glanced to where Eadulf was helping Fidelma to her feet.

'This needs a lot of explanation, sister,' he said. Then, more kindly, 'Are you hurt?'

Eadulf had taken charge, fussing a little over Fidelma and pouring her a goblet of wine.

She turned it away.

'Agatho is the one who is hurt.'

They turned to him. Sister Athelswith was hurrying forward to staunch the bleeding.

Agatho was now laughing, in spite of the knife still embedded in his shoulder and the blood soaking his clothes. He was crooning in his shrill voice.

'Who, except the gods, can live time through forever without pain?'

'I will take him to Brother Edgar, our physician,' Sister Athelswith offered.

'Do so,' agreed Fidelma with a sad smile. 'Brother Edgar may well be able to treat the knife wound but I fear there is little he can do to treat this poor man's mind.' As the elderly *domina* escorted Agatho through the door, Fidelma turned back to the others and grimaced.

'I had forgotten how strong and swift Sister Gwid could be,' she said almost apologetically. 'I had no idea that she would react with violence.'

Abbess Abbe looked moodily at her.

'Truly, are you telling us that these horrendous murders were committed solely by Sister Gwid?'

'That is what I am telling you,' affirmed Fidelma. 'Sister Gwid has now given you proof of her guilt.'

'Indeed,' Abbess Hilda agreed, her face still showing the shock of the revelation. 'But a woman . . . to be of such strength . . . !'

Fidelma glanced at Eadulf and smiled. 'I will have that wine now.'

The anxious brother handed her the goblet. She drained it and handed it back.

'I knew that Gwid seemed to worship Étain and preened herself whenever she was near. I was in error to think that she had sought Étain's friendship out of mere respect. We are all wise after the events. Gwid had studied under Étain at Emly. Étain became the object of adulation by Gwid, a lonely, unhappy girl who, incidentally, had spent five years as a slave in this kingdom, having been captured from her own country as a small child.

'Apparently Gwid was upset when Étain left Emly for Kildare. She could not follow because she was bound in the abbey for another month. When she was free to follow Étain she found that Étain was coming to Northumbria to take part in this debate. She therefore took passage from Ireland to Iona.

'It was there, at Iona, that I met Gwid and she claimed that she was Étain's secretary in order that she could journey with us to Streoneshalh.

'But the indications of what was really happening were before my eyes the whole time. When I saw Étain she seemed hesitant about acknowledging Gwid as her secretary. In fact, Athelnoth indicated that Gwid had followed Étain here not because Étain had sent for her but from her own motivation. He thought Étain had given Gwid the job once she arrived out of pity. Naturally he did not go into detail as to how he knew this because he did not want to reveal his relationship with Étain.

'But this was confirmed by Seaxwulf, who was Wilfrid's secretary. He told me quite clearly that Gwid was not really Étain's confidant nor privy to any of the negotiations Wilfrid was conducting with Étain. We were all so horrified to learn of these negotiations that we forgot this main point.'

Fidelma paused. She poured herself another goblet of wine and sipped it reflectively.

'Gwid had developed an unnatural adulation for Étain, a passion that Étain could never return. And Étain had told me yet I did not see it. She told me that Gwid, who is a good Greek scholar, spent more time worshipping the poems of Sappho than construing the Gospels. Knowing Greek, I should have known immediately the implications of that remark.'

Oswy interrupted.

'I do not know Greek. Who is Sappho?'

'An ancient Greek poetess, surely,' Eadulf interposed.

'A lyric poetess born at Eresus on the island of Lesbos. She gathered a circle of women and girls around her and her poems are full of the passionate intensity of her love for them and theirs for her. The poet Anacreon says that it was because of Sappho that the name of the island, Lesbos, connotes female homosexuality.'

Abbess Hilda appeared distressed.

'Are you telling us that Sister Gwid developed a . . . an . . . an unnatural love for Étain?'

'Yes. Gwid was desperate in her passion. She demonstrated her love by giving Étain copies of two of Sappho's poems. Étain gave one to her own lover, Athelnoth, presumably to explain to him what was happening. He indicated as much to us. The other she kept. At some stage, just before the opening of the synod, Étain told Gwid that she could not respond to Gwid's love – that, indeed, she loved Athelnoth and, after the synod, they were going to cohabit in a double house.'

'Gwid went berserk,' interposed Eadulf hurriedly. 'You saw just how quickly she lost her temper? She was a strong woman, physically stronger than a lot of us, I'll warrant. She attacked Étain, a slightly built woman, and cut her throat. She took Étain's betrothal brooch, given her by Athelnoth, and tried to take back the two poems that she had given Étain. She could only find one, for the other was already in Athelnoth's keeping.'

'I remember that she arrived late in the *sacrarium* on that first day of the debate,' Fidelma said. 'She had been hurrying and was red in the face and breathless. She had just come from killing Étain.'

'While Étain remained celibate, Gwid was more or less content to remain her doting slave. Just being near her was probably enough. But when Étain told Gwid that she loved Athelnoth—' Eadulf shrugged.

'There is no rage so powerful as hate born of scorned love,' Fidelma commented. 'Gwid was a powerful young woman but she was intelligent and cunning as well, for she cleverly tried to implicate Athelnoth. Then she realised that Étain must have given him the other poem. And rage again possessed her. That Étain could betray love and hold her up to ridicule before this mere man! Indeed, she even told me that she considered that Étain had found absolution for what Gwid saw as her sin in this murder. Oh, not so directly was this said but I should have interpreted it correctly when it was said.'

Oswy was bemused.

'So Gwid also felt compelled to kill Athelnoth?'

Fidelma nodded.

'She was strong enough, after she had knocked him unconscious, to hoist his body on to the hook in his *cubiculum* to choke him to death and make it seem like suicide.'

'But,' interposed Eadulf again, 'Sister Athelswith heard the sounds of Athelnoth being killed and came to the door. Gwid had time to hide under the bed as the *domina* came into the *cubiculum*. She saw Athelnoth at once and ran off to raise the alarm. Gwid was now in a dilemma. She had no time to look for the vellum with her second poem on it.'

'But how did Seaxwulf come to get the brooch and poem, the other brooch and poem?' Wighard enquired. 'You said that Gwid had taken this from Étain's body.'

Sister Athelswith slid back into the room and motioned Fidelma to continue.

'Brother Seaxwulf suffered an affliction. He had the mind of a magpie. He loved to pick up pretty things. He was rebuked and chastised for attempting to steal from the brothers' *dormitorium*. Wilfrid had him beaten with a birch stick. Later, in spite of this, Seaxwulf must have searched the *dormitorium* of the anchoresses. He had an eye for pretty jewellery and discovered Étain's brooch among Gwid's personal things. He found it wrapped in a Greek poem called "Love's Attack". He took them both. The poem intrigued him. He looked it up in the *librarium* and found that it was a poem by Sappho. He even asked me about the custom of exchanging gifts between lovers. I did not see what he was driving at until too late. Seaxwulf must have suspected Gwid. When he knew Athelnoth had been killed he came to tell me. He found me in the refectory with sisters close by. In his anxiety to be understood he addressed me in Greek to arrange the meeting. But he forgot that Gwid, who was sitting within earshot, knew Greek better than he did. It was a fatal mistake. Gwid had to silence him.

'She followed him, knocked him on the head and then killed him in the wine cask by holding him under the liquid. I came along too soon for her to search the body. In my surprise at discovering the body I slipped and fell off that stool by accident knocking myself out. My cry brought Eadulf and Sister Athelswith into the *apotheca*. They took me to my *cubiculum*. This gave Gwid time to retrieve Seaxwulf's body and drag it along the passage to the *defectorum* on the cliff edge and throw it into the sea. Not before she searched it, of course.'

'So why had she missed the brooch and poem on Seaxwulf's body?' demanded Abbess Hilda. 'She had enough time while she was dragging his body from the cask and transporting it along the tunnel.'

Fidelma smiled wryly.

'Seaxwulf followed the latest fashion. He had a new-style *sacculus* sewn into his *tunica*. This was where he had placed both the poem and the brooch. Poor Gwid did not know of the existence of the *sacculus*. But she was not worried, having disposed, as she thought, of the body and any evidence it held by throwing it into the sea. She did not realise that the tide would wash the body close inshore along the harbour within six to twelve hours.'

'You say that Sister Gwid was able to drag the body of Seaxwulf through the tunnel to the sea. Was she really that powerful?' demanded Hilda. 'And how did she, a stranger, know of the *defectorum*'s existence? It is for our male brethren only and usually only male guests are informed of its existence.'

'Sister Athelswith told me that, to keep male modesty intact,

261

the sisters who worked in the kitchens were told about it so that they would not wander along it by mistake. After Étain's death, Sister Gwid took to working in the kitchens to occupy her time.'

The elderly *domina* coloured.

'It is true,' she confessed. 'Sister Gwid came to ask me if she could work in the kitchens while she was here. I felt sorry for her and agreed. The mistress of the kitchens obviously warned her about the male *defectorum*.'

'We were distracted, for a while, by the politics of your son Alhfrith,' Eadulf conceded. 'We were misled for some time believing that he or Taran or Wulfric might have been involved in the matter.'

Sister Fidelma spread her hands with a gesture of finality.

'There you have it.'

Eadulf smiled grimly.

'A woman whose love is scorned is like a stream dammed by a log, deep, muddy and troubled and withal revolving with powerful turbulence. Such was Gwid.'

Colmán sighed.

'Publicius Syrus said that a woman loves or hates, she knows no other course.'

Abbess Abbe laughed scornfully.

'Syrus was a fool like most men.'

Oswy rose to his feet.

'Well, it took a woman to track down this fiend,' he observed. Then he grimaced. 'Even so, had not Gwid been of a volatile temper, all you had was circumstantial accusations. True they all fitted into a complete pattern but if Gwid had stood and denied everything could you have convicted her?'

Fidelma smiled thinly.

'We shall never know that now, Oswy of Northumbria.

But I would say yes. Do you know much about the art of calligraphy?'

Oswy made a negative gesture.

'I have studied this art under Sinlán of Kildare,' went on Fidelma. 'It is easy to the trained eye to spot individuality in the penmanship of a scribe, the way the letters are formed, the polished unicals, the cursive script. The poems were clearly, in my opinion, copied by Gwid.'

'Then we should be grateful to you, Fidelma of Kildare,' Colmán said solemnly. 'We owe you much.'

'Brother Eadulf and I worked as one on this matter,' replied Fidelma awkwardly. 'This was a partnership.'

She smiled quickly at Eadulf.

Eadulf returned the smile and shrugged.

'Sister Fidelma is modest. I did but little.'

'Enough to make these facts known to the assembly before I give my decision this very morning,' replied Oswy decisively. 'Enough to take the sting out of my words, trying to dispel the suspicion and mistrust that pervades the minds of our brethren.'

He paused and laughed ruefully.

'I feel that some weight has lifted from these shoulders of mine, for the slaying of Abbess Étain of Kildare was done not for Rome or for Columba but in the name of lust, which is the meanest of motives.'

Chapter Twenty

The *sacrarium* was unusually quiet as Oswy rose from his seat and looked around at the rows of expectant faces. Sister Fidelma and Brother Eadulf, now their task was done, felt oddly detached from the synod and, instead of returning to their seats on the benches of their respective factions, they stood quietly together by a side door watching the events as if they were no longer part of them.

'I have made my choice,' Oswy stated. 'Indeed, there was no choice to make. When all the argument was spent, it came down to one matter. Which church had the greatest authority – that of Rome or that of the Columban rule?'

There was a murmur of anticipation. Oswy raised a hand to silence it.

'Colmán claimed the authority of the Divine Apostle John. Wilfrid claimed the authority of the Apostle Peter. Peter is, in the words of the Christ Himself, the keeper of the gate of Heaven and I have no wish to go against him. I desire to obey his commands in all things in case when I come to the gates of the Kingdom of Heaven he, who, by the testimony of the Gospels themselves, holds the keys, should turn me away and there be no one to open for me.'

Oswy paused and looked around the hall, which was unnaturally still.

'Henceforth, the church in my kingdom of Northumbria shall follow the rule of Rome.'

The silence became ominous.

Colmán rose, his voice heavy.

'Lord King, I have tried to serve you well these last three years, both as abbot at Lindisfarne and as your bishop. It is with a sorrowful heart that now I must resign these posts and return to my native land where I can worship the living Christ in accordance with my conscience and the teachings of my church. All those who wish to follow the ways of Columba will be welcome to join me in my voyage from this land.'

Oswy's face was firmly set but there was also sadness in his eyes.

'So be it.'

There was a murmuring as Colmán turned and left the *sacrarium*. Here and there, members of the Columban church rose to follow his dignified figure.

Abbess Hilda stood up, her face also sad.

'The synod is at an end. *Vade in pace*. Depart with the peace and grace of our lord Christ.'

Sister Fidelma watched as the benches began to empty. There was hardly a sound now. The decision had been made and Rome had won.

Eadulf bit his lip. Although he was of the Roman faction he seemed to find sadness in the decision, for he glanced unhappily at Fidelma.

'The decision is political,' was his verdict. 'It was not made on grounds of theology, which is sad. Oswy's greatest fear is political isolation from the southern Saxon kingdoms over whom he wishes to extend his domination. If he had adhered to the teachings of Columba and his fellow Saxons had adhered to Rome, then he would be marked as bringing an alien culture to their land. Rome is already as much a political power in the kingdom of Kent as it is a spiritual power. The Britons to the west and the Dál Riadans and Picts to the north all threatened our borders. Whether we be men of Kent, or Northumbria, or Mercia or Wessex or East Anglia we are still of one language and one race. We must still contend for the supremacy of this island against those Britons and Picts who would drive us back into the sea.'

Fidelma stared at him in surprise.

'You are well versed in the undertones of political motivation, Eadulf.'

The monk grimaced wryly.

'Oswy's decision was couched in the language of theology but, I tell you directly, Fidelma, his decision was made in the hard reality of political concerns. If he had supported the Columban cause then he would have incurred the enmity of the bishops of Rome. If he supported Rome then he would be accepted by the other kingdoms of the Angles and Saxons and they will then join forces to assert supremacy over this island of Britain and, perhaps one day, the lands beyond. That, I believe, is Oswy's dream. A dream of power and empire.'

Sister Fidelma bit her lip and exhaled deeply.

So this was all it had meant? No more than power politics. No great intellectual decision or theological broadening of the mind. Oswy was just concerned with power, as all kings were in the final analysis. This great Synod of Streoneshalh was no more than a charade and had it not been for such a charade her friend Étain might well be alive. She turned abruptly away from Eadulf, tears suddenly rimming her eyes, and strode off to be alone for a while, walking along the cliff tops outside the brooding abbey. It was time to give way to the grief she had felt for her friend, Étain of Kildare.

267

* * *

The bell was tolling for the *cena*, the final meal of the day, when Fidelma crossed the cloisters to enter the refectory. She found Brother Eadulf waiting anxiously for her.

'The pro-Roman bishops and abbots have met,' he told her, speaking awkwardly, trying not to notice the redness around her bright eyes. 'They have held a convocation and decided to elect Wighard as the replacement for Deusdedit.'

Fidelma showed little surprise as they turned in step into the great dining hall.

'Wighard? So he will become the next Archbishop of Canterbury?'

'Yes. It seems that he is thought to be the obvious choice of successor for he has been Deusdedit's secretary for many years and is knowledgeable on all things relating to Canterbury. As soon as the synod disperses, Wighard is to go to Rome to present his credentials to the Holy Father there and ask his blessing in office.'

Fidelma's eyes glistened a little.

'Rome. I would love to see Rome.'

Eadulf smiled shyly.

'Wighard has asked me to accompany him as his secretary and translator for, as you know, I have already spent two years in that city. Why not come with us and see Rome, Sister Fidelma?'

Fidelma's eyes brightened and she found herself seriously contemplating the idea. Then the colour came hotly to her cheeks.

'I have been too long away from Ireland,' she said distantly. 'I must take the news of Étain's death back to my brethren in Kildare.'

Eadulf's face fell in disappointment.

'It would have been nice to have shown you the holy places of that great city.'

Perhaps it was the wistfulness in his voice that made her suddenly annoyed. He presumed too much. Then she relented her anger almost as soon as she recognised it. It was true she had grown somehow accustomed to Eadulf's company. It would seem strange to be without him now that the investigation was over.

They had barely settled at their table when Sister Athelswith came up and informed them that the Abbess Hilda wished to see them after the serving of the *cena*.

The Abbess Hilda rose from her chair as Sister Fidelma and Brother Eadulf entered her chamber and came forward with hands outstretched to both of them. Her smile was genuine, but there were deep etches around her eyes which marked the strain of the last days and the final conclusion of the synod.

'I have been asked to thank you both on behalf of Colmán and of Oswy the king.'

Sister Fidelma took her hand in both of hers and inclined her head while Eadulf bent to kiss Abbess Hilda's ring according to the Roman practice.

Abbess Hilda paused for a moment and then gestured them to be at their ease. She seated herself before the fire.

'There is no need for me to say what a debt this abbey, indeed, this kingdom, owes you both.'

Fidelma saw the sadness behind the abbess's face.

'It was a little service,' she replied softly. 'I wish we could have concluded the matter sooner.' She frowned. 'Shall you leave Northumbria now, like Colmán?'

269

Abbess Hilda blinked at the unexpected question.

'Me, child?' she responded. 'I have spent fifty years here and it is my country. No, Fidelma, I shall not go.'

'But you supported the rule of Columba,' Fidelma pointed out. 'Now that Northumbria has turned to Rome will you still find a place here?'

The abbess gently shook her head.

'It will not turn Roman overnight. But I will accept the decision of the synod to follow Roman ecclesiastical custom, although my heart sympathises with Irish usage. Yet I will remain here at Streoneshalh, at Witebia – the pure town – and hope it remains pure.'

Brother Eadulf stirred uncomfortably and wondered why he continued to feel sad. After all, his side had won the great debate. The *unitas Catholica* had triumphed. Rome's rule now extended across the Saxon kingdoms. Why, then, should he feel that something had been lost?

'Who will take over from Colmán now as bishop?' he asked in an attempt to rid himself of his melancholy.

Abbess Hilda smiled sadly.

'Tuda, although educated in Ireland, has accepted Roman orthodoxy and will be bishop of Northumbria. But Oswy has promised that Eata of Melrose will become abbot of Lindisfarne and so that shall be.'

Eadulf was puzzled.

'But Eata also supported the rule of Columba.'

Hilda nodded agreement.

'He now accepts Rome according to the decision of the synod.'

'And what of the others? What of Chad, Cedd, Cuthbert and the others?' Fildema asked.

'They have all decided that their duty lies in Northumbria and they will abide by the decision of the synod. Cedd has gone to Lastingham with his brother, the abbot Chad. Cuthbert is to accompany Eata to Lindisfarne as the prior.'

'So the changes have been tranquil?' mused Fidelma. 'No religious war threatens Northumbria?'

Abbess Hilda shrugged.

'It is too early to say. Most of the abbots and bishops have accepted the decision of the synod. That is for the best. Though many have chosen to accompany Colmán back to Iona and perhaps on to Ireland to form a new settlement. I do not believe that the peace of the kingdom is threatened from any religious quarter. Oswy's army dealt swiftly with Alhfrith's rebels. While Oswy mourns the death of his first-born son, he is more secure in his kingdom than ever.'

Eadulf raised an eyebrow laconically.

'But there is still a threat?'

'Ecgfrith is young and ambitious. Now that his elder brother, Alhfrith, is dead, he is demanding that he be made petty king of Deira under his father. But his eyes are already on Oswy's throne. And we are surrounded by hostile nations, Rheged, Powys, the kingdom of the Picts – all are eager to be at our throats. And Mercia always stands ready to take revenge. Wulfhere the king does not easily forget that Oswy slew his father Penda. He is already establishing Mercian domination south of the Humber. Who knows where danger will threaten from?'

Fidelma regarded her sadly.

'Is that why Oswy departed so soon to join his army?'

Abbess Hilda suddenly gave an uncharacteristic wry grin.

'He goes to join his army just in case Ecgfrith entertains the notion that his father is as weak as Alhfrith once claimed.'

There was an awkward silence. Then Abbess Hilda gazed thoughtfully at Eadulf.

'The bishops have chosen Wighard for the new Archbishop of Canterbury. I understand Wighard will shortly set sail for Rome. Are you accompanying him?'

'He needs a secretary and interpreter. I have been to Rome and will be joyful to visit the city again. I shall, indeed, go with him.'

Hilda turned inquisitive eyes to Fidelma.

'And you, Sister Fidelma. Where do you go now?'

Fidelma hesitated and then shrugged.

'Back to Ireland. I need to take the news of Étain's death and the decision of the synod back to Kildare.'

'A pity that your talents will be separated,' observed Abbess Hilda slyly, glancing from Fidelma to Eadulf. 'Together you have made a formidable pair.'

Brother Eadulf's face reddened and he coughed nervously.

'The talent was entirely with Sister Fidelma,' he said brusquely. 'I did little but lend physical assistance when needed.'

'What is to happen to Sister Gwid?' cut in Fidelma brusquely.

Abbess Hilda's eyes hardened.

'She has been dealt with in our Saxon way.'

'What does that mean?'

'She was taken out and stoned to death by the sisters of the abbey as soon as Oswy made his decision known.' Abbess Hilda rose abruptly before Fidelma could reply and articulate her sudden feeling of revulsion.

'We will see each other again before you depart on your separate journeys. Go with God. *Benedictus sit Deus in donis Suis.*'

They bowed their heads.

'*Et sanctus in omnis operibus Suis,*' they responded as one.

Outside Fidelma turned on Eadulf, her anger boiling over. The Saxon monk reached out a hand to catch her arm.

'Fidelma, Fidelma. Remember that this is not your land of Ireland,' he said hurriedly to quell the hot-tempered words that welled in her. 'Here things are done differently. A murderess is stoned to death, especially one who kills for such a shameful crime as lust. This is the way it must be.'

Fidelma bit her lip and turned away. She was still too full of resentful belligerence to articulate the sudden distaste she felt.

It was not until the following day that she saw Brother Eadulf again in the refectory as the bell finished tolling for the serving of the *jentaculum*, the breaking of the fast.

Even before she was seated, the elderly *domina* Sister Athelswith came hurrying up to her.

'A brother from Ireland has just arrived in search of you, sister. He is in the kitchens for his journey has been long and he is dusty and famished.'

Fidelma glanced up with interest.

'He has come from Ireland? Searching for me?'

'From Armagh itself.'

Fidelma stared in amazement before she rose and went in search of the traveller.

The man was exhausted and covered in the dust of travel. He was seated in a corner of the abbey kitchens tearing hunks of bread and slurping milk as if he had not eaten for many a day.

'I am Fidelma of Kildare, brother,' she announced.

He gazed up, his mouth still full of food.

'Then I have something for you.'

273

Fidelma ignored the man's ill manners, as he spoke with his mouth full and particles of his meal slipped from his mouth.

'A message from Ultan of Armagh,' the monk said, thrusting a package at her. She took it, turning in her hands the vellum-wrapped bundle, which was tied with a leather thong. What could the archbishop of Armagh, the leading churchman of Ireland, want with her?

'What is it?' she asked, wondering aloud rather than seeking an answer, for obviously the answer lay in the package.

The messenger shrugged between the mouthfuls of food he was masticating.

'Some instructions from Ultan. You are requested to proceed to Rome to present the new Rule of the Sisters of Brigid for the blessing of the Holy Father. Ultan asks me to beg you to undertake this embassy for you are the best qualified and the ablest advocate of the Sisters of Brigit of Kildare, the Abbess Étain notwithstanding.'

Fidelma stared at the man, hearing his words but not really comprehending them.

'I am to do what?' she asked, scarcely believing her ears.

The monk glanced up, frowning as he took another bite of bread into his mouth. He chewed several times before answering.

'You are to present the *Regula coenobialis Cill Dara* to the Holy Father for blessing. It is the request of Ultan of Armagh.'

'Requesting me to go to Rome?'

Suddenly Sister Fidelma found herself hurrying along the vaulted cloisters of the abbey back to the refectory. She did not know why her heart was beating more rapidly or what made the day so suddenly pleasant and the future full of excitement.